WHEN LOVE ENTERS . . .

"No, no, no, my sweetest, I am not trying to be kind. I do want you, with all my heart, all my soul. I want to protect and cherish you. Please, please, my own darling, you have no need to be afraid when I am with you. You will come, will you not?"

Her trembling had not ceased, but she said, "Yes, I . . . I will if you really want me."

"My own darling, my beloved, how many ways can I say it to make you believe me? I love you, Eugenie. I have been in torment these last weeks because I could never tell you what was in my heart. Do you believe that I love you?"

She stared into his eyes. "I do believe you," she whispered. "And . . . I love you, too. I have loved you ever since I first saw you."

"Eugenie . . ." Thurston lifted her and, holding her against him, carried her to the waiting coach.

"Reading THE VIRTUOUS MISTRESS was a real pleasure."

—Elizabeth Mansfield

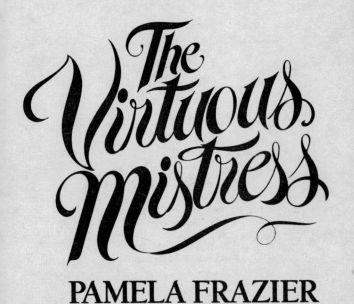

The Virtuous Mistress

PAMELA FRAZIER

BERKLEY BOOKS, NEW YORK

THE VIRTUOUS MISTRESS

A Berkley Book/published by arrangement with
the author

PRINTING HISTORY
Berkley edition/February 1988

ISBN: 0-425-10641-1

A BERKLEY BOOK ® TM 757,375
Berkley Books are published by the Berkley Publishing Group,
200 Madison Avenue, New York, NY 10016
The name ''BERKLEY'' and the ''B'' logo
are trademarks belonging to the Berkley Publishing Corporation

PRINTED IN THE UNITED STATES OF AMERICA

10 9 8 7 6 5 4 3 2 1

The Virtuous Mistress

PROLOGUE

ON A WARM April day in the Year of Our Lord 1802, the Countess Eugenie de Villiers danced in a grassy spot not far from Cheyne Walk, where the old, lame street musician, his cane hooked over one arm, played his violin. The music, a sprightly gavotte, beguiled her, mesmerized her. From head to toe she gave herself to its strains, leaping and whirling, a pattern of movement she had invented. Her patched cotton skirts swirled about her, showing portions of her thin but shapely little legs, and her pale gold hair, loosed from the tight, hurtful braids that her Aunt Vivienne had wound around her head earlier that morning, now fell over her shoulders to the middle of her back, save when at a movement of her head, locks of it strayed across her face.

Some few people stopped to watch the child, amused at her concentration and her apparent obliviousness to what was going on around her. A poetically inclined youth, who had hoped to stroll by the banks of the adjacent river and derive inspiration from its pellucid, sun-dappled waters, was momentarily brought to a standstill watching Eugenie. He thought her the very spirit of the burgeoning spring and decided to write a quatrain.

An older man, with less poetic thoughts, stopped to watch, his hooded eyes traveling from her head and down her slender body to her small, bare feet, which were, he thought, beautifully formed, slender of ankle and high of arch. A glance about him brought the welcome notion that the child was alone. Another glance, again at the child, corroborated an earlier feeling that she was no more than eight—possibly the daughter

1

of some laborer or, better yet, a vagrant. Certainly there was none to claim her, not at this moment. He had but to approach her, and quickly too. There were many who would pay for this dainty morsel—pay well and in gold. Smiling, he moved forward to stand in her pathway so that she was forced, albeit reluctantly, to stop.

"Well, my pretty," he said in a drawl, "you are quite an accomplished daughter of Terpsichore."

The little girl blinked up at him but did not answer.

"Are you a mute, then?" he inquired hopefully, thinking that a mute could not protest, could not scream, and would present rare sport until the novelty and the bloom wore off. He was too absorbed in his thoughts to realize that the music had ceased until the street musician came to his side.

"Mais non, monsieur, she is not a mute. I have my grandchild instructed so that she to strangers does not speak. As you can see, she is most obedient."

The stranger, one Henry Jenner, turned quickly, his eyes narrowing. "Ah, the little one is your grandchild, then?"

"Yes, my youngest," the musician acknowledged, his hand bearing down on the child's thin shoulder.

He received a suspicious glance from Jenner. "Well, you are blessed in your progeny, or, rather, grand-progeny." His smile acknowledged his own witticism but drew no answering smile from the old musician. Intent on his objective, he continued doggedly, "It must be taxing playing on the street in all kinds of weather, especially for a violinist as accomplished as yourself." His gaze lingered on the latter's clean, but much mended, garments.

"I do not complain." The musician shrugged.

"And nor would you complain were there more money in your purse than the groat or halfpenny they throw you." Jenner waved his hand at the tree-shaded street.

"No one would complain had he a heavier purse," the musician responded, his eyes narrowing.

Old Pierre was pinching her shoulder. Eugenie wondered why. Indeed, as she listened to the conversation of the two men, she was surprised almost to the point of interrupting —but not quite. Her Aunt Vivienne held strong views on the subject of obedience, and Eugenie, who had been by nature loquacious, had learned in many very hurtful ways not to interrupt when her aunt and her friends were conversing. The old musician, Pierre, was not a member of her family in name, but certainly he was her elder, and so was the other man whose eyes she did not like, though she could not have explained why. She wished he would go away. She longed to dance to the music that old Pierre played. It was seldom that she escaped the vigilance of her Aunt Vivienne, but on this particular morning her cousin Etienne had been detailed to watch her, and as usual he had wandered off, leaving her to seek out the violinist who was her good friend, even though they had rarely passed more than the time of day. Consequently it was most confusing to hear him claim a relationship that did not exist. She listened intently now as the stranger said, "Your purse could be weighted with gold."

"Gold?" the violinist repeated. "I do not understand, monsieur."

"I expect you are caring for her in the absence of her mother," Jenner pursued, his thin lips quirking into a smile.

"Her family is dead, sir. The Terror." Pierre explained.

"Ah, yes, the Terror . . . horrible. So many French suffered the guillotine. I expect you might have been a vicomte, or a marquis, or at the very least, a chevalier, *n'est-ce pas?* And now you are reduced to playing the violin in the streets of Chelsea Village—but that is foolish, my friend, when you could live luxuriously."

"I—could live luxuriously?" Pierre raised his eyebrows.

"Yes, I am sure you understand what the word means."

"Ah, yes, monsieur, I the word know. It means that if I sell my child, here, to you . . . and you present her to such clients who can afford to pay the price you ask for her services, I will be well rewarded. Am I correct, monsieur?"

Jenner took a step backward and then stopped, eyeing the man warily and then smiling. "You are remarkably astute, my good man, but the street brings wisdom, does it not? And you will not even need to bargain with me. The sum I will offer must, I know, astonish you and . . ."

"Villain," old Pierre said softly. *"Canaille,* I beg you will be off and quickly before this bow leaves the violin strings and plays its tunes on your buttocks. . . ." He made a sudden movement, and the horsehair bow whistled through the air and struck Jenner on the back.

"Damn you!" he said, springing away. "I could . . ." His fists were clenched, and his hooded eyes were very menacing now.

"I suggest that you can do nothing, monsieur." The musician's cane was in his hand, and he made a movement with the top of it, drawing out a length of steel that sparkled blindingly in the sunlight and sent a pattern of red dots dancing before Eugenie's eyes. Even so, she could mark and smile with relief at the stranger's hasty departure.

"Oh"—Eugenie smiled up at the violinist—"you made him go away. I am glad. I did not like him. He had odd eyes."

"You are singularly astute, my child." Old Pierre was frowning.

"Astute?" she repeated. "What does that mean?"

"It means 'wise,' my child."

"Oh." Eugenie nodded. She gave him a puzzled look. "But Monsieur Pierre, we are not related, are we? My aunt . . ."

"No, child, we are not related," he assured her. "But come, we must go now to your aunt. You will give me her direction, please."

"Must we?" Eugenie looked at him nervously. She swallowed visibly. "I should not be here . . . it was your music brought me as before."

"I know . . . and you have music, too, child. It is here." He touched her head and pointed to her feet. "And there. You like to dance, yes?"

"Yes, very, very much." Eugenie raised glowing blue eyes to his face. "It is the music . . . your music, you see."

"I see," he agreed. "And it would be well if your aunt also saw . . . much more than she does at present. Please, you will give me her direction."

"She will be angry. She does not like it when I speak to strangers."

"But strangers we are not," the violinist persisted. "We have seen each other many times, and occasionally we have passed the time of day. It is very important, child, that you let me speak to her."

Eugenie had been taught to obey. And when her elders spoke to her in such commanding tones, she had perforce to listen. She did not expect that her aunt would look with favor on the elderly musician. She would not approve his ragged garments, and after he had gone, there would be another beating. She said reluctantly, "Very well, monsieur. You will come with me, please."

Vivienne de Champfleury was the granddaughter of one Monsieur Alphonse Thiboust, a banker of dubious heritage who had managed to give his daughter, Alys, a dowry sufficient to snare one Comte de Monvel.

De Monvel had, his father-in-law was fond of saying to Alys, "not two *sous* to rub together." Still, his great name, coupled with his aristocratic disdain of the banker, was enough to sway the old man in his favor, and Alys Thiboust, a pale, pretty girl, became Madame la Comtesse. They lived in the comte's ancestral château, refurbished and furnished by the banker who, being distressingly plebian in conversation and manner, was welcomed neither by his son-in-law nor by his daughter. Fortunately he died before his grandchild Vivienne was born, and consequently the comtesse had not the embarrassment of inviting him to the christening of a daughter, whose black eyes were, in shape and depth, a replica of his own.

As she grew older, Vivienne de Monvel's resemblance to her grandfather increased. In addition to his dark eyes, she had his low brow and, worse yet, his broad shoulders and short, chunky figure. Fortunately there was also enough of the Thiboust money to provide her with a dowry large enough to tempt a de Champfleury, one of the oldest, if not the richest, families in Normandy. They were married in the year 1787 when Vivienne was eighteen. She remained in Normandy with the aging Comtesse de Champfleury while her husband happily spent her dowry in Paris, returning occasionally to pass a night or two with his bride.

Vivienne lost her first child, a daughter. In 1795, when her son Etienne was eight months old, her husband and the comtesse's daughter, Madeleine de Villiers, and her husband, the Comte Eugene de Villiers, were guillotined.

Vivienne, clad in farm woman's garb, drove a cartful of straw through the North Gate of Paris. On the way she jested loudly and crudely with the soldiers who guarded the gate. They, in turn, laughed and never questioned her peasant heritage. Had they not seen a thousand similar in appearance gathered to watch the daily spectacle at the Place de la Revolution? Many of the female observers knitted, but Vivienne's fingers, short and capable, were obviously better suited to her duties as a farmer's wife. They did not even question the straw in her cart. They believed her when she told them it was to preserve the eggs and other produce she sold each day.

It was not until she was very far away that she allowed her mother-in-law to emerge from the straw where she had lain, one trembling hand over the mouth of little Eugenie and the other clamped down on Etienne, who had been inclined to wriggle and whimper—sounds that fortunately were lost in the laughing exchange between his mother and the soldiers. Vivienne might have set Etienne on her lap, the comtesse had contended, but her daughter-in-law was taking no chances. Though his features were hardly formed yet, Etienne, fair and delicate, had inherited only his mother's dark eyes. Other than that, he took after the de Champfleury side of the family and, possibly, the de Monvels.

Eventually Vivienne reached Ostend and then England. She sold the jewels that also had been hidden under the straw and bought a house in Chelsea, a street away from Cheyne Walk. It had a parlor, a dining room, a kitchen downstairs, and three rooms upstairs. Vivienne appropriated one of the rooms for herself and Etienne. The comtesse and Eugenie occupied the other room. The third room was where she worked on the garments she eventually obtained from various mantua makers, utilizing her skills with the needle, learned at the convent.

She worked very hard for the pittance she earned. The labor did not improve a temper that had always been short. She expressed herself loudly when she lost it and made life difficult for her frail, grieving mother-in-law, and equally difficult for her small niece by marriage. Even Etienne, the one person in her life she adored, felt the sting of her slap and cowered under her virulent scoldings.

Consequently it was with many qualms that Eugenie knocked timidly on the door of her aunt's house, hoping against hope that either her grandmother or her cousin would admit her, explaining that her aunt was away from home in London. She swallowed nervously as the door was jerked open and Vivienne de Champfleury stood glaring up at the tattered musician.

"I 'ave nothing for beggars," she began in her heavily accented English. Her eyes fell on Eugenie. "You . . . *tu es méchant . . .*"

"Madame," the musician said pacifically. He continued in French. "I have brought your niece home."

"Have you?" Vivienne snapped. She continued in the same language, "And where did you find her, monsieur?"

"She has come often to hear me play." He indicated his violin case.

"I have seen you!" Vivienne's voice rose, and she began to breathe quickly. Eugenie recognized these as bad signs and drew closer to the violinist. "You play in the streets!"

He was not unaware of Eugenie's movement and could easily guess the reasons behind it. He said, "Yes, madame, I play in the streets, but perhaps I had best introduce myself. I am Pierre de Lascelles, and at one time I was connected with the Paris Opéra. But of that, no matter. I understand the dance—"

"The dance?" Vivienne echoed. "Why do you talk of the dance?"

"If you will bear with me, Madame," old Pierre said evenly.

"Monsieur"—she eyed him contemptuously—"I have not the time, and if it is money you wish, I have not that, either."

"Tante Vivienne!" Eugenie could not stop her protest even though she knew it would only fuel her aunt's fires.

"And you"—her aunt's hot eyes fell on her—"why did you run away from your Cousin Etienne?"

"I did not run away from him," Eugenie cried indignantly. "He left me!"

"Liar!" Vivienne screamed shrilly.

"Madame." The musician spoke in a commanding tone of voice that brought Vivienne's glare to rest on him. Before she could launch into another diatribe, he continued in the same tone, "I beg you will listen. Your niece should not be dancing in the street!"

"Dancing? She was dancing in the street?" Vivienne repeated incredulously, her black eyes narrowing.

"She is a natural dancer," the musician said quickly. "She cannot resist the music."

"She can and will, or I will know the reason why!" Vivienne glared at Eugenie. "You"—she caught Eugenie by the shoulder—"dancing . . . a de Villiers, a Champfleury, become a spectacle. . . ."

"Madame, I beg you will listen! She is, as I have told you, a

natural dancer. It is an accomplishment that comes early and
cannot be resisted. And I can make of her a real dancer, a great
dancer.'' He spoke quickly, earnestly, aware of a need to
command the attention of this shrew. ''She has an innate sense
of rhythm, and under my tutelege she could, in a few years
only, become a great artist.'' He paused, reading doubt and
derision in the woman's eyes. ''And she would make much
money.''

''Money? That one?'' Vivienne said sarcastically.

''There is a great demand for French dancers, madame.
Since the troubles with Napoleon, few have made their
appearance here in London. They are not allowed to emi-
grate.''

''Napoleon, that beast!'' Hatred shone in Vivienne's eyes.
Yet if there were hatred and anger, there was also a spark of
interest in their dark depths. ''Money?'' she repeated. She
stared contemptuously at her niece. ''This one could make
money?''

''Not at first, madame, but within a few years I would say
that she might easily make a fortune.''

''A fortune?'' Vivienne's gaze indicated that he had lost his
senses. ''She is only eight.''

''I promise you, madame, that if she were to become a
dancer, she will—before she is eighteen—have all London at
her feet.''

Vivienne's laughter was loud and ugly. ''Sure, you are
pleased to jest, monsieur.''

Reading the mixture of contempt and anger in her aunt's
face, Eugenie shrank back against the musician.

He was not unaware of the movement and put a comforting
hand on her shoulder. His own anger was rising, but it was
necessary to keep his temper if he was to convince this
termagant of his sincerity and, at the same time, preserve the
poor child from the beating he guessed her aunt was itching to
give her. He said evenly, ''I do not jest, madame. There are
not many who possess the natural grace of this child. I have
had the opportunity to see many young dancers. She could
easily be of their number. There is a school for dancers. In a
matter of a few years she will be able to join them. And by the
time she is thirteen, she will be bringing gold into your
coffers.''

''Gold?'' Vivienne repeated, her eyes narrowing.

"Gold," he said firmly.

"She will not be thirteen for five years, and meanwhile she is only another mouth I must feed. I have no money for lessons."

"I will teach her for very little, madame. I will teach her for the cost of a loaf of bread and a bottle of wine. When she is ready, she may share some of her earnings with me, if she chooses."

Eugenie, listening as she had never listened before to the conversation of her elders, stared up at her aunt's face. It seemed to her that some of her anger was fading away. Yet there was doubt. Vivienne said, "A loaf of bread and a bottle of wine each day, monsieur?"

"With each lesson. I would begin with three a week," he said, nodding.

There was another pause while Vivienne regarded him narrowly, the workings of her mind visible on her face. He read doubt and contempt—but also he read speculation. He would have been glad to teach the child for nothing but guessed that her aunt would not respect him for it and, indeed, might even suspect his motives, unconsciously connecting him with the monster from whom he had just rescued her niece.

"Very well," Vivienne said grudgingly. "We will see how she does, monsieur, but if at the end of the month she does not show progress, the lessons will be at an end."

"A month it is, madame," he said.

"Oh, Aunt Vivienne!" Eugenie breathed.

"Get inside," her aunt said with a look that boded ill for her. She stared at the musician. "A month only, monsieur", she said emphatically.

"I promise you, madame, you will not regret it," he said with a courtly bow. He smiled at Eugenie. "I should like to start tomorrow." His eyes found Vivienne's face again. "If that is agreeable with you, madame?"

"It is agreeable," she snapped. "At what hour?"

"At two in the afternoon."

"Very well, monsieur, and we shall see what we shall see."

"I will bid you good afternoon, madame," he said with another bow.

Later that evening Eugenie, lying on the hard little bed in the room she shared with her grandmother, was very hungry but, at the same time, much relieved. She had gone to bed supperless, as a punishment for slipping away from Etienne and lying about it. Etienne, of course, had convinced his mother that the fault had been hers, but at least she had not been beaten. Evidently her aunt was of the opinion that a dancer must needs be sound of wind and limb.

Grandmother had protested mightly over Monsieur de Lascelles's offer. "A Champfleury and a de Villiers must not dance for the public!" she had cried in accents of utter horror.

"A Champfleury and a de Villiers must eat," Vivienne had said shrilly. "And if she can earn more than a few *sous* for her supper, the better it will be. I, for one, do not believe she has a chance of being a dancer, but I also am willing to be shown, if there is something to see. As it is now, it is I who bear the burden of the entire household on my shoulders—am I a beast that I should be so encumbered? No, no, and no! I say that if there is a chance that she can earn good money, we must take it."

"There was a Champfleury who rode out with Henri IV—" Eugenie's grandmother had begun.

"And who is now dead with Henri IV and Louis XIV. Our France is no more. That we live is a miracle—but we do not live, we merely exist. If this child can contribute . . . I say that it is all to the good!"

Eugenie smiled as she thought of the events of the day, and her hunger vanished, to be replaced by excitement. She was going to be a dancer, a real dancer—and life suddenly had a meaning!

PART ONE

CHAPTER ONE

THE LIBRARY AT Seabourne Hall was a long, narrow room with high windows facing the justly famous rose gardens. An Aubusson carpet in soft rose and gold covered the floor, and its color was picked up by rose-colored damask draperies. One wall was completely given over to shelves containing the famous Seabourne Collection.

It had been amassed over several generations and included, among many treasures, a Gutenberg Bible and a Book of Hours, handpainted on parchment by a fourteenth-century monk of undisputed artistry. At the far end of the room was a fine desk brought from Italy and inlaid with mother-of-pearl. Over a wide fireplace, flanked by marble caryatids, hung a portrait of a lady in medieval costume, but that, of course, was a fancy of the artist, Sir Joshua Reynolds, who had thought she bore some resemblance to an Italian madonna.

Thurston Sorrell, standing in front of the desk, threw a regretful glance at the lady of the portrait. Even though he had been a mere six years of age when she had reluctantly died, remembering him and his elder brother Tom in one of her last breaths, her very last being used to whisper the name of her beloved husband, the present Viscount Seabourne, he still missed her.

"And so you are determined upon acquiring town polish, Thurston?" the man behind the desk said half humorously, half caustically.

Dark eyes of a vaguely almond shape and very like those of the portrait met cool, gray, judgmental eyes. His father's question was, Thurston thought, manifestly unfair, given the fact that he had, upon leaving Oxford, come directly home to spend the entire summer and most of the autumn at the hall. Furthermore he had not been idle. He had devoted a great deal of his time learning estate management against the time when he would settle down at the Bastle, a property in Northumberland inherited from a great-uncle on his mother's side of the family.

He said gently, "I thought I might visit London, sir."

Despite his son's soft response, the set of his broad shoulders, coupled with the way he held his head, suggested to Lord Seabourne that Thurston's months of country living were indeed at an end. "I see." His eyes strayed to the window. It was near the end of November, and the trees had turned red and gold. That he had kept his younger son away from the temptations of the city considerably longer than he had originally anticipated, should have pleased him more than it did. He was reasonable enough to be aware of that. Yet the thought of all that awaited the lad in London was enough to bring a frown to his eyes and another word of caution to his lips. "If you are determined on seeing your Uncle Simon, I beg you will not let yourself be tempted—" He broke off, frowning at his son's laughter. "Might I know what I could have said to stir your risibility, Thurston?" he inquired coldly.

Thurston hastily swallowed another burgeoning laugh. "I am sorry, Father, but were I of a less steady mind, I vow your repeated injunctions regarding my wicked uncle would fast drive me into his camp."

"Are you of so steady a mind?" Lord Seabourne murmured, half to himself.

"Do you not know that I am?" Thurston countered, his candid brown eyes lingering on his father's face.

Lord Seabourne said reluctantly, "You are most unlike him, but you are but one and twenty, and the town itself is full of temptations."

"I mean to avoid them, sir," Thurston said determinedly. "I do not believe I would care for my uncle's mode of life. To my mind it is much too hectic. Actually I will probably be home in the spring, and then it will be time to stay at the Bastle."

Lord Seabourne loosed a sigh of relief. "It is time and past that someone lived there again, lad."

Thurston did not miss the note of urgency in his father's tone, and there was a touch of impatience in his manner as he answered, "I must go to London, sir, if only for three months."

"Very well. If you must, you must," Lord Seabourne said in a long-suffering tones. His voice, however, became brisker as he added, "You may send your bills to Mr. Quincy Delamere, who is my man of business in the city. I will give you his direction. He will supply you with the ready, but I beg of you, go to Brooks and Boodles, but remember, you are not a gambler and—" He broke off, smiling wryly. "There is an echo in my head. I fear I am, in effect, saying the very same words that my father said to me. Consequently I will cease the homilies—take what you want from London and, of course, visit Simon, but I depend upon that intelligence that won you such high marks at Oxford—" Again he broke off, this time with a chuckle. "You can see that I am full of advice which, again, if you are anything like me when I was your age, you will not heed."

Thurston looked fondly at his father. "I beg you will not worry about me, sir. I have no wish to follow in my uncle's footsteps. I can think of nothing duller than the ceaseless pursuit of pleasure."

Lord Seabourne said thoughtfully, "You might be surprised to learn that long ago Simon himself was of the same mind."

Thurston regarded his father with considerable surprise. "You do astonish me, sir. Might I know what it was that transpired to change his mind?"

"A cruel disappointment. The young woman he wanted to marry died suddenly. He could love no other. The men of our family are often so constituted. . . ." Inadvertently Lord Seabourne's eyes strayed to the portrait of his late wife.

"Do you still miss her so very much, Father?" Thurston asked compassionately.

"I imagine that I will never cease to miss her. I wish you might have known her better. However, the relationship of mother and son is intrinsically different from that of husband and wife. It is a matter of sharing the same memories, laughing at the same jokes . . . and occasionally it is not speaking at all but looking at each other and knowing . . ." Lord Seabourne

sighed and added, "But I am becoming overly sentimental. Go
to London when you choose, Thurston, and enjoy yourself in
any way you see fit."

"I do thank you, Father," he returned gratefully.

A few minutes later Thurston, emerging from the library,
saw his brother Thomas in the hall and sighed, not wishing any
unpleasantness after his salutary conversation with his father.
Tom resented his going to London just as he resented everything else about him—as if, indeed, it was his fault that he
topped Tom by three inches and was dark instead of fair and
with strong rather than insignificant features. Both their like-
nesses could be found among the paintings of their ancestors in
the portrait gallery at the far side of the house, and furthermore
Tom did resemble their fair, gray-eyed father but, unfortunately, did not possess his fine features or his height. Yet though he
was short, Tom was well proportioned and athletic and, of
course, as the eldest son, would inherit Seabourne Hall and the
title as well—compensations that ought to have satisfied him.

Thurston said, "Good afternoon, Tom. Have you been to
see the fair Serena?"

Tom nodded, saying curtly, "She made a great point of
asking after you and seemed much cast-down when I told her
that you were probably going to London at the week's end."
He added, "Are you?"

"I am going *tomorrow*," Thurston emphasized.

"And with father's blessings, I take it?"

"As long as I do not fall into Uncle Simon's evil ways.
About Serena—"

"What about Serena?" Tom interrupted with a touch of
belligerence.

"I may be wrong, but it occurred to me that you had
misconstrued a friendly reaction. There is nothing between
Serena and myself, as you are well aware. There never has
been."

Tom reddened. "Did I suggest that there was?"

"I had that impression," Thurston said gently. "I did not
tell her that I was leaving for London, so I expect that she was
merely surprised."

Tom loosed a long breath. "I expect she must have been."
He managed a smile. "After all, I imagine she thought you
would be remaining for the ball announcing our engagement. It
is only a month away. I wish you would be there."

Thurston smiled back at him. "I do not think you will miss me, but I promise that I will return for the wedding, provided that it takes place in February, as planned."

"And if it does not?"

"Then I will send you my good wishes."

"Do you really wish us well?" Tom demanded bluntly.

Thurston stifled a sigh as he read the suspicion in his brother's gaze. "We were only *children* when we made that silly pact," he said insistently. "How could Serena wed both of us? She would have had to be a Mohammedan, and then it would be the man who would have two wives."

"I have always believed . . ." Tom began ponderously.

"And I have always believed that she preferred you, Tom," Thurston told him emphatically.

"She was mighty glad to see you when you returned this summer."

"I was also very glad to see her. She has grown exceedingly pretty, but I am not in love with Serena, and my dear Tom, I assure you that she is not in love with me. She is marrying you."

"The match was arranged by our parents, and well you know it," Tom said resentfully.

"Tom"—Thurston spoke with a patience he was far from feeling—"if you could see yourselves together, you would not question Serena's affections—and now, will you please excuse me? I must direct Curran concerning the garments I intend to take with me."

Tom came closer to Thurston, and taking his hand, he said, "I will be up to see you off, and never think that I do not wish you well."

"And never think that I do not wish the same for you, Tom." Thurston smiled. "But you have already had my assurances on that."

It was a great relief to leave his brother, and rather than going upstairs to confer with his father's valet, Thurston came outside. There was a cool wind blowing, and showers of leaves were falling like golden rain from the tall old trees that edged the pathway through the gardens where he had chosen to stroll. Head down, he walked slowly, thinking about Tom's continuing resentment. It was really ridiculous.

Tom would inherit the hall. He, on the other hand, must needs hie himself up to the chill vistas of the border country

—to the Bastle, a strongly fortified house almost as large as a castle.

In his mind's eye he could envision its gray stone walls and its slate roof. There were small towers, too, with slits in them to allow the passage of arrows in those years when the Scots and the English settled their disputes with war machines, with dirks and swords, bows and arrows, maces and catapults. Furthermore the elderly uncle from whom he had inherited had cherished a passion for its warlike past. He had a fine collection of weaponry and had restored discomfort to rooms which during the passage of a century had become more and more modern in aspect. Wallpaper had been stripped off, exposing the rough stone walls beneath and floors were denuded of carpets and strewn with straw. The furniture ran to deal tables and hard wooden chairs. Tom would not have enjoyed it, nor would have Serena.

The hall, on the other hand, had risen in Queen Elizabeth's time and had endured sundry alterations during the reigns of James I, Charles I, and, inadvertently, during the time of Cromwell, when the stables had been razed and some of the tenant cottages knocked down. However, during the reign of Charles II, when the family returned from France, a disciple of Sir Christopher Wren had remodeled the whole of the lower floor.

Thurston sighed as he envisioned the changes made by that architect and others employed in subsequent reigns, subservient to the wishes of each owner. If he were Tom, he would follow his father's example and leave well enough alone, but he had a strong feeling that Tom intended to put his stamp on it too. He sighed again, thinking how much he preferred the leafy vistas of Somerset or, to be more specific, the town of Butleigh, which lay only five miles from the hall. King Arthur of Round Table fame had supposedly preferred Somerset too. He smiled at the fancy. There were several counties that claimed the legendary monarch and, of course, despite the fact that his mighty skeleton had been exhumed from a grave in Glastonbury some centuries ago, it was doubtful that he had ever existed at all.

Serena, he remembered, believed that he had—little Serena, who used to be Guinevere to Tom's Lancelot while he, as the younger son, was either the Green Knight or Mordred—to be felled in mock battle by a "sword"-brandishing brother. He wondered about Serena. He had seen very little of her in the last few months. In fact, he had had the feeling that she was purposely avoiding him. That had hurt him—they had all been such good friends when they were little, but since he had come home from Oxford to find her betrothed to Tom, she had become extremely elusive.

In fact, her attitude had reminded him of the days when they were children and she and Tom were always exchanging secrets, for all that she was four months younger than himself. Consequently the jealousy that he had sensed in his brother appeared particularly misplaced. Even if the match had been arranged between their parents, Tom had always loved Serena, and when they were all three of them together, she had always seemed to favor him.

He frowned. There had been, he recalled, a time when he had envied Tom almost as much as the latter appeared to envy him at present. In those days, before he had left for the university, it had seemed extremely unfair that his elder brother should have had both the estate and Serena—the arrangement having been concluded when they were aged three and a half and four. However, four years away and seeing other females had not only cured his heartache, but also it had put Serena in a proper perspective.

She was pretty, but no prettier than a certain little chambermaid at an inn some two miles outside Oxford. Her name was Meg, and she had been the first to warm his bed and, being far more experienced than the green lad he had been, had instructed him in the ways of love. Naturally he never would have learned that from a Serena, who must needs be seen and admired but never subjected to the interesting familiarites he had enjoyed with Meg. He smiled a trifle ruefully. There had been a time when he had fancied himself in love with Meg, but then, one night he had discovered her being equally instructive to another undergraduate. He laughed. He had been badly hurt by her defection—until a week later he had discovered another equally cozy and willing damsel.

"Thurston."

He came to a startled stop when he saw Serena standing on the path, a few feet away from him, looking unexpectedly lovely in a close-fitting brown coat that was almost the same color as her eyes. Her corn-colored hair was almost hidden by a high-crowned hat. She did not need the additional height it provided;—she was almost as tall as Tom—nearly eight inches over five feet, but the hat was becoming and she really looked quite beautiful. Moving toward her, he bowed over the hand she held out to him. "Serena, my dear, how very good to see you!"

"And you, Thurston, on this last day." She raised her eyes, and their glances locked. "I thought you might be staying longer, but Tom tells me that you are leaving tomorrow."

"Yes, tomorrow morning, early," he acknowledged.

"It's cold weather to be traveling so far."

"It was considerably colder up north," he said.

"You were at the Bastle a long time."

"Not as long as I was here," he said. "I wish we might have seen more of each other, Serena."

"Do you? I think you must be funning me. Tom has said that you have been very busy."

"I could always make time for a ride or a chat with you, Serena."

"But you did not," she said, a faintly accusing note in her voice. "I expected that you would come visiting with Tom. Mama and Papa were surprised by your absence."

She was regarding him intently, and there was something in her eyes that made him uncomfortable. He said, "You have been much occupied with Tom. I have already congratulated you on your forthcoming nuptials, but let me do so again."

"I thank you, Thurston." She blinked rapidly and put a hand up to her eye. "Oh, dear, I think something must have just flown into my eye. It seems to be tearing."

He moved toward her. "I will try to take it out," he said solicitously.

"No, Thurston," she said, protesting quickly. "I . . . will be able to blink it away, I think." She opened and closed her eyes twice. "There, it is done. May I say that I hope you will find London to your liking? But of course, you have already been there, have you not?"

"Only for a day or so with some friends from the university. We attended a lecture on Astronomy at the Royal Society. I wanted to be ready for London."

"And are you?" she asked.

"I would, of course, say that I am, but only time and the city itself will tell."

"I have never been in London," she said thoughtfully.

"You must have Tom take you there on your honeymoon, my dear."

"I think he has it in mind to go in another direction —Scotland, perhaps."

"Will it be Edinburgh?"

"I think it might be the Highlands. However, nothing has been decided—save the date of the wedding. February twenty-third. It is exactly three months from today. I do hope that you will be able to attend."

"I shall make it my business to be there, my dear. After all, I will need to see my brother through . . ." He paused and felt his cheeks grow warm.

"The fatal ceremony?" she questioned lightly.

He laughed. "I meant, of course, that I would be his best man, and I can think of nothing less fatal than being your groom, my dear Serena."

"I will write and remind you of those words—if I hear that you have decided to remain overlong in London." She favored him with a challenging smile.

"I have given myself three months only, my dear. I can think of nothing that would prevent me from attending that wedding."

"I understand that London is full of temptations." The challenging smile had changed to a penetrating look.

"None so tempting as seeing you and Tom properly married, I assure you."

"A great deal can happen in three months," she responded musingly. "But . . . I must go." She held out her hand. "I wish you well."

Again he kissed her hand. "And I will say the same to you, my dear Serena."

"Do enjoy London, dearest Thurston." She withdrew her hand from his grasp and hurried away.

He stared after her until she was lost amidst the trees. He had found their encounter unsettling. Indeed, it had seemed to him that neither of them had said exactly what they meant, mainly because he had followed her lead and found it elliptical in ways he did not wish to consider further. In fact, he wished that they had not met, and at the same time he was even more pleased that he would be on his way to London in the morning . . . the early morning.

* * *

"Well, well, well." The Honorable Simon Sorrell smiled genially at his nephew. "I am indeed pleased to see you, my lad."

They were sitting in a chamber that was small but elegant. Striped satin draperies hung at the windows, and a couch was covered in the same material. Thurston noted an ebony desk with a curved top in one corner of the room and a Dresden china clown on a small marble mantelshelf. A painting depicting a fanciful Grecian landscape hung above it. The carpet beneath his feet was soft, and the air was heavy with the scent of two huge bouquets of hothouse roses in vases set on a small table and on a console table in the hall. His uncle's surroundings were almost effete, Thurston thought, save for the pair of crossed foils hanging on one wall. "And," the Honorable Simon continued, "I am pleased to discover that you have more than fulfilled your earlier promise."

"My . . . earlier promise, sir?" Thurston inquired confusedly.

"I am speaking of your appearance, of course. I had hoped that you would favor your mother's side of the family, and I see that you do have much of the look of the beautiful Elvira—her eyes and her cleft chin. As for the rest of your features, they seem to be largely your own and mighty pleasing too."

Thurston reddened. He wished that he might return the compliment, but while his uncle was a well-looking man, the way of life so decried by his father had made its mark on a face that had endured some twenty-odd years of drinking and wenching. At forty-eight his cheeks were flushed, and so was his nose. His eyes were bloodshot, and there were streaks of gray in his hair—the latter hardly visible, however, amidst his blond locks. He contented himself with saying, "You are kind, sir."

"On the contrary"—his uncle raised the quizzing glass that hung around his neck and surveyed his nephew through an eye rather unsettlingly magnified—"I am never kind, but on occasion I can be honest. I would say, my lad, that you are quite the most personable of the brood. In the proper setting —I speak of garments rather than chambers—you would and undoubtedly will cut a dash. I will give you the names of my tailor, my haberdasher, and my boot maker, to which you must repair immediately, as soon as you are settled."

"I am settled for the nonce, sir," Thurston said. "I am

staying at Ibbetson's Hotel.''

"Ah, Ibbetson's." The Honorable Simon pulled a face. "A quiet spot, fit for clerics and scholars only." He cocked an eye at his nephew. "Do you—er—wish to be quiet, young Thurston?"

His uncle looked as if he had just swallowed something very disagreeable, Thurston thought. He said hesitantly, "I do not know that I wish to remain there—but the one time I was in London with some of my friends from Oxford, we stayed there."

"Ah, you would." Mr. Sorrell grinned. "It is known to be quiet and inexpensive. However, if you are minded to set this town by its ears, as it were, my boy, my advice is to either hire a house or take lodging in a more central and fashionable location. As it happens, I know of some elegant rooms just off St. James's Square, which can be had for forty guineas a week. That might be considered a trifle dear, but I imagine that you are not short of the ready."

"No, I am not. I would like to see them," Thurston said eagerly. "Are they near the British Museum? I should like to visit it while I am here, and also St. Paul's and the Tower and Westminster—"

"Ah, very commendable," his uncle said, interrupting. "One should view these sights at least once. I hope, however, that you will want to accompany me to the opera—Tuesday week when it opens for the season."

Thurston's eyes glowed. "Oh, yes, sir! I am extremely fond of music. Handel and Arne . . ."

"I, too, but this will be some Italian trifle. I misremember the name, but it is notable mainly for its ballet, and Mademoiselle de Montfalçon will be putting the Vestris's nose out of joint with her dancing—the most charming little creature in the world. I vow, we are all at her dainty feet! I have secured a box directly over the stage, so that you will be able to enjoy her charms to the fullest." He cocked an amused eye at his nephew. "I am speaking relatively, of course. The poor child is surrounded by dragons."

"Dragons, sir?"

"There is a most disagreeable woman drags her from the theater before she has even a chance to grace the Green Room. I presume you know what a Green Room is, Thurston?"

"Yes, sir. It is where the actors receive their public, and 'tis green because after the bright lights of the stage the color is easier on the eyes," Thurston said glibly.

Simon Sorrell gave him an astonished stare. "I vow! You do have a fund of useful information. I never knew that. Yet I imagine that in my way I might also contrive to be instructive. If you will take my advice, you must first see to your garments—or rather I will, if you do not mind me accompanying you like a bear leader?"

"No, sir, not in the least," Thurston said eagerly. "I should be delighted."

"Very well, we will commence on the morrow. And I insist that you remove from Ibbetson's!"

"I will, sir, at once," Thurston said gratefully.

"In fact, if you are not too weary, I will show you those rooms."

"No, sir, I am not in the least weary," Thurston assured him excitedly.

His uncle's smile contained a modicum of bitterness. "And you traveling near two hundred miles at a pace that would have left me bedded for a week. Ah, youth, it is something that no one appreciates until it is gone. Do you have a valet, by the way?"

"No, sir, I usually—"

"But you must have one," his uncle said, interrupting yet again. "If only to manage your cravat." He bent a critical eye on the mass of white cloth under his nephew's chin. "I do not say that you must emulate a Brummel . . . poor man, he is by way of being much in disfavor at this time, but no matter, you must achieve *style*. You are not in the country now. I will have my man Jacob send you someone of his acquaintance—there's no one more knowledgeable, I assure you." Mr. Sorrell rose. "And now, lad, come with me, London awaits your pleasure!"

Thurston was thinking of his uncle's words some seven days later as, feeling not unlike a lad let out of school, he walked in the direction of the British Museum. It had been a week of fittings—for the tight stockinette trousers, the highly polished Hessian boots with their bright gold tassels that he was currently wearing, as well as for the dark brown coat that his tailor declared was nearly a match for his eyes. Over it hung the many-caped overcoat, also brown, that he liked even though his valet, a knowledgeable young man named Graves, told him that it was not absolutely the latest style. Still, as he had observed, they were being worn. He was also wearing a tall black beaver hat, and as he had left his new lodgings, Graves had pronounced him "all the crack." He sighed, wondering if, in time, he would become used to the stylish tightness of his garments and the scratchy folds of his admirably tied cravat, which was making it difficult for him to lower his chin. During his four years at the university and his seven months divided between Somerset and Northumberland, he had given very little thought to his garments other than choosing his favorite browns for jackets, coats, and boots, and buying the softest buckskin for his breeches.

Here, he thought with some annoyance, dressing seemed to be an art, an expensive one, too, even if one did not aspire to be a dandy. He grinned. Graves had told him that Beau Brummel took five baths a day and was never seen before noon because of the ritual of dressing. He had added that some few of the Beau's cronies were admitted to his dressing room to watch their idol at this particular endeavor. The valet had spoken wistfully as if, indeed, he wished his new master might emulate that sartorial perfection.

Thurston laughed merrily enough to startle a number of fellow pedestrians and move a beggar to hold out a trembling hand for largesse. Thurston automatically dropped a coin into his hand as he went on walking and thinking about his experiences of the past fortnight. These were enough to make him wish that he were still at the hall, and he had quite decided that three months in the hectic city would be more than enough. Despite parental warnings, he had found it impossible to refuse all of his genial uncle's invitations and had, with considerable misgivings, thrice accompanied him to Brooks, spending wearying evenings at the tables—evenings which, in fact, did not end until four in the morning and on two occasions had necessitated his practically carrying his inebriated uncle to his waiting post chaise. Furthermore he had been shocked at the amount of money Simon Sorrell had dropped.

He, himself, drinking only water, had managed to win almost as often as his relative lost. He was richer by a thousand pounds, and of course he had to admit that it was exhilarating to see the gold and bank notes piling up in front of him. It had not, however, been particularly pleasant to see the distress written large on the face of a man who had challenged him to a game. The others with whom he had played had seemingly taken their losses as casually as had his uncle, who had later congratulated him, calling him a "downy bird" and a "knowing 'un."

Yet if he were richer and, for the nonce, had no need to call upon Mr. Quincy Delamere, he could not like the fact that he had, in effect, turned night into day and slept three mornings away. He could imagine his father's disapproving looks, and undoubtedly he would have prophesied that despite all warnings, he was placing his own feet squarely in his uncle's footsteps. With that in mind, he had, last night, refused an invitation to a private party given by one Lord Carlisle, whom his uncle had described as a most convivial sort and "one you should know, my lad." Ignoring Mr. Sorrell's remonstrances, he had retired early, determined on seeing some of the sights that had originally drawn him to London. First on his list was, of course, the British Museum, which was within walking distance of his new lodgings.

He felt particularly exhilarated that morning. He had already been riding in the park, and rather than finding the sun at its zenith when he awakened, he had seen the golden orb rise in the frosty skies. Then he had returned to his lodgings—the rooms that were his for the large sum of five pounds a week. That they consisted only of a large bedroom, a living room, a study, a cubbyhole for his servant, and a small kitchen made them rather cramped. However, they were charmingly furnished, and as his uncle had said, the location was unexceptional.

The Honorable Mr. Sorrell had also added with a sly look that should he care to entertain a female companion, the bed was large and soft enough for a night of dalliance. It had been on the tip of his tongue to tell his uncle that "dalliance" had no part in his current itinerary, but he had not yielded to that temptation. He would have only encouraged his uncle to burden him with introductions to a series of females whose amorous expertise was in direct ratio to their overripe charms.

"Stay away from highborn females, lad," the Honorable Simon had warned. "See them more than once, the old tabbies'll have you wedded and bedded before you can blink. Now I know a little bit o' muslin new to the game. Her name's Bess Blaine, and she does minor roles at Drury Lane. She's not demanding. A trumpery locket or bracelet will please her, and she's a cozy armful for a day, a night, a week . . . and will not act out a Cheltenham tragedy when you part. And meanwhile you will have learned much that will be to your advantage.''

He had no need for instruction. He wanted . . . but he was not sure what he wanted. No, that was not entirely true, he reflected. He did not want to be pressed into an involvement with any woman. The condition of being heart-whole and fancy-free suited him. He frowned, wondering why he should suddenly think of Serena—as she had stood there in his path that day at the hall—with questions in her eyes and, later, tears? *Had* there been questions? The tears . . . and why had she been there at all?

He did not want to dwell on Serena, his brother's promised bride. There had been a time, but the time was past, he reminded himself. Still, he was glad that he had spent several months at the Bastle—away from temptation. Did she tempt him, or was it merely the affection born of a long friendship that had invaded him at that moment in the garden? Undoubtedly it was the latter, and when he returned to officiate as his brother's best man, he would dance one dance with the bride and go on his way. Would he ever marry?

Unlike Tom, there was no pressing necessity. He was not bound to furnish heirs to the title and the hall. He grimaced. His heirs must needs shiver in the cold winds that howled across the Scottish border. As for a bride . . . he could not imagine that any of the damsels he had glimpsed in London would look with favor on the steep, gray sides of the Bastle or on a spot where neighbors were situated leagues rather than miles away—and snowbound for most of the winter. The uncle who had deeded him the house had died a bachelor and . . . He paused in his thinking as he saw the tall mansion known as Montague House after its former owner, the Duke of Montague, and which was now called the British Museum.

It was an immense structure with high stone walls stretching almost the length of a city block. There were towers on two sides, and a third, in the center, was surmounted by a cupola. Its style was Louis XIV—that much he had learned from a London guidebook purchased in Oxford some two years earlier.

As he entered the courtyard he saw that the sheds built to

house the Egyptian artifacts captured from Napoleon's forces in Alexandria were still there.

Among the spoils, he recalled, was the supposed tomb of Alexander the Great, a claim that, he had no doubt, had originated in the mind of the conquering Napoleon. Naturally the self-styled emperor must needs subjugate the dead as well as the living monarchs of the world. And would that he, too, soon join the ranks of the departed.

On this grim if heartening thought, Thurston strode into the main hall and, after signing his name in the register, moved toward the great staircase. Two more Egyptian monuments in black marble, covered with hieroglyphics, dominated the hall. He paused to study the strange pictures, wondering what they meant. Unfortunately, unlike such ancient languages as Latin and Greek, there existed no key to the Egyptian writings.

Moving forward, he lingered beneath a large stone ram's head from Thebes and, approaching the staircase, admired a mahogany model showing the bridgeworks at Blackfriars. However, that interested him less than the paintings on the ceiling depicting an overconfident Phaeton driving the chariot of the sun through the heavens. On reaching the second floor, he went into the first room and was further titillated by Phaeton's fiery fall. Then, as he started to look at the other exhibits, he heard a low voice protesting, "I beg you will stop annoying me, sir. I am *not* alone. My cousin will soon be returning."

"Your . . . cousin?" Laughter reached him; low, ugly laughter. "Do you have a cousin, my love? Then I beg you will let us seek him together."

"Please, sir, let me alone!" The soft voice now held a note of panic.

Thurston stepped forward hastily and saw a small, slender female confronting a tall, husky man who was grinning down at her in a way he found most offensive. His features were coarse and his nose bulbous. He had mean little eyes and a full, loose mouth. He was not badly dressed. Probably, Thurston thought, he was a well-to-do member of that class his uncle called collectively: "cits."

As he reached them he heard the man say, "Now, come, little ladybird, if you think you can up your price by these remonstrances, you have the wrong bird in your pretty little net."

The female's back, which was all that Thurston could see of her, stiffened. She said coldly and with just the touch of an accent Thurston decided must be French, "You insult me, sir."

"I doubt that," her tormentor said with a drawl. "Next you will be telling me that a lone bit o' muslin such as yourself is here to gaze at the exhibits."

"I am *not* a bit o' muslin, as you are pleased to put it. I am a respectable female. My cousin is below and will be returning soon—now I ask you to go or else I will scream."

"Scream away, my lovely." The man seized her arm.

"I think," Thurston said coldly, coming to his side, "that you are annoying this young lady."

"Oh, is that what you think, young sir?" The man regarded him belligerently. "Well, I will have you know that his 'lady' is my—"

"I am nothing to him," the girl cried. She turned and fixed large, imploring blue eyes on Thurston's face. "My cousin left me to look at the preserved fish in the basement."

"Cousin!" Her unwanted companion laughed. "A likely story. She has been here upward of fifteen minutes without her—cousin as she chooses to call him. She is here for the same reason that other unaccompanied females are here, and I am quite willing to pay her price."

The girl flushed. "It is not true!" she exclaimed hotly.

"Of course it is not true." Thurston visited a cold stare on the face of the other man. "Obviously, sir, your powers of discernment are at a very low ebb, and I will thank you to be on your way at once!"

"Oh? And supposing I refuse?"

Brown eyes met choleric blue eyes steadily and coldly. "I do not suspect you will refuse, sir," Thurston said evenly. "It would not be wise." He was pleased to see the bully pale and step back.

"Very well, and be damned to you," he growled. "I'm not about to bruise my bone-box for the likes of her. Indeed, I wish you luck with the little doxy." He turned on his heel and strode away hastily.

"Oh, I do thank you, sir," the girl whispered.

Thurston, gazing at her upturned face, experienced a shock. She was quite the most beautiful girl he had ever seen. In addition to her huge blue eyes, she had a straight little nose and a pointed chin with the suggestion of a dimple. Her mouth was neither too full nor too thin—indeed, it was in perfect harmony with the rest of her features. Her close-fitting bonnet hid most of her hair, but a few pale gold tendrils had escaped to curl about her forehead. Her skin was very white, but there was a lovely color over cheekbones that were high, giving her a faintly foreign look, but, he remembered, she was foreign, French, and one of the highborn émigrés, come to England after the Revolution, he guessed. Everything about her breathed refinement, and he noted that her garments were not new. Her coat was worn, and her close-fitting velvet bonnet also showed signs of wear. He discerned a flush on her cheeks and noted that she was now looking down as if embarrassed. He, too, flushed, realizing that he had been staring at her.

He said, "I wish I might have given that rogue the beating he deserved!"

"Oh, I am glad you did not, sir. You might have been hurt," she breathed.

"And he, too, might have been hurt," Thurston said grimly. "But I heard you mention your cousin. Shall we see if we can find him down in the basement?"

"Oh, no," she protested. "He has looking at those horrid exhibits, and they are all so ugly."

He felt a surge of disappointment at that hasty refusal, thinking that, after all, her "cousin" might be as that bully had suggested, a ploy to meet a likely-looking man or, rather, customer. Still, it was impossible, he found, to connect her with such predators. The innocence reflected in those blue eyes could not be feigned. He said, "Would you care to look at some of the exhibits up here—while you are waiting?"

She shook her head, saying regretfully, "I do thank you, sir, but Etienne said I must await him here. We have already been through the rooms. It is my fault that I am alone—I could not bear to look at those horrid, spiny things floating in the jars—fish and eels." She shuddered.

"Well, then, shall we both look for your cousin?" Thurston asked. "You may remain at the door of the—er—fish chamber."

"Oh, dear, you need not bestir yourself to fetch Etienne," she protested. "You must see the rest of the museum. It is very interesting."

"I can wait," he responded, wanting more than ever to

believe in the presence of her elusive cousin.

"If you choose," she said shyly, "but again . . . ah!" she suddenly exclaimed. "At last, here he comes."

Thurston, looking in the direction in which she was staring, saw a short, dark young man striding toward them. He darted a suspicious glance at Eugenie and said sharply in tones also coated with a slight French accent, "Have I not told you, Eugenie . . ."

"This gentleman, Etienne," the girl said, interrupting, "was kind enough to fend off a most disagreeable man. Why were you so long, pray?"

"Long?" he echoed indignantly. "I was gone no more than ten minutes."

"I must disagree," Thurston interposed. "I have been here over ten minutes, and part of the time was devoted to dealing with a rogue who was bent on seduction—to put it bluntly."

"That is true," the girl whispered. "I was terrified."

Etienne glared at Eugenie. "Did I not tell you to remain in a corner and speak to no one?" he demanded irritably.

"I did not speak to him!" Eugenie retorted indignantly. "*He* spoke to me—and this gentleman was kind enough to send him packing."

"That is no more than the truth," Thurston assured him. "He was most unpleasant and intimidating—besides being twice the size of your cousin. She was in real danger, young sir."

Etienne favored him with a sulky look. "Well," he said grudgingly. "I do thank you for having rescued her, and now we must go. Come, Eugenie!" Putting an arm around her, he hurried her out of the room.

"Wait!" Thurston cried, and started after them.

"Sir! What are you about, pray? Do you not look where you are going?"

Thurston, coming to a startled halt, found himself looking down at an elderly man and woman. "I . . . I am sorry."

"Sorry!" shrilled the old man. "You nearly knocked us down!"

"Indeed, he did. I think we should call the guard." The old woman glared up at Thurston.

"I am extremely sorry, sir and . . . madame," he repeated. "I—I was trying to catch up with my friends," Thurston said, stuttering. "I hope I did not hurt you."

"You ought to be ashamed," the old man said raspily. "This is not proper museum behavior, certainly."

"You have my apologies, sir." Thurston strode forward, and reaching the top of the stairs, he looked down, hoping to catch a glimpse of the cousins and saw them at the entrance. "Please," he called loudly, gaining glares from several other patrons who were mounting the stairs. "Please," he called a second time as he hurried down to the ground floor. Unfortunately, by the time he came into the courtyard, there was no sight of them—nor did he see them when he reached the street.

He loosed a long breath, feeling almost ill with frustration. If he only knew her full name—but he did not. He knew only that she was called Eugenie and that her cousin's name was Etienne and that, in common with Romeo, he had fallen in love with her at first sight. Unlike Romeo, however, he had no chance of scaling the orchard walls or any other walls to find her. He did not know where she lived and, undoubtedly, in a city of this immense size, the chances of seeing her again did not exist!

CHAPTER TWO

"HOW MANY TIMES . . ." Etienne began as the hackney turned into their street.

"How many times are you going to tax me with that?" Eugenie retorted. "If you had not remained for fully twenty-five minutes in that cellar, I would have spoken neither to that great bully nor to *him*."

"I told you," her cousin said self-righteously.

"I remained in the corner. I neither spoke nor looked at anyone. *He* approached me. I told you what he said—now let there be an end to it!"

"That other one . . ." Etienne growled.

"Would you have had me be silent when it was he who rescued me?" Eugenie glared at her cousin.

"I hardly think that you could term it a 'rescue.' I cannot believe that you could have been ravished in the British Museum."

"We do not know what might have happened if he had not interfered." Eugenie shuddered, unwillingly reminded of an incident long, long ago when Pierre de Lascelles had rescued her from one, whom she now knew to be a procurer. "I have told you what he accused me of . . ." She shuddered again. "He asked me my *price!*"

"You should have told him 'above rubies.'" Etienne grinned.

"I do not think it was amusing," Eugenie said coldly. "And you did not thank that other young man properly. You dragged me off . . . I do not even know his name."

"It is not necessary for you to know his name," Etienne

retorted. "And were you primed to give him your name as well? That would have been a fine kettle of fish! I saw the way he was looking at you. I vow he was as moonstruck as Jean-Paul." Etienne widened his eyes and let his mouth hang open.

"If you do not desist, I shall tell Aunt Vivienne what happened," Eugenie said warningly.

"Oh, will you?" Etienne appeared undaunted by her threats. "You say one word, my girl, and I will tell her that you were flirting with two strangers, and guess which one of us she will credit?"

"You are abominable!" Eugenie hissed.

"And you are stupid," Etienne retorted. "You *were* flirting with that man."

"I was not!" she said, flaring.

"I know what I saw," Etienne growled.

The hackney pulled to a halt before Eugenie could answer her cousin. Actually, she thought bitterly as they walked toward the front door of their house, she had no redress. If Etienne were to tell her aunt that she was flirting, she would box her ears first and ask questions afterward. *And* she would not believe the answers!

Despite the money that had swelled the household coffers since she had joined the corps de ballet at the King's Theatre, money Eugenie never saw, her aunt continued to decry her profession. Ironically enough, she who had encouraged her niece in this endeavor was almost as vociferous as her late grandmother had been on the subject of a de Villiers with Champfleury blood running blue through her veins dancing on the stage! And now that she had been promoted to solo roles, her aunt's comments were even more caustic—this because of the multiplicity of notes and flowers that had arrived at the theater all last season and had continued to arrive during the months that the King's was dark. Her aunt destroyed the notes and parceled out the flowers among the other girls. On occasions when there had been jewelry as well, she had sent it back without delay and with no accompanying note.

Etienne interrupted Eugenie's thoughts by unlocking the front door. "Now remember . . ." he hissed as they came inside.

"You need not worry," Eugenie muttered, hoping against

hope that her aunt was still in the city. In another few moments
that particular hope was realized, and she was able to go to the
tiny room she had occupied since they had first arrived in
England. It was a great mercy not to face the barrage of
questions that were her portion every time she stirred out of the
house. Her aunt appeared to believe that the young men who
sent her the flowers, and the older ones who offered the
jewelry, had somehow divined her direction and were lying in
wait for her. Furthermore, each time a jewel was brought to
her dressing room, Vivienne appeared to believe that she had
encouraged the sender.

"If Jean-Paul or his mother, the Comtesse de la Vigne, were
aware of your sly looks at the boxes—and do not trouble to
deny it, I have seen them with my own eyes—she would forbid
the banns!"

"Am I supposed to dance with my eyes closed?" Eugenie
had retorted once—only once. She put a hand to her cheek,
feeling in retrospect the stinging blow her aunt had given her.
She could also hear the storm of invective that had followed.
She had been accused of having the morals of an alley cat!

"I suppose," her aunt had railed, "you would like to go to
one of those young men who stare at you each time you appear.
You imagine, I expect, that they look upon you as 'the nymph'
or 'the goddess' they mention in their foolish notes. You would
see how quickly they would bring you to earth! You do
remember what happened to that stupid little bit of muslin you
called friend—Mary Clare?"

Poor, poor Mary Clare.

Eugenie winced as she thought of her best and, until
recently, her only friend among the dancers. She was the child
of a fond and foolish mother who, Eugenie suspected, was no
better than she should be. She accompanied Mary Clare to the
theater each night and ordered that she remain in the house
until she could return for her. However, there were many times
when Mary Clare waited in vain and, at length, called a
hackney and went home alone. It was only natural that
eventually she would find one who would accompany her to
that home, or at least make the offer. She had been wise
enough to refuse—until the rainy night when a particularly
personable young nobleman had offered to drive her there.
Despite Eugenie's warnings, she had shyly accepted the offer.

Since there were performances at the King's Theatre on Tuesdays and Saturdays only, Eugenie had not seen Mary Clare until the following Saturday. She had arrived without her mother and with the young nobleman, looking half defiant, half pleased. A large diamond glittered on her finger, and she had worn a sable tippet. Her mother had come to fetch her after the theater, screaming at her and letting everyone know what they had guessed already—that Mary Clare had not returned home for four nights. The older woman had demanded the name of her lover and, receiving no satisfaction, had slapped Mary Clare on either side of her face, calling her ''doxy'' and warning her that she would live to rue the day!

Inevitably her words had proved prophetic. Mary Clare had continued wearing beautiful clothes, continued her liaison with the nobleman, and continued dancing until she swooned on stage and had been carried off, weeping later because her lover had deserted her. She had been expecting his child, and it died with her when she threw herself under a passing carriage.

Eugenie shuddered, and then she shuddered again as in her mind's eye she saw the handsome face and stalwart body of the young man who had come to her aid in the museum. The feelings he had aroused in her had been unlike any she had ever experienced. She had heard him call after her and had had an almost overwhelming desire to tear herself from Etienne's grasp and run back to him. Now a sob escaped her; she would never see him again and should not want to see him.

Was she not betrothed to the Comte de la Vigne, dearest Jean-Paul, who had shyly told her that though their marriage had been arranged by her aunt and his mother, it was much to his liking. And she, knowing no other young man, had been able to admit that she, too, was satisfied with the arrangement. She was no longer satisfied! Beside that darkly handsome young man who had stood between her and that beast in the museum, Jean-Paul, almost as fair as herself, had suddenly become naught but a shadow! It was wrong to wish that the stranger of the museum might attend the ballet, wrong to hope that he might see her, recognize her, and come back to the Green Room, but what would be the use of that? She would, as always, merely pass through there—to be escorted to a waiting gig by either her cousin or her aunt, and unfortunately it was generally her aunt.

"I would stay and I would speak to him," Eugenie whispered defiantly, and then an unfamiliar anger possessed her. It did no good to speculate on what might happen if he did attend the ballet and did recognize her. She was not in command of her life—no, not even though she had, since the age of fourteen, when she had become a member of the corps de ballet, contributed more money to the household than had her aunt in all her years of laboring for the mantua makers! The monies she earned were pocketed by Aunt Vivienne, and she had not so much as a *sou* to spend on her clothes! Save for the coat and gown she wore to the theater and nowhere else, her garments were made-over hand-me-downs or fashioned from the scraps her aunt received from the mantua makers for whom she still worked. *He* must have noticed them, must have believed her poor, even poverty-stricken!

Suddenly the walls of her room were blurred by tears. Flinging herself down on the bed, Eugenie began to weep as she had never wept in her entire life, not even when her dear grandmother had died, not even when her equally dear dancing master, Pierre de Lascelles, had died. Indeed, it seemed to her that if she could not see the stranger of the museum again, life would be joyless, meaningless, and a heavy burden.

"Well," the Honorable Simon said as he and his nephew settled themselves in a box at the King's Theatre. "Can you imagine a better location than this—to view *Alcestis?* And, if you tell me that in years past seats were situated on the stage, I will say that it is far better to watch the dancers—er, the ballet—from this vantage point. We are right over the stage, as you can see."

He frowned as he looked at his nephew's brooding visage. "I vow that you are in a rare taking, my lad. In fact, I do not believe I have ever seen so virulent a case of the green sickness. If it continues, I will suggest that you be blooded!"

Thurston essayed a laugh that died a-borning, as in his mind's eye he saw the lovely face that had not ceased to haunt his waking hours and disturb his nights since what he was beginning to call their "fatal encounter" in the museum.

His uncle's efforts to rouse him from his near stupor had been largely unsuccessful. Of what use was it to visit the Houses of Parliament or to wander through St. Paul's or even to meet the Prince Regent, as they had last Saturday at

Boodles? His Royal Highness had been both gracious and cordial. He had welcomed Thurston to London and invited him to a ball at Carlton House for Thursday week. The invitation had arrived this morning.

Yet though he had professed himself delighted to attend, he could think of the ball only in terms of the beautiful girl from the museum. If he could have gone to a country dance with her or been her partner for a cotillion—he was sure she must be grace itself on the dance floor—he would have been delighted. As it was, delight and excitement were two words that had seemingly deserted his vocabulary. He doubted that he would ever use either of them again. He had returned to the museum on four separate occasions, wandering through the rooms, seeing nothing—not even the famous, if illegible, Magna Carta in a library full of rare volumes that must have fascinated one who at Oxford had been called a "budding bibliophile." Yet nothing had attracted him, and though he had seen and had even been approached by several unattached females, his search had been in vain. And would she remain in his mind forever? It was a daunting thought—to wander through life always looking and never, never satisfied.

"Ah, there she is!" his uncle murmured, passing a quizzing glass to Thurston.

His nephew regarded him blankly. "Who, sir?"

"The little Wilson . . . that box across the house. A sweet armful, our Harriett, if a bit overblown by now."

Thurston, seeing an attractive young woman in an extremely low-cut gown ablaze with jewels, looked with lackluster eyes upon a face that while not precisely beautiful, was bright and animated. He returned the glass to his uncle with a long sigh. "She is not to my liking."

"You do not know her. I can tell you that you'd be well advised to court her. She is known to be very kind to young men, and she is certainly experienced in the art of dalliance. If anyone could help you forget this unknown, fair . . ." He paused as his nephew regarded him with a burgeoning horror. "But what's amiss, lad?"

"I love her," Thurston said in a low, trembling voice. "I will never love anyone else and to . . . to mention *her* in the same breath with that . . . that courtesan . . ." He shuddered and rose. "I must go."

"I beg you will sit down!" Mr. Sorrell said sharply. "The curtain is rising." He caught the bottom of his nephew's coat. "And I charge you, remember where you are, please."

"I . . . am sorry, sir." Flushing, Thurston sat down, only half hearing the overture. The curtain rose, and applause greeted an artful set showing the great court of King Admetus's palace. He gazed at the scene with the same disinterest he had accorded music, which, until this moment, he had really loved. And then, as the mourning Alcestis appeared with her troop of dark-clad maidens, Thurston sighed. He could wish the opera were beginning rather than ending. He longed to be out and away.

"Ah," his uncle whispered. "She is here, the little Montfalçon, and look, she has been given a solo. There, you must watch. I tell you, she is the very essence of grace." He thrust his glass at Thurston. "Look . . . there, third from the left. Is she not a picture?"

He had need to remember his manners, remember that he was his uncle's guest. He looked in the direction Mr. Sorrell had indicated and dutifully brought the glass to his eye and stiffened, barely stifling a cry of amazement, as his incredulous gaze fell on the upturned face of the girl he had seen in the museum! As he stared at her she whirled, and kneeling before the sorrowing queen, she lifted supplicating arms, and as his uncle had said, she was the very essence of grace!

"Who is she?" he demanded hoarsely.

"Her name is Marie . . . Marie de Montfalçon. Of course, it is an assumed name, assumed for the stage. But is she not beautiful?"

"Marie de Montfalçon," Thurston whispered. "And she . . . she is an opera dancer?"

Simon Sorrell regarded him amusedly. "Yes, of course. She does not sing. Those that sing do not have her grace of movement. Mademoiselle de Montfalçon is advancing rapidly in her career, for all this is only her second season as a soloist. When she was merely one of the corps de ballet, she stood out from the others, and now . . . I have it on very good authority that the Vestris would like to spread broken glass beneath her feet." He lowered his voice. "I wonder if the dragon who guards her will be as vigilant this season? We will go to the Green Room after the performance and hope for the best.

Would you like that, my boy?"

"Yes," Thurston said. "I would enjoy meeting an opera dancer."

Mr. Sorrell patted his nephew on the back. "Ah, am I to hope that you are recovering from your recent malaise? I thought that so many flowers from the . . . garden of love must help to raise your spirits."

"Are they?" Thurston demanded.

He received a blank look. "Are they . . . what?"

"Flowers from the . . . the garden of love?"

"Bless you!" Mr. Sorrell laughed low in his throat. "Of course they are. I doubt that there is one amongst that throng on stage—with the possible exception of La Vestris and the little Montfalçon, who has not a marquess, a viscount, or a baronet on her string. But I beg you will turn your attention to the stage." He glanced at his nephew and smiled. He had no need to proffer that bit of advice. The lad was staring at the bevy of beautiful young girls as if he were in a dream of pleasure. He chuckled to himself. There had been moments in the past few days when he had been well on the way to believing that the madness of love, something he had always imagined to be apocryphal, might have, after all, several grains of truth in it, but judging from his nephew's swift recovery, it was obviously a fable. He turned his attention to the stage and the lovely little Mademoiselle de Montfalçon and the warming fantasies her slender form and beautiful face invariably invoked.

Alcestis was a long opera, even though some part of its score had been cut in order that the ballets might be extended. Thurston, sitting impatiently through three acts dealing mainly with the heavyset soprano's efforts to exchange places in Hades with her more slender mate, was happy only when he could glimpse the incredibly beautiful girl who had, he could still admit, stolen his heart at the museum. Yet blended with his exultation at finding her again was a strain of disappointment. She had seemed so shy, so gentle, and so *innocent*! Could innocence exist in such an atmosphere, he wondered dismally, and could not rejoice at an answer based on all his uncle had not scrupled to tell him regarding the lives of actresses and dancers. There were also his memories of Oxford soirees wherein various of his friends had spoken of wild weekends in London with one or another fair, frail maiden from the theater or the opera. As a group, they had much in common with Miss Wilson, who was allowing all manner of liberties from her current escort who, his uncle again told him, was a duke.

Yet on the other hand, Mademoiselle de Montfalçon was certainly well guarded. In addition to her hasty departure from the museum, there had been his uncle's disgruntled mention of dragons. And was Uncle Simon interested in her? The answer to that question was only too obvious. He shuddered. To imagine this nubile beauty suffering the caresses of a dissipated, middle-aged man, whose previous excesses had, in effect, added years to his age, revolted Thurston. However, he could cheer himself with the thought that Simon Sorrell's pursuit had proved as futile as his own on that day at the museum.

"Well, they have taken their bows, my boy." His uncle's voice cut through the applause. "Will you wish to accompany me back to the Green Room?"

Thurston arose with alacrity. "Oh, yes!" he said eagerly. "I . . ." Then, meeting Mr. Sorrell's amused gaze, he felt singularly gauche. In a belated effort to achieve some modicum of sophistication, he drawled, "I should like to see some of the performers and give them my congratulations." Unfortunately, before his uncle could respond, he added with an excitement he could not suppress, "Would it be possible to . . . to meet some of the . . . uh, them."

"Sometimes yes, sometimes no," Mr. Sorrell answered. "I myself am interested in but one. I need not tell you which."

"The little Montfalçon," Thurston muttered.

"Quite! And this season I mean to beard the dragon in her den." So saying, he moved out of the box.

Thurston, following him along the corridor, was conscious of a deep desire to confront him and shove both fists into his jaded eyes, while another wiser part of his mind attempted to assure him that an opera dancer hardly merited such a show of anger.

The Green Room was an oblong chamber hung with portraits of actors and singers from the past and present. Thurston recognized a pastel of Garrick and another of John Kemble. There was also a current portrait of Madame Catalani. A marble bust on an adjacent bookcase proved to be that of Shakespeare. There were several chairs pushed against the walls, but no one was occupying them. It would have been difficult indeed to remain seated with so many people, mainly gentlemen, milling about, eager eyes fixed on the door through which the performers must come.

Thurston wondered if there was enough space for them to emerge and wished that he and his uncle had the privilege of visiting Miss de Montfalçon in her dressing room—but even had they been allowed to go backstage, Mr. Sorrell, through the bribing of the stage-door custodian, had learned that her quarters were strictly guarded by either her cousin or his mother, the formidable Madame de Champfleury, a name, his uncle had said, obviously must be assumed, for no opera dancer could claim a relationship to one of the most ancient and aristocratic clans in France.

"Ah," Mr. Sorrell said, "there she is."

His thoughts dispersing immediately, Thurston looked eagerly about the room, and, seeing no one resembling the dancer, asked disappointedly, "Where?"

"That woman near the door. Lord, Lord, to think that she is related to that beautiful creature! Unless I miss my guess, she has more than a *soupçon* of peasant blood, and in her eternal black, she certainly dresses like a peasant!"

"There . . . such a dragon," Mr. Sorrell grumbled. "I think of Pluto guarding the gates to Hades, or rather of his three-headed dog, or perhaps Argus of the hundred eyes might be a better description—for surely she sees all."

"Where is she?" Thurston demanded, still confused by the ever-increasing number of people milling about him.

"I beg you'll not have me resort to the vulgarity of a pointing finger," his uncle drawled. "She is, as I told you, pressed against the wall—by the door."

Finally Thurston spotted the squat, dark woman in her sable garments, and noting the set of her mean little mouth, his heart fell. "That woman is . . . *her* aunt?"

"Yes, indeed, a blood relation, I understand. If she did not lay claims to being a refugee, one could almost imagine her sitting by the guillotine and watching the heads roll. However, I understand from an—er—acquaintance, who also dances in the corps de ballet, that she is not above venting her spleen on her niece. She has the reputation of being half guardian, half jailer. And directly when Mademoiselle de Montfalçon comes through the door, you will see her spring into action. Ah—and here she comes!''

She was wearing a dark cloak and a close-fitting satin turban of a blue that was a match for her beautiful eyes. Several rounds of applause and cheers greeted her, and she was quickly surrounded by a group of admiring young men who had, perforce, to move back quickly as the short, dark woman, one hand clasping her niece's arm, barreled her way through the assembled gallants, dealing hurtful jabs with both elbows, effectively discouraging and dispersing them.

The girl with her did not look to the right or to the left but kept her eyes lowered as if, in the company of her formidable guardian, she were afraid to open them—but open them she must! Hardly aware of what he was doing, Thurston pushed and shoved his way toward her, unmindful of angry remonstrances and a few cries of pain. Finally he was close enough to say, ''Mademoiselle de Montfalçon!'' in tones loud enough to bring him a fiery glance from her chaperone and a startled look from the girl, a look of immediate and delighted recognition.

''You!'' she exclaimed, and smiled up at him, only to be pulled back by her suddenly furious companion. In another few seconds the girl and her charge had gained the door and were gone.

''Good God!'' Simon Sorrell's voice was loud in Thurston's ears. ''You will not be telling me . . .''

There were tears in Thurston's eyes as he nodded. ''Yes, it was *she*,'' he said huskily. ''And she . . . she knew me.''

''That was obvious.'' His uncle nodded. ''obvious to me and obvious to her watchdog. I think you were guilty of a tactical error, my lad. Unless I miss my guess, the guards will be doubled around the prisoner.''

In the carriage that was bringing them back to Chelsea, Vivienne, her hand hurtfully tight on Eugenie's arm, said angrily, ''Who was he?''

''I do not know,'' the girl said with a sigh.

''Do not tell me that!'' her aunt snapped. ''He knew you, and you knew him. I want to know how and when, you little fool!''

"I am tired, Aunt Vivienne. It was a long evening. I wish to rest," Eugenie murmured.

"You will not rest until I hear the whole of it from you. *Where* did you meet him? If I must keep you up until dawn, I will have the truth!"

"There is no truth!" Eugenie flashed, hating her aunt as she had never hated her before. She knew that eventually she must needs tell her the truth, but in a careful way, so as not to implicate Etienne. It was bad enough with one enemy in the house. If Etienne were to become her tormentor as well, her dancing might suffer. A thought that both shocked and pleased her went through her mind—if she and that young man were together as Mary Clare and her lover had been . . . But that way lay destruction! She cried out in pain as her aunt's hard hand descended on her cheek.

"I have asked you a question. I demand an answer," Vivienne shrilled.

"I . . ." Eugenie began, and paused. The carriage was drawing to a stop. As she and her aunt descended the steps she had a craven desire to flee—but that, of course, was impossible. There was no place to go but into the house, which was as much a prison as if there were bars at the windows. She went inside, her aunt following her, and then there was the ritual of removing her good bonnet, her good cloak, and her one good gown and giving them into her aunt's keeping.

Finally, arrayed in her peignoir, she steeled herself to face and parry her aunt's questions. Still, she stiffened as Vivienne, entering the room, sent the door slamming against the wall. She confronted Eugenie, her black eyes radiating ire and suspicion. "And now, I charge you, tell me about the man—and I warn you, I shall know if you are lying."

It was an old threat, one that had terrified a younger Eugenie, who, no matter what punishment lay in store for her, had always blurted out the required response. And as she had, when she was younger, Eugenie looked down, saying meekly, "I met him once . . . only once . . . at the British Museum. Etienne and I were arguing, and he thought I was being intimidated by a stranger. He tried to intervene, but Etienne explained the situation and the man apologized and went on to look at the exhibits."

"That is all?" Vivienne demanded suspiciously.

"It is all," Eugenie said. "I expect he must have been extremely surprised when he saw me tonight."

"You are sure that is all?" Vivienne pursued.

"I would swear to it on my mother's head," Eugenie said steadily. "Now . . . may I please go to bed, Aunt Vivienne? I am very tired."

Her aunt's hard, black gaze lingered on her face. "Yes," she said grudgingly, "you may go to bed. However, if I see you so much as exchange a word with that young man—"

"I do not know him," Eugenie said, glad that she was now telling the truth.

Her aunt's eyes still remained on her face. "I will question Etienne also, and if there is something that you have not yet told me, best reveal it now or it will go hard with you. Of all things in this world, I most abominate liars."

"I have told you everything that there is to tell," Eugenie said steadily.

As Vivienne left the room Eugenie could not restrain a fit of trembling. Never before had she lied to her aunt, but as the woman had implied, the repercussions would undoubtedly be most uncomfortable were her falsehoods revealed. Consequently it was necessary to compound her so-called crime and alert her cousin to her deviations from the truth. She did not believe that her aunt would approach Etienne on the matter until the morning. She had worked hard all day, and undoubtedly she would retire as soon as she entered her chamber.

Some ten minutes later Eugenie, listening tensely for footsteps in the hall beyond her door, decided that she had gauged her aunt's actions accurately. She had gone to bed.

Opening her door cautiously and wincing at a rusty squeal of unoiled hinges, she lifted her head, straining to hear any untoward sounds from her aunt's chamber, which lay two doors down the hall. Satisfied that she still heard nothing, she crept across the corridor to the larger chamber that Etienne occupied. Going inside, she heard the sounds of deep breathing, interrupted every so often by a light snore. It took some few minutes to rouse her cousin, and several more to placate him for having interrupted his slumbers. Yet after she had recounted her conversation with his mother, he was obviously relieved.

"That was clever of you to make up such a tale and on the spur of the moment," he said admiringly.

"It was necessary," Eugenie whispered. "And you promise you'll not betray me when she questions you tomorrow?"

"Of course I will not," he assured her. "Do you suppose I want the flat of her hand on my face?"

"I did not think you would," Eugenie murmured. "And it must remain our secret."

"It will be ours alone, my dear," he promised fervently.

Once in her room again, Eugenie, crawling into the hard little bed she had occupied during all her years in the house, lay awake a long time, caught in the grip of the excitement she had managed to conceal from her aunt. One of her very fondest hopes had been realized. *He* had come to the opera, and *he* had seen her dance and had come backstage afterward—but would he come again?

Judging from the chagrin she had seen reflected on his countenance, she was sure he would . . . and then? She sighed. Even if he were to come, her aunt would be there, girding her loins for battle. Yet there were times when Etienne accompanied her—and it might not be difficult to persuade him to let her at least talk to . . . but she did not even know his name. Still, if they were to converse, undoubtedly he would introduce himself and it would be lovely to exchange a few words with him. However, as soon as this hope filled her mind, she groaned. The fact that he had approached her would render her aunt very wary, and it was unlikely that she would permit Etienne to accompany her.

No, she would come herself and guard her as if she were a prisoner. And in effect that was exactly her status in this household—a prisoner in a prison. It was a thought that had occurred to her earlier in the evening, she recalled bitterly. Yet she had heard that all prisons were not as fast as they were purported to be, and the fact that they *had* met again was propitious—especially since she had read disappointment in his eyes when her aunt had so hurriedly whisked her out of the Green Room.

Though generally she was not conceited, Eugenie thought it quite possible that he might want to see her again. Certainly she wanted to see him again, and after all, they had met accidently the first time because Etienne had been in the cellar of the museum. It was not impossible, given her cousin's penchant for wandering off on his own, that circumstances might unite to facilitate another such encounter. With a little gurgle of happy laughter she slid under the covers and was quickly asleep.

CHAPTER THREE

ON A SATURDAY night in the second week of January, Thurston arrived at his uncle's house and was greeted by his butler with a properly regretful look. On taking Thurston's hat and cloak, he said, "Mr. Sorrell is not feeling his best, sir. He asked if you would come up to his bedroom."

Thurston said concernedly, "Is he very ill?"

"It is a quinsy, sir, no more."

Hurrying up the stairs in the wake of the butler, Thurston found his uncle lying in bed, a handkerchief to his nose. "I am sorry you are not well, sir," he said, hoping against hope that his uncle had not canceled his box at the opera.

"I thank you for your solicitude," Simon croaked. "You will take my box tonight, of course, though I wonder you are not weary of so fruitless a quest. Sir Lancelot confronted with dragons and ogres fared better, I'm thinking."

Thurston grimaced. "I live in hope that that creature she calls aunt will break her leg or, better yet, her neck."

Simon laughed weakly. "Such vehemence, my dear Thurston, and so much stamina as well. I am fond of music and I confess to a similar fondness for some of the stage decorations, but even I would balk at two operas a week for . . . how long has it been? Six weeks, as I live, and I imagine you are prepared to remain there as long as the season lasts . . . and with so little encouragement too. I vow, it boggles the mind!"

"To see her is enough," Thurston said softly.

"Ah, youth, ardent youth . . . but you are not quite the loser, are you? It seems to me that you are bent on proving the truth of that old adage—'Lucky at cards, unlucky at love.'

Damn me if I would not prefer the former—if I could have such a winning streak! 'Tis amazing that you can find anyone brave enough to play with you!"

"I have lost from time to time," Thurston reminded him. "You will remember Thursday last . . ."

"You have won considerably more than you have lost. Why, man, you have become tolerably rich, which makes me believe in that old adage, 'To him who hath shall be given.'"

Thurston said somberly, "But I do not have what I want the most."

"And you've not seen others equally fair? It seemed to me that you were developing a liking for little Miss Wickwarre, a charming girl. I would cite her background, save that it could make no impression on you."

"Miss Wickwarre? Do I know her?" Thurston demanded confusedly.

Simon chuckled. "You stood up with her for the cotillion at Almack's last Wednesday night. She is fair . . . reddish curls, brown eyes."

"Oh, yes, I remember. She has very little to say for herself." Thurston shrugged.

"My dear lad, had she the wisdom of a Voltaire, would you have listened?" Simon questioned. "You are besotted with this creature. Indeed, I begin to believe that she has cast a spell on you."

"You are also fond of her, sir," Thurston countered.

"Yes, I admit that I do find her most enchanting to watch, but I have ceased knocking my head against stone guardians. Tonight would have been my first visit to the opera in three weeks, if you will remember—and I have not attended both performances in any week since the season began. Indeed, my poor Thurston, I have come to the conclusion that the more you present yourself there, the stronger will be the chains that bind your fair one. That woman, it would appear, has her own ax to grind. I am sure of it, the damned peasant! And remember that she is blood aunt to that child—but, of course, you do not want to marry her, do you?"

Thurston reddened. "I wish to know her better, sir. And yes, if she is all that I happen to believe she is, I think I might very well wish to wed her."

"You have lost your senses!" His uncle sat up straight. "My dear lad! One does *not* marry these charming little creatures.

They are butterflies or, rather, mayflies. They live for a day and *pouf*!" Simon snapped his fingers. "They vanish and another takes their place."

Thurston glared at Simon. "She is not of their ilk, sir. Can you not see how far above the others she is?"

"Come, lad, I admit she's beautiful. She is also graceful, a fine little dancer, and bound to go far in her profession, but I beg you will be sensible. I know you consider yourself her knight errant and would wear her garter on your sleeve, but you'd be advised to make her your mistress rather than your wife—that is, if you can ever manage to foil her resident dragon."

"The fact that there is a resident dragon has served to convince me that she is no ordinary opera dancer—actually I needed no convincing. Her manners, her appearance, everything about her tells me that she is gently bred, a lady."

"She might well be a lady or, rather, of gentle birth, born, of course, on the other side of the blanket. Furthermore I have an idea that the crone who guards her is angling for a higher bidder than yourself, lad. She will want a title, and I would not be surprised were she primed to capture a marquess or even a duke. However, I would bet this house and all that it contains that her plans do not include matrimony."

"I think I must be going, sir," Thurston responded coldly. "I hope you will be feeling better soon."

"And I hope that you enjoy the opera. It is a great pity that you cannot enjoy *la petite* Mademoiselle de Montfalçon as well." Simon grinned.

Thurston, moving to the door, closed it quietly behind him. Simon chuckled. It pleased him mightily that his handsome young nephew had had to endure twelve performances —tonight would mark his thirteenth evening at the opera house, and given the double onus of the number and the aunt, he did not imagine that he would be any more fortunate on this night than he had been on all the others. "A stone wall," he muttered, and slid down under the covers, wondering when Thurston would weary of his vain pursuit. He had laid a bet on it with one Sir John Hammond and had also established a time limit of fourteen weeks, comprising twenty-eight performances in all. He could, he thought, have let it run for the length of the season, so sure was he that the girl's tyrannical aunt would never miss a Tuesday or a Saturday.

"Ah, Eugenie, 'ave you seen 'im?" Teresa Mancini, a dancer who had once dressed beside her when they were in the corps de ballet, stuck her head into Eugenie's tiny dressing room. Her eyes, as black as her hair, sparkled with merriment. " 'E's alone tonight. The older 'un's not wi' 'im."

Eugenie, breathless from her chores as a Fury in the second act of *Orpheus et Euridice*, looked up and blushed. "Yes, I did," she admitted.

" 'E's so 'andsome," Teresa continued. "An' yer aunt's not wi' you tonight."

"No, she's prostrate with one of her headaches, but alas, my cousin is here in her stead," Eugenie explained with a sigh.

"But per'aps 'e'll let you talk to 'im." Teresa winked. "I would not mind exchangin' a word or two wi' yer cousin. Per'aps I might even flirt wi' 'im."

Hope rose and fell in Eugenie's breast. "No, he will make me leave as soon as I have changed my clothes. He is much too afraid of Aunt Vivienne to be of any help."

"Oh, poor Eugenie," Teresa said sympathetically. "I do think it's a fair shame the way she keeps you under lock 'n key like a prisoner. You ought to rebel . . . if 'twas me, I'd tell 'er a thing or two."

Eugenie laughed wryly. "I have not the ammunition to wage such a battle."

Teresa also laughed. "Well, I do 'ope you'll be able to speak wi' 'im, at least. Per'aps yer cousin'll be late."

"No, he will not be late," Eugenie said regretfully. "He is in the Green Room. My aunt insisted that he remain there throughout the performance."

" 'E's not there now." Teresa grinned.

"He's not?" Eugenie asked in some surprise.

"No, I 'ad reason to go there a few minutes ago 'n it's empty."

"Well, he did want to do something other than accompany me to the theater tonight. He and my aunt had quite a few words over it, but in the end he capitulated. He might have slipped out for a nonce, but you may be sure that he will return before the final curtain," Eugenie said, ruthlessly snuffing out the spark of hope that had risen in her breast.

Her cousin would not dare let her speak to the man she now

knew as Thurston Sorrell, thanks to a huge basket of roses that had arrived for her on the day after their brief meeting in the Green Room.

Her aunt, of course, had read the card and immediately connected him with Mr. Simon Sorrell, whose flowers she had been sending back all last season and part of this one. She had not hesitated to place his relative in the same category, and she had taken a special pleasure in sending back the flowers. Furthermore, since Mr. Thurston Sorrell repaired to the Green Room after every performance, her aunt had actually helped her dresser remove her garments as hastily as possible. Sometimes her face stung as with a rough rag her aunt ruthlessly wiped off her makeup. And meanwhile the time was drawing closer when she must needs wed Jean-Paul. Her aunt and his mother were speaking about a May wedding—and May was only four months away!

Of late, each time she had gone to church on a Sunday, she had prayed that something would happen to forestall their plans.

"I do not want to marry him . . ." she murmured.

"Marry him?" Teresa echoed, her eyes wide. " 'E's not like to ask you, love. 'Tisn't often a fine gentleman like 'im'd marry one o' us."

Eugenie looked up and blushed. She had forgotten that Teresa was still there. "I was not thinking of him," she explained. "I am betrothed."

"Oh, are you?" Teresa asked delightedly. "Well, an' am I to know 'oo 'e might be?"

"His name's Jean-Paul."

"I expect 'e's French like yerself?"

"Yes, he is."

"Well, that's all right 'n tight, isn't it, an' if ye'd like to pass the other along to me, I'd not be complainin'." Teresa laughed. "I'd best go," she added. "I've got to be a Lost Soul . . ." She went out humming a snatch of the music to herself.

Eugenie laughed and then sighed. She was more than a little envious of Teresa and the other girls in the ballet. Most of them came and went as they pleased—though eventually they might be constrained by a lover or, on occasion, a husband. Yet even so, they did have fun! Their talk was of fine cafés and intimate suppers in private houses. Often they compared notes, and

their laughter was low and insinuating. She had heard scraps of
conversations that had brought a blush to her cheek and at the
same time had aroused her curiosity concerning love between
man and woman—but, of course, it was not really love; it was
merely amorous dalliance, and she must needs remember the
sad fate of Mary Clare.

Still, for every Mary Clare there was a wise Teresa who
drifted from lover to lover like a bee among flowers and
seemed never the worse for the experience. She, on the other
hand, was treated like a prisoner—for all she was considered
one of the best dancers in London, the equal of Marie Vestris,
who hated her accordingly. Yet she had not one good gown to
her name, and even the cloak she wore to the theater was three
seasons old. She could not imagine that matters would change
once she was wed. Jean-Paul might love her, but he had
already exhibited signs of jealousy and had insisted that once
they were wed, she must not dance.

"But dancing is my life!" she had told him, only to have
him laugh and say, "I will be your life, my love."

If courtesy had not prevented it—courtesy and considera-
tion for his feelings—she would have answered, "But you are
not my life and never will be. I am in love with someone else. I
am in love with a man I see only from afar but who dominates
my dreams each night, and every time I see him, I feel like one
who, having been lost in the desert, has come upon a spring of
fresh water." She sighed, and chiding herself for being
foolishly romantic, she called to her dresser and prepared for
the next act.

Etienne was not present when Eugenie came into the Green
Room, and at first she did not see Thurston Sorrell, either
—and while she stood looking for him, gradually she became
surrounded by numbers of gentlemen all complimenting her on
her performance. It was an experience she could not like, and
one that her aunt had always spared her. However, at this
moment she was unprotected, and men with avid eyes and
hands that clutched her arm or crushed her fingers and with
voices that all said the same things, combined to confuse her.
Then, suddenly, there was a tall presence behind her, protecting her, easing her out of the crowd, not heeding the protests
that followed, and someone said, "Miss de Montfalçon has
promised to let me take her home."

A protest rose to her lips. "My cousin," she murmured in a

voice so low that it was lost amidst the babble of congratulations, of protest, and then, almost before she knew it, she was outside in the cool, frosty air, and Thurston Sorrell was leading her to his waiting carriage.

"My cousin will call for me," she said, albeit reluctantly.

He came to a stop just at the door his footman was holding open for them. "Your cousin appears to have deserted the fort," he said half humorously, half tensely. "And it is up to his second in command to see you home. May he? I should have asked before, but it was necessary to rescue you first."

She looked up into his dark eyes and thought she saw little flames in their black depths. All manner of words came to her lips, but she could only voice six of them. They were, "Thank you, I should be delighted."

"Would you like to go home immediately, or might you not prefer a small repast?" He paused, but before she could respond, he continued, "In my lodgings there is chicken and champagne."

A negative trembled on her lips, but she could not bring herself to utter it. He was mentioning food she seldom ate, and though she did drink wine, she had never tasted champagne. It was far too dear for her aunt's purse, but actually none of this really mattered. It was the tantalizing thought of spending a little time with him, after all these frustrating weeks of seeing him from afar or being summarily hustled out of her dressing room by a determined and hostile Aunt Vivienne. She said hesitantly, "I should like that, I think, but I must not stay very long."

"You will not stay long, I promise you," he said on a breath, hardly believing in her acceptance. Indeed, he could compare himself to the sculptor Pygmalion who, gazing so long at his marble creation, saw her suddenly become a living, breathing entity! And had Pygmalion, in common with himself, wanted to take her in his arms and never let her go? And had he, again like himself, felt that he was living in a dream from which he must all too soon awaken?

Thurston's lodgings were in the front of the house and were reached through a private entrance at its side, a convenience he had never appreciated quite so much as when he produced his key and let Eugenie into the small hall. A candle was burning on a table set against the wall, its flame illuminating the door to

the sitting room. He held it open for Eugenie. She hesitated a
brief second before moving across the threshold into a room
rendered less shadowy by the candelabra on the mantelshelf
and by the mirror that backed them.

On a table beside a long sofa was the repast he had
mentioned and which Graves had prepared every opera night
only to remove it in the morning, untouched. Thurston did not
feel hungry now. He wanted only to gaze at the girl whom he
had, until this enchanted moment, seen but once. He could not,
would not, count the times he had watched her from his box at
the opera or glimpsed her so briefly in the Green Room
—watching impotently while her aunt ruthlessly dragged her
out.

Indeed, he was hard put to believe that he was not dreaming,
but of course, he was not. She was there, looking shyly about
her. The flames from the candles were reflected in her eyes,
and he, removing her cloak, wanted to put his arms around her
and kiss her, not once, but many, many times! But again he
could not, because were he to embrace her, he might not be
able to let her go, this vision that had become a disturbing and
exciting reality.

He could scarce trust himself to speak, but the silence was
lengthening between them. He put her cloak over an adjacent
chair and said, "Will you not sit down?" He indicated the
couch.

"Thank you," she whispered.

Pygmalion's Galatea might have spoken thus, he thought, in
the voice she would have been using for the first time, unaware
of its potential, just as she was equally unaware of her power
over the sculptor—but he must not continue thinking in this
vein; it was passing ridiculous! "Will you let me serve you
some chicken?" he asked.

"Y-yes." Eugenie, aware that she was still standing, sat
down and was surprised at the softness of the couch. "That
. . . would be very nice," she continued hesitantly, over the
second thoughts that were passing rapidly through her mind,
thoughts dominated by her aunt and what she would have
thought had she been able to see her. She could envision her
anger and her shrill denunciations. She would need to endure
those when he brought her home that night. Indeed, she must
tell him that she could not remain there any longer, and

certainly she never ought to have agreed to come with him in the first place. Had she been swayed by Teresa's airy talk about cozy midnight suppers? No, she must needs be honest with herself! He and he alone had been the deciding factor. She had fallen into the habit of looking for him each time she danced, and he dominated her dreams and her waking hours as well.

She had been scolded more than once by the dancing master at the theater, who had sarcastically demanded if her wits were wandering when she failed to obey one or another of his instructions. Now, that which she had never believed possible had happened! They were together in this room, and she was half excited, half fearful, as she accepted a plate of sliced chicken and a glass of sparkling wine. He, too, had a glass of that bright wine, and now he raised it, saying, "To the most beautiful girl in the world."

"Oh." Eugenie had raised her own glass, but she said blushingly, "I could never drink to that. I . . . I will drink to you." She took a sip of the bubbling liquid and stared at him in surprise. "Oh, this is delicious . . . it must be like drinking sea foam!"

He regarded her in surprise. "Have you never drunk champagne, then?"

"Champagne?" she echoed. "Will you tell me that this is *champagne?*"

"It is"—he smiled—"or on this night I think I should prefer to call it nectar."

"Nectar?" she questioned.

"Surely you have heard of Jove's nectar, the nectar of the gods? That is what we are quaffing this night."

"Oh!" she exclaimed. "Now you are teasing me."

"No," he said gravely, his gaze catching and holding hers. "I am telling the truth. Will you have more?"

"Yes, it is good." She watched as he filled her glass again. "Teresa has told me about champagne, and she is quite right."

"Who is Teresa?"

"She is also a dancer—my best friend since Mary Clare . . . left." She frowned, wishing that she had not thought of Mary Clare at this precise moment—when nothing ought to cloud her happiness.

He had heard sadness in her tone, and it seemed to him that a shadow had passed across her face. He did not want her to be sad, not on this night. "To you!" he said gaily as he lifted his glass.

"But I will not drink to me!" she protested again. "I will drink to you."

"Let us touch glasses," he said, holding up his glass.

"Yes, we must." She loved the sound of that touching. It was like a tiny crystal bell. She loved the delicious bubbles that slid down her throat. And then, to her surprise, the glass was empty again. She had thought she was only sipping it. "It must dissolve like the dew on the grass," she told him. "The champagne."

"It does," he agreed, and filled her glass a third time. Again they touched glasses; again they drank to each other.

"You are so graceful," he said suddenly. "Everything you do . . . every movement you make, is grace personified. And on the stage you are an houri come to life . . . no, that is not a proper comparison. You are a fairy, Titania! How long have you been dancing?"

She looked at him in bemused surprise, and then was brought up short by her own surprise. She had imagined that he knew how long she had been dancing, that he knew everything about her, but though she had seen him every Tuesday and Saturday since the opera house had reopened, she had spoken to him only once, and that had been in the museum.

"I have been dancing since I was very little, though not professionally then." She began to tell him about her dearest Pierre. He listened very attentively, interrupting only when she described the procurer, whose face she had never forgotten. "Your dear Pierre should have killed him," he growled. However, he smiled as she explained her rescue but surprised her by commenting, "It seems you exchanged one manner of slavery for another."

"Oh, no, I love to dance," she said, sipping champagne from a glass that never seemed to become empty. "Love to dance . . . loved old Pierre. He died, you know." Tears filled her eyes. "First Grandmère and then Pierre . . ."

"And left you with that woman." He frowned.

"Yes, Aunt Vivienne . . . hate her. *Moi, je danse pour rien* . . . Every *sou* I earn, she takes. I have no clothes, *et maintenant* she will make me to marry Jean-Paul."

"Jean-Paul?" he asked quickly.

"*Oui*, Jean-Paul . . . le Comte . . . but I do not care."

"But I care," he said strongly. "She cannot make you marry him."

She gazed at him vaguely. "She will. They speak of a date and my bridal clothes, which she will make out of scraps. But I do not want to marry him. . . ."

"You will not marry him!" he said strongly. "You are mine."

"Oh, *non, non, non,* I belong to Tante Vivienne, must go to her now, you know. It is late, I think. . . ." She stood up quickly, and much to her surprise, the room appeared to be whirling around her. "Everything is . . . is going around." She stood on her tiptoes and whirled. "Around 'n' around 'n' around . . ." She giggled and fell unconscious at his feet.

Awakening to a headache that seemed pounding in back of both eyes, Eugenie opened them with difficulty and looked vaguely at a beige wall with a dark brown molding. Slowly the thought seeped into her consciousness that she ought not to be looking at such a wall, nor should she be feeling the smoothness of satin under one hand and a woolly blanket over her—a blanket but no rough cotton sheet beneath it. She moved and felt rather uncomfortable. Her skirt had worked its way up almost to her waist, but why would she be wearing a skirt in bed? She must still be dreaming. No, she could not be dreaming; she was definitely awake and looking ahead of her again. She blinked against a thin line of sunlight creeping through the heavy damask draperies at a window she had only just noticed, a window that had no right to be in her bedroom. . . . With a little squeak, she sat bolt upright, oppressed by a flood of fragmented images that increased the ache behind her eyes and sent a lump into her throat. The wall facing her was not in her bedroom, not in her house—*she* was not in her house. Where, then, was she?

"Where?" she murmured aloud.

"Ah, you are awake," commented a voice she knew, or rather thought she knew but could not quite place.

"Yes," she answered out of habit as she puzzled over the voice and then gasped as at the same time she realized that it was a man's voice and not the voice of Etienne. She looked up to find Thurston Sorrell, no longer in well-cut evening clothes but in a brown jacket, a high, marvelously tied cravat, a white shirt, a brocade vest, and stockinette trousers fastened under black boots. He was looking down at her gravely.

"Ohhhhh." The fragments of consciousness came together, providing illumination and, at the same time, sheer terror. "I . . . I have been here all the night?" she questioned in rising accents and wondered why she had asked him that question when she knew the answer. Before he could respond, she said, "I *have* been here all the night. Why did you not take me home?"

"My love"—he seemed as distressed as she—"I could not. I have not your direction, and even if I had known it, I could not have done so." He knelt beside the couch where she lay. "I beg you to forgive me. It was the champagne. I should not have given you so much of it and would not had I not been foxed."

"The champagne," she said. "Teresa told me that it . . . it can befuddle one?"

"Teresa is quite right," he said regretfully.

"I was . . . befuddled?" she whispered.

"You became unconscious," he explained. "I would have put you to bed, but I did not wish to . . . to take such a liberty. I fear your gown is sadly wrinkled."

"My gown," she repeated. A dry laugh escaped her. "That is the least of my worries. My aunt . . ." She put a trembling hand to her pounding throat. "She will . . ." She shuddered as images of Aunt Vivienne's distorted face streamed into her mind.

"She will do nothing," he said staunchly. "I will assume full responsibility for what has happened, unless . . ." He paused and swallowed.

"Unless?" she questioned.

He seized her hands. "Unless you would rather remain here with me, my dearest."

She looked down at him. His head was bowed. There had been longing in his tone, and also shame, for his inadvertent contribution to the situation in which she now found herself. It was not his fault, she knew. The blame rested securely on her shoulders. She had listened too closely to Teresa—to talk that had sown rebellion in her breast and a wish to be free of the tasks that were her portion when she was not dancing, the sewing and the mending of the garments her aunt brought home from the mantua maker. She wanted to enjoy herself; she had wanted to be with the young man, who seemed to love her, no matter what the consequences were, and perhaps Etienne could share some of that blame. Still, a pride she had not known she possessed rose in her mind.

She was not Teresa, a nameless waif from the streets. In her own right she was the Comtesse de Villiers, and her mother, unlike Vivienne, had been *born* a de Champfleury. Those with such a heritage did not cower in fear at facing a punishment, no matter how unmerited, and she would be punished. Aunt Vivienne would beat her, but she had been beaten many times before with switches, sticks, and fists. Undoubtedly this punishment would be worse than all the others put together. However, she could face it. Facing it was bred in her bones. According to her grandmother, the parents she had never known had gone to their deaths by guillotine with great bravery. They had held hands in the cart that bore them to the Place de la Liberté, and each had mounted the steps to the great blade as calmly as if they were going sight-seeing on some Paris street.

She said resolutely, "No, I think you must take me home, my dear. I will explain the situation to my aunt."

He rose. With a mixture of regret and admiration he said, "I will have my valet press your gown. There is water for your ablutions in the bedroom. As soon as you are ready, I will take you home, but you must also let me speak to your aunt."

"As you choose," she said gratefully, knowing instinctively that he had been hoping against hope that she would remain with him. He could not desire it any more than she, but she did not want to dwell overlong on her feelings. She slipped off the couch and hurried into the bedroom.

Despite her resolutions, Eugenie, staring out of the window of Thurston's post chaise, felt a pounding in her throat. Her aunt had not been well the previous night. She had been in a vile humor, and consequently she would be doubly angry at what had happened, but then, she was always angry. She wished she did not need to dwell on that coming confrontation. It would be pleasant to rejoice in Thurston's company for the last time and to experience, perhaps, his kisses on her mouth. She wished that he would kiss her. Just to be near him was exciting, and a kiss—but she dared not dwell on that. Indeed, it was well that he had not, for after today, she would probably never see him again. Her aunt would not relax her vigilance until she was forced into Jean-Paul's arms.

No, she thought suddenly. She would not marry Jean-Paul. She would not allow them to force her to it. It would be a betrayal of the love she had already given to the man beside her, the love she could never take back, never in her life! She tensed as the carriage drew to a stop.

Air bubbles of fear had joined the pounding in her throat. Eugenie swallowed convulsively as, with Thurston behind her, she went up the steps to her front door. Once more she was remembering the violent headaches from which her aunt suffered intermittently. They rarely lasted longer than a night, but afterward she seemed to hold everyone to blame for her suffering. Eugenie had a fugitive wish that she might run back to the post chaise and have Thurston drive her to the other end of the earth, but lacking that alternative, she hoped that it would be Etienne who would answer the bell she had just pulled. However, it was Aunt Vivienne, clad in deepest black, who appeared at the door. Her face was grim, but her eyes were blank as if she were indeed looking at a stranger.

"Yes?" she inquired coldly.

Eugenie drew herself up. "Aunt Vivienne," she began, only to have her aunt shake her head.

"Why do you call me by such a name? I do not know you."

With an audible gasp Thurston stepped forward. "Please, you must listen. Your niece—"

"I have no niece," came the stern retort.

Eugenie looked at her in horror. A pulse began to pound in her throat, and her heart was pounding heavily as well. She had seen and experienced her aunt's anger many times, but she had never seen her in this present mood. Her face looked as if it were carved from stone, and her tone of voice was that of a judge pronouncing sentence upon a malefactor. "But . . . Aunt Vivienne, if you would heed me, I—"

"What have you to say to me, you little whore?" Vivienne demanded contemptuously in French. "You, coming here with your lover! You ought to be stoned in the public square—you, fresh from your bed of shame and degradation!"

"It is not true!" Eugenie cried.

"Madame!" Thurston moved forward. "You have no right to speak to your niece in such a way. She has done nothing wrong. Last night your son did not come to fetch her . . . ."

Vivienne glared at him. "You lie. He was there from the beginning of the performance and waited for hours!"

"He was not there!" Eugenie cried. "I waited and waited."

"He was not there, Madame," Thurston said firmly. "Your niece—"

"I have said that I have no niece. I disown her. She is not fit to stand on my threshold. She is fit only to lie down with swine such as yourself. Have her and welcome. I have no use for trash." With a lightning move she thrust out both hands and brought them against Eugenie's shoulders.

With a startled cry the girl fell back and was caught by Thurston, who held her against him. "Damn you, you might have killed her, you ill-conditioned old witch!" he said in a low voice.

Vivienne drew herself up, saying icily, "One cannot kill the dead. She is dead, do you hear? She is dead." She moved back and closed the door. There was the sound of a bolt being shot into place.

"Oh, my love," Thurston began.

Eugenie looked up at him blankly, and breaking from his sheltering arms, she ran to the door. "She cannot lock me out!" she cried. "My clothing, my shoes . . . my *dancing* shoes. I must have them. And where . . . where can I go?" She pounded on the door. "Aunt Vivienne, hear me! I beg you to listen. I have done nothing, nothing wrong—do you hear, nothing! I fell asleep only, I slept the night on the couch . . . alone, alone, *alone,* do you understand? I am innocent of any wrongdoing. Let me in, let me in, let me in!" She knelt on the stoop, pulling futilely at the unyielding door. "Let me in!" She began to sob.

"Love . . ." Thurston caught the hysterical, frightened girl in his arms. Helping her to her feet, he held her against him. "It is useless, my poor love, do you not see? She has made up her mind, and you are more fortunate than you know . . . to be away from that terrible woman! I cannot believe that she is sane."

She looked at him blankly. Her fury had at last drained out of her. She said dully, "But my clothes are inside, everything that . . . that belongs to me, my books, the miniature of my mother, everything, do you not see? And there is no p-place for me to go and no money. I have nothing. All that I have earned, she has taken. Oh, God, God, what will happen to me?"

Anger such as he had never experienced in all his twenty-one years consumed Thurston. He gladly would have strangled the woman, and at the same time, to realize that this poor child had lived all her life with that cold, heartless tyrant filled him with horror. "My dearest love." Unmindful of a gathering knot of passersby, he kissed Eugenie's hair and her tear-wet cheeks and her woeful mouth. "You must calm down. Have you forgotten me, quite? You've not to be afraid when I am with you." He smoothed her tangled hair. "You will come with me, my love?"

He was not sure that she had heard him. She was still trembling and uttering frightened little cries. "I do not know what will happen now . . . I do not know."

"My angel, my dearest, listen to me," he said huskily. "I love you, have loved you from the first moment I saw you. I want you." He put his hand under her chin, tilting her face toward him. "Please, my own darling, come with me, live with me. Let me care for you."

She stared up at him. "You . . . cannot want me. You are trying only to be kind."

"No, no, no, my sweetest, I am not trying merely to be kind. I do want you, with all my heart, all my soul. I want to protect and cherish you. Please, please, my own darling, you have no need to be afraid when I am with you. You will come, will you not?"

Her trembling had not ceased, but she said, "Yes, I . . . I will if you really want me."

"My own darling, my beloved, how many ways can I say it to make you believe me? I love you, Eugenie. I have been in torment these last weeks because I could never tell you what was in my heart—there was always that woman hanging over you like some monstrous spider, weaving her web about you. But she is gone and we may both forget her. Will you try to do that?"

"Yes, I . . . I will try."

"And you do believe that I love you?"

She stared into his eyes. "I do believe you," she whispered. "And . . . and I love you too. I have loved you ever since I first saw you."

"Eugenie . . ." Thurston lifted her and, holding her against him, carried her to the waiting coach.

In the hour that followed the confrontation with her aunt, Eugenie, trying to sort out her feelings of anger, of confusion, and of love and gratitude, was largely unsuccessful. Even after

Thurston had taken her to an inn and bought her a sweet-tasting liqueur to calm her nerves, she was hard put to reassemble her thoughts. The suddenness of her expulsion from the only home she had ever known had not only shocked her, it also had drained her and confused her. She had never been very happy there—that home had once contained her grandmother, who had told her tales of her parents; and old Pierre Lascelles had come to see her there; and in her hard little bed she had read her beloved books, some of them the property of the parents she had never known. The books had formed a link with them, and now that link was broken. Undoubtedly her aunt would burn those books, as she had often threatened to do.

Tears rolled down her cheeks and were patted away by Thurston's linen handkerchief. "Come, my dearest darling," he said softly. "There is much that we must do."

She was startled to find that the coach had stopped. Then Thurston was lifting her down, and she found herself on a street where there were many little shops. She did not know why they were there, but nothing else mattered, for he was with her.

The next few hours passed like the dreams she had dreamed when reading Perrault's *Cabinet des fées*. The beggar maid had been transformed into a princess, through the enchantments of a fairy godmother, who had bought her gowns, beautiful gowns, some of a silk so fine that it might have been spun by enchanted spiders.

Price was never mentioned by the mantua makers who displayed the materials and suggested styles. However, she knew they were expensive from her own experience with those women for whom her aunt worked. He did not appear to consider the cost. He only insisted that they be finished as quickly as the seamstresses could work, and he made appointments for fittings. Then he bought her shoes and shoes and shoes of a kid so soft, it seemed to caress her feet, and there were dozens of pairs of silk and lisle stockings.

She came out of her half stupor to protest his extravagance, but he refused to listen and continued to buy her hats and gloves and reticules. By the time they reached his lodgings, she had a new cloak, a sable scarf, and a pearl necklace as well. There was also nightwear of the finest lawn and a silken negligee. Yet even while she was riding the crest of excitement, she was not entirely free from a lingering anguish and anger. Furthermore, though she hated to acknowledge it, even to herself, she was also experiencing fear—a fear that increased with each purchase and each fleeting, knowing smile she had glimpsed in the eyes of the women who served them. Something her dear *grandmère* had often quoted came back to her.

"Who can find a virtuous woman? For her price is above rubies."

If only her grandmother were alive and still with her, but she was not. There was only Aunt Vivienne, who was no relation at all, and she had a feeling that despite the fact that she had done nothing wrong save to drink too much champagne and fall asleep on Thurston's couch, her aunt's actions had within them the seeds of her own doom.

Arms came around her, and she was held close against her lover's body. He rested his chin on her curls. "You must be hungry, my sweetest." He pointed to the table his quiet, self-effacing valet was setting. "Come and have something to eat."

She wondered if she could eat and, a second later, wondered when she had sat down at this table, now covered with a snowy cloth and fine china. She could not seem to marshal her thoughts. The events of the past few hours swirled through her head like a brightly colored stream of indefinable objects. However, she did feel better when she had eaten some part of a delicious casserole. She also found, to her surprise, that she could face the valet, who was serving them with equanimity, even though the man must be aware of their relationship or, rather, their relationship to be. Yet as that thought came to her, she felt an urge to rise and run from the room, from the house . . . where? There was no *where*. There was only here, here where all her questions concerning the ways of men with the women they loved were soon to be answered. She knew some of those answers, had heard them in the chatter of the girls in the dressing room she had shared with them until she rose to the rank of soloist. Something Teresa had once said came to mind: "Never tell a man you love him."

Through her lengthy eyelashes she looked at the man seated across from her and found him looking at her ardently. "I . . ." She paused, confused.

"What is it, my love?" he asked.

"I do not know," she murmured. "I have forgotten what I meant to say."

"I hope you are not afraid of me," he said with great concern.

"No . . . never, never of you." Almost without thinking, she stretched out her hand.

He clasped it, studying her. "You seem unhappy. Are you?" His gaze darkened, and before she could respond, he added, "You must not think of that woman or what she told you. She is nothing to you."

"Very well," she said. "I will not think of her. I will think only of you. I mean . . ." She paused, wondering if she had said too much, but it had been the truth.

"I hope you mean exactly what you just told me, my very dearest."

"Am I?" she said on a breath. "Your . . . very dearest?"

"You have been so ever since that day in the museum. I suffered the tortures of the damned when your cousin hurried you away so quickly and I thought I might never find you again. Then, when I saw you at the ballet, I began to believe in miracles." He was still holding her hand, and his grasp tightened. "If I could tell you what . . . what it means to me . . . to have you sitting across this table from me here, in my home, but you will soon know what I cannot express in words alone."

Soon . . . soon . . . soon . . . the word echoed like a drumbeat through her mind, and the man across from her seemed to waver as if, indeed, she were seeing him reflected on the surface of some rock-disturbed pool. Her thoughts were tending in such strange directions, such uncharted ways. She wanted . . . but she was not sure what she wanted.

"You look frightened, my love," he said softly. "I do not want to frighten you or . . . or hurt you. If you do not wish to be with me, you have only to tell me and . . ." He paused. "I wonder if you understand what I am saying."

She nodded. "I do understand." In the ears of her mind there was laughter, the bawdy laughter of the girls in the ballet. And there were the confidences of Mary Clare in the days before she left . . . but she did not want to think of Mary, not at this moment. "I do understand," she repeated, and put out her hand. "I want to be . . . with you."

He brought her hand to his lips. "Oh, my dearest." Then, releasing her, he put a glass in her hand. The color and the bubbles told her that it was champagne, and he, too, was holding a glass. "We will toast each other only once. To you, my dearest Eugenie."

"To you, my dearest Thurston," she murmured, and clicked glasses with him. Then she drank and felt the glass being lifted from her hand and set down on the table. He lifted her in his arms and bore her into the bedroom.

She was conscious of a blending of excitement and fear as, clad in one of her new nightdresses, she lay close to Thurston in the wide bed. Again, she had heard enough gossip among the girls of the ballet to know why he had come up behind her as she finished combing her long hair and kissing her lingeringly, had carried her to this bed—but she knew very little more because with sly looks at her, their talk had become whispers, punctuated with giggles.

She loosed a little breath of surprise as in the dim light from the single candle on the night table, she saw that his arms and shoulders were bare. In another moment she felt his fingers at the little buttons on her nightdress. It was being eased off, and her face was hot with confusion and embarrassment until the bed sank under his weight and she found his lips on her mouth in a kiss, unlike any kiss she had ever experienced, an invading, exciting kiss that lasted until she was nearly breathless. Then there were other kisses on the hollow at the base of her throat and on her breasts, and in being passive, she was finding a need to return his kisses and his caresses, a need to twine her fingers in his hair, a need to arch against him, a need to say, in spite of all that well-meant advice, "I love you, love you, love you. . . ."

"And I," he said ardently, "I will love you until my dying breath."

Then neither of them had any more need for words.

CHAPTER FOUR

THEY HAD TWO days of discovery, which amounted to forty-eight hours of ecstasy. Yet now, Eugenie, flushed and looking incredibly lovely, yet at the same time, mulishly stubborn, faced Thurston.

"It is a ballet they have not performed lately. I must rehearse this afternoon." She held up her new ballet shoes. "You bought these, Thurston. Surely you expected me to use them!"

He hardly remembered being asked to purchase them. He could compare his mind to a slate newly wiped. He said, "But you do not need to dance, my dearest. You are with me now."

She said patiently, "Do you not understand, Thurston? Dancing is my life. Without it I am only half a person."

"But, my love . . ." He paused, realizing that he had exhausted all his arguments. He tried to examine his feelings, but they were amorphous. He knew only that he feared to let her out of his sight. Indeed, since they had become lovers, he had been beset by all manner of strange fears concerning her, whom he loved as he had loved no one in his life, and she, by every look and every gesture, had seemed equally fond.

She was incredibly giving, incredibly responsive. To think of these last two days was to realize the full meaning of paradise. He could liken her to Eve, an innocent Eve who had never hearkened to the subtle whispers of the serpent. There had been moments when he had wished himself as innocent, but these had passed quickly, as he became the teacher and she his shy little pupil—but shy only at first. Later she proved incredibly responsive to a passion she could match with her own. Yet at this moment she appeared so stricken, so unhappy. He could not bear to see that look on her face. He must needs capitulate. "Very well, I will not stand in your way, my lovely, but I beg you will let me come with you."

The sadness fled. Dropping her shoes, she ran to him and caught his hand. "But of course you may come. You will sit in the theater, and later you will tell me if I pleased you . . . or you will be a stern Aunt Vivienne and say that I need to point or—" She was silenced by his hand over her mouth.

He said tenderly, "I would not dare attempt to criticize perfection. I could not be so bold."

She pushed his hand away gently and smiled up at him. "Could you not, Monsieur Thurston? Me, I have found you quite bold on occasion."

He laughed and drew her closer into his embrace. "Only in areas where I am knowledgeable," he said, and covered her face with kisses. "Stay with me this afternoon," he begged.

"I shall be with you always, but I must dance," she said seriously. "I am a soloist. It is wonderful to be a soloist, and to be with you is even more wonderful. May I not be twice blessed?"

"Of course you may," he said, feeling ashamed of himself for trying to press his advantage again. It was not out of jealousy, he told himself, it was part of a prevasive fear that this incredible happiness might not last. Yet why should it not? He had known from the first that he wanted to marry her. Yet he must needs discuss the matter with his father. It might mean a quarrel and a subsequent separation, and there was also the matter of the Bastle. He could not imagine her in the wilds of Northumberland! He would like to sell it and find a more felicitous spot, and he would—But at this moment, to leave her even for half a day was a painful thought. Were he to see his father, he might have to be gone as long as a fortnight.

"Why are you frowning?" Eugenie asked anxiously. "Are you very angry with me, my love?"

"No, my dearest, I could not be angry with you. Do you not know how very much you mean to me? But go now—get ready and I will escort you to rehearsal."

"Oh, Thurston." She flung her arms around him, kissing him joyfully.

"My dearest," Thurston said when he finally lifted his head, "that was a very dangerous thing to do—it might keep you from rehearsal."

"No," she said positively. "Now that you know how much my dancing means to me, you will not interfere. Do you imagine that I do not know you? We dancers are not automatons or puppets pulled by strings. It takes intelligence to be a dancer."

"Agreed—and beauty and grace and charm," he said, kissing her again. "But let us go, lest temptation overtake me and turn me into an ogre."

The theater looked very strange without the chandeliers ablaze or the footlights burning on stage. From being a place of scarlet and golden splendor, it was now dark, cavernous, and so cold that Thurston was concerned for Eugenie's health and said so.

She giggled. "Were I to perish by such means, my love, I should have been dead before I reached my tenth year."

"You have been dancing so long?" he demanded incredulously.

"I have been dancing since I could walk, but I began lessons when I was eight. Have I not told you about my darling Pierre?"

"Your . . . darling Pierre?" he repeated with a frown.

"My teacher." She sighed. "He is dead and I do miss him."

"Oh, your teacher," he said, and was glad that the darkness of the auditorium had prevented her from seeing the anger he knew was reflected in his eyes.

"I will tell you about him after rehearsal."

"Yes, you must."

"I do hope it will not be too tedious for you to watch us. Rehearsals are not very interesting. Indeed, they are often quite tedious."

He took her hand and brought it to his lips, "Nothing that you could do would ever prove tedious to me, my beloved."

"Oh," she breathed. "I do love you so much—so much that it frightens me." She stood on tiptoe to kiss him and then hurried up the stairs to the stage.

She had not known quite how she would feel as she met her friends among the dancers. She did not have any really close friend—mainly because her aunt had refused to let her fraternize with the other girls.

"They are scum," she had said harshly, "not fit to kiss the shoe of a de Champfleury."

She had not, Eugenie remembered resentfully, hesitated to require a de Champfleury to do the most menial tasks at home, scrubbing the floors and ironing on the days when she was not rehearsing, but she would not dwell on the past. The past had gone out of her life. She would never again see that coarse, common woman who gave herself the airs of a great aristocrat. With a sudden flash of insight she realized that it was her very heritage that Aunt Vivienne—herself a quarter peasant—hated and resented. That and the fact that for the first nine years of her life she had been forced to support her. Well, she had been paid in full—and how it must have pleased her to thrust her into the street. But she was not in the street! For the first time in her eighteen years of life she was wearing fine silks and jewels and furs, a sharp contrast, indeed, to the rags she had left behind. But more important than that, she was with a man with whom she had fallen in love the very first time she had seen him. She had thought never to see him again, but she had, and ecstacy had suddenly become much more than a word printed in a book!

"Eugenie!" Teresa came up to her, her dark eyes alight with merriment and pleasure. "But who was it I glimpsed below in the auditorium?"

Meeting her friend's laughing eyes, Eugenie blushed and blushed again as she said, "H-he wanted to . . . to watch a . . . rehearsal." Her cheeks had grown warm and grew warmer yet as she saw a knowing look in Teresa's black eyes. Yet if she were embarrassed, she was not ashamed, she decided defiantly.

"Ah, my dear," Teresa murmured. She embraced her and, moving back, said, "I am so happy for you. You must tell me all about it."

Eugenie nodded, not committing herself because she knew that she could tell no one about anything. The happiness she was experiencing must not be a subject for gossip and giggles and gleeful comparisons. She said merely, "We are very happy."

"You look very 'appy," Teresa stated. "'Appier 'n I've ever seen you, 'n' it's a pleasure to think we won't 'ave to see that sour-faced old 'arridan anymore. She 'as a look 'd sour

milk. Besides,'' she added with a giggle, ''it's much nicer to
'ave so lovely a lover.''

''Please''—the ballet master came toward them—''an end
to gossip . . . to work, to work, ladies.''

Thurston, sitting in the second row, watched entranced as, at
the comand of the ballet master, the girls dutifully went
through their paces. They worked very hard, he thought
concernedly, and he could not approve of the way the man
spoke to them. His manner bordered on the contemptuous, and
once, when Eugenie was singled out, he was hard put not to
interrupt the proceedings and tell him that he was out of line.
Fortunately second thoughts intervened before he could take
action. A few minutes later he was deeply thankful that he had
heeded those inner promptings as the man praised Eugenie for
her grace in making a complicated turn.

He was so enrapt in watching the proceedings that he was
not aware of the two young men who had entered the row in
which he was seated to place themselves, one on either side of
him, until one of them said in a low, trembling voice,
''Scoundrel, I would like to cut your heart out.''

''And I would be glad to be your second,'' muttered the
other youth.

Thurston, whose eyes had grown used to the semidarkness,
recognized Etienne, but the other who had spoken first was a
stranger. He said calmly, ''I do not know you, sir.''

''You know me.'' Etienne snarled.

''Yes, I know that you failed to meet your cousin at the
opera house Tuesday last.

''I did not fail; I was there, but you had stolen her away,''
Etienne hissed. ''You kept her with you all the night, damn
you.''

''She took no harm of me,'' Thurston snapped. ''I shudder
to think what might have happened had she been forced to go
home alone!''

''You dare say that, you who have made her your whore,''
muttered the other young man.

''She is not my whore,'' Thurston retorted in a low, furious
voice.

''Liar, seducer,'' came the furious retort. ''She was mine,
my bride-to-be. The banns were to soon to be read, and
now . . .''

''Come, come, Jean-Paul,'' Etienne said soothingly. ''You

are better off without her.''

"Who are you?" Thurston looked at the young man named Jean-Paul.

"He is the Comte de la Vigne," Etienne said curtly. "And he is . . . was . . . betrothed to my cousin.''

Thurston said loudly and incredulously, "I do not believe it.'' He rose to his feet.

Etienne also stood up. "You can believe it. It was all arranged. Ask her . . . she'll not dare deny it, and if she does, she is lying. She and the truth are strangers.''

Thurston turned on him, "It is you who are lying—as you lied about meeting her the other night. She was alone and waiting for you.''

"I would have come," Etienne growled. "I . . .'' He paused as his companion glared at him and leapt to his feet.

"You *would* have come?" he questioned. "You were not there?"

"I . . . I was not far away," Etienne muttered defensively. "I arrived only minutes after she left . . . with him.''

"Damn you!" Jean-Paul cried. "Now we have the truth of the matter—you left her alone. Great heavens, I have a mind to call you out.''

"How did I know that she would go with this man?" Etienne retorted. "He is the one whom you must challenge!''

"What is happening down there?" the ballet master demanded irritably.

In that same moment Eugenie, who had heard some of the altercation and recognized her cousin's voice, rushed down into the auditorium. "Etienne—" she began, then stopped in shock. "Jean-Paul, what are you doing here?"

"You can ask me that?" he demanded furiously. "You whom I would have married in June?"

Eugenie stepped back. Her heart began to pound heavily. She had forgotten about Jean-Paul and the arrangements to which she had agreed so reluctantly. She said in a low voice, "The marriage was none of . . . of my desiring. I was not consulted.''

"You were agreeable!" Jean-Paul cried. "You told me you were.''

"Only after my aunt would give me no peace," she retorted. "I did not want it. I never wanted it. I was never in love with you. I did like you, but each night I prayed that something would happen to prevent our marriage. That is the truth!''

Jean-Paul caught her by the shoulders. ''And something has happened, has it not? You have become this man's—''

''I warn you!'' Thurston pushed him back and put his arm around Eugenie. ''Say no more unless you want your words, with your teeth, pushed down your throat.''

''It is not what you think, Jean-Paul,'' Eugenie cried. ''I love him. I love him with all my heart—with all my being.''

''Mademoiselle de Montfalçon!'' the ballet master thundered. ''We are waiting for you. As for the rest of you . . . gentlemen, get out, get out of this theater before I have you thrown out!''

Eugenie hesitated a second and then with an imploring look at Thurston she hurried back onto the stage.

The three young men strode up the aisle, Thurston behind Jean-Paul and Etienne. On reaching the lobby, he said coldly, ''Well, what is it to be, Monsieur le Comte, swords or pistols?''

Etienne said quickly, ''I will be your second, Jean-Paul.''

Jean-Paul, turning toward Thurston, shot a contemptuous look at Etienne. Addressing Thurston, he said, ''I have decided that, after all, I do not wish to fight for this woman. They say that in the night, all cats are gray. I wish you joy of her, monsieur.'' Turning on his heel, he went toward the outer doors with a protesting Etienne close behind him.

Thurston walked slowly back into the auditorium and sat down in the rear of the great house. The episode had left a bad taste in his mouth, and it had raised questions he did not want to consider. He had forgotten about Eugenie's betrothal. She had, he recalled, told him about it that first night, but she had been three parts befuddled by the champagne. It had not seemed really serious, but certainly it was serious to young Jean-Paul. Still, she had assured him that it had been none of her desiring.

''Mademoiselle de Montfalçon!'' The ballet master's irate voice reached him. ''You are not attending, and that pirouette was *clumsy!*''

Thurston looked up in time to see Eugenie, head lowered and shoulders dropping, nod. ''I am sorry,'' she said in a small voice.

Thurston's heart went out to her. He wished that he might

give the ballet master a piece of his mind—several pieces. Undoubtedly she had been disturbed by the sudden appearance of her fiancé. He frowned and unwillingly conjured up an image of Jean-Paul. The young man had looked stricken—at least at first. He could not blame him for that, nor could he blame him for refusing his challenge. Undoubtedly he considered himself betrayed, and in a sense he had been—though inadvertently. He could not imagine Eugenie willfully ignoring so strong a commitment. Had she? No, of course, she had not. He was positive that she was telling him no more than the truth when she had said the marriage was none of her desiring.

Her aunt would never have heeded her objections. That woman, Madame de Champfleury, as she called herself, was probably impressed by his title. Yet judging from the young man's garments, there was little money to match it. Undoubtedly he, in common with Eugenie, had been born of émigré parents. And what had her family been like? They had, he realized, never discussed her mother and father. Undoubtedly she was an orphan. Had they perished during the Terror? Were they aristocrats? Eugenie had all the earmarks of an aristocrat —still, he could not imagine that a girl of such lineage would have been allowed to dance in the ballet, and certainly nothing about the aunt suggested nobility.

"Thurston! Oh, you *are* here!"

He looked up quickly to find Eugenie standing beside him. It was too dark to see her expression, but he had heard distress in her voice. "Of course I am here, my love." He rose and stepped into the aisle, putting an arm around her and finding her body taut. "Did you imagine that I would leave without you?"

"What happened with Jean-Paul?" she asked bluntly. "You will not have a duel?"

"No, no, of course we will not," he said soothingly.

"Oh, I was so frightened," she whispered. "And you . . . what can you think of me? I should have told you about him, but . . . I had forgotten about the arrangement. Always I tried to put it out of my mind. I did not want it—ever. Do you believe me?"

"Of course I believe you, my dearest love." He dropped a kiss on the top of her head. "Are you finished with the rehearsal?"

"Yes, it is at an end—we will have another one tomorrow in

the morning. I hope you do not mind.''

"No, I do not mind. I was entirely wrong to want to keep you all to myself. Such talent belongs to the world!''

"I could wish it were nearer to the end of the season.'' She sighed. "I would like to devote all my days and . . . nights to you.''

"When at last the opera house closes, we will go on a long journey, perhaps to Northumberland. It is cold country but beautiful in the spring and summer . . . and Scotland, too, is beautiful then.''

"I would like to go anywhere with you,'' she said softly.

"My dearest.'' He dropped a kiss on her cheek. "Where do you want me to take you now?''

She moved against him. "May we go to your home?''

"No,'' he said fondly. "We will go to *our* home.''

"Oh,'' she whispered. "I do love you so much. Until I met you, I was only half alive.''

"And I,'' he murmured, all his faith restored if indeed he had ever lost even a morsel of it, "I was not alive at all. . . . I was an automaton moved by a metallic mechanism.''

"And so this is why you did not come to visit me more than once on my bed of pain?'' Simon drawled, eyeing Thurston's happy face with an anger he was just barely managing to contain. He was well on the way to bitterly regretting that evening he had first taken him to the opera.

Thurston blushed. "I am sorry that I was neglectful, sir, but I hope that now you know the reasons, you will understand. You are looking much better.''

"I am feeling much better,'' Simon said. "I have had a fortnight in which to recuperate and two days beyond that.'' He smiled sourly. "I would gladly change my fortnight for yours . . . you have all the earmarks of a happy benedict, though I trust you have been wise enough to avoid the meshes of matrimony.''

Thurston looked down. "We are not married yet.''

"Yet?'' His uncle frowned. "There is a certain sinister significance to that reply that I cannot like. One sows wild oats, my dear Thurston, but one does not remain to harvest them.''

Thurston had moved to a window. "I love her,'' he said, staring down into the darkening street. "And she loves me.''

"Of course she does, the dear child," Simon said indulgently. "From all you have told me about her aunt and from what I, myself, have seen of the creature, I can imagine that poor little Eugenie looks upon you as a second Sir Lancelot. Sir Lancelot, I might mention, did not find it necessary to bestow a betrothal ring upon the numbers of distressed damsels he managed to rescue from durance vile."

Thurston turned back from the window, a black frown on his face. "You cannot diminish her or what I feel for her with this talk, Uncle Simon. I do not believe I wish to hear any more of it. I will bid you—"

"Hold, lad!" Simon raised thin brows. "I am a surrogate for your father while you are in London. I am merely trying to see this situation from his point of view. In his shoes I am quite sure I would not welcome an opera dancer into the hall."

"He does not need to welcome her into the hall," Thurston said stiffly. "Tom is the heir and soon to be married."

"Ah, yes, but there is always the possibility—"

"Was there such a possibility in your case?" Thurston retorted.

"No, but I have enjoyed being a black sheep, as it were. I do not think it is a color that becomes you, Thurston. You are fond of your father and he is fond of you. My parent . . . your grandfather, who fortunately died before you had a chance to know him, was not fond of me. Consequently it was easy for me to forsake the family fold. Will it be as easy for you to dwell in the wilds of Northumberland . . . and how will your bride-to-be take to the howling winters?"

"I have it in mind to sell the Bastle."

"Ah." Simon raised his eyebrows. "Then you are serious about the little Eugenie."

"Has anything that I have said led you to believe that I am not serious?" Thurston demanded angrily.

"No, unfortunately I am of the opinion that you imagine yourself to be in love with her—"

"I imagine nothing!" Thurston interrupted.

Simon raised a placating hand, "Heed me, lad, I am sure that even Eugenie would agree that it is not *comme il faut* to marry your mistress. French women understand these situations."

"I do not care whether it is *comme il faut* or not. I love her as I have never loved anyone in my entire life. And . . ."

"Your . . . entire life?" Simon repeated. "It seems to me that you are but one and twenty. That is not a great age, certainly."

"I will be twenty-two in April—that is little more than two months from now. And my age does not matter. I am quite old enough to know my own mind and my own heart."

"A man in love never knows his own mind—however well he might imagine he does. And he does not think with his heart," Simon said sagely. "I advise you to ponder well on this decision. Remember that marriage is not a matter of a few delightful moments—it lasts a lifetime."

"A lifetime is not long enough to spend with her," Thurston said ardently.

"I see," Simon responded dryly. "And what does she think? Unless I miss my guess, she understands the arrangements far better than you. It might not even be her first!"

Thurston turned shocked and angry eyes on him. "How can you say such a thing?" he demanded with a mixture of indignation and fury. "I have told you what happened with her aunt, and you, yourself, have had experiences with the woman!"

"Again, you do not know the French mind. The aunt might be merely a clever actress, endeavoring to—er—engage your pity as well as your love and thus insure the relationship."

"No!" Thurston exclaimed. "You did not see her on that day. You did not hear her! The woman's a monster, and Eugenie was a complete innocent when she came to me. She had been with no man before me. She was a virgin."

"With blood on the sheets to prove it? My dear lad, there are ways of obtaining little vials of blood. . . . Have you ever read that charming and instructive little masterpiece by John Cleland. 'Tis entitled *Fanny Hill*."

"May you go to hell with your insinuations!" Thurston shouted. "I will bid you—"

"Hold, lad, I expect I must believe you and give you both my blessing."

Thurston regarded him coldly. "I believe that you are mocking me."

"No, on my honor I am not. I was only testing you, lad."

"Testing me?"

"Shall I say, rather, that I was testing the strength of your love, and I see it really is love and not mere infatuation. Consequently I can only offer you my blessings and my sincere congratulations.''

Thurston loosed a long breath. "I . . . thank you, sir.''

"And will you join me in my box tonight?''

Thurston hesitated. His uncle's earlier comments still angered him, but he had finally capitulated, and furthermore his box was directly over the stage, affording him an excellent view of the dancers—or rather one dancer. He said, "I thank you, Uncle Simon—in these circumstances I will be pleased to join you. But now I must go.''

"I will say God's speed, my lad.'' Simon smiled.

Once alone, Simon's smile faded quickly. He smote his fist against his palm, mentally cursing Eugenie's cousin for failing to meet her at the theater on that fatal night. He directed another string of invective at her aunt for her unyielding attitude.

"Damned foolish woman,'' he muttered, and then he cursed the moment when he had first invited his nephew to share his box at the opera, but as his anger died down, he found himself waxing philosophical. He could not have foreseen that meeting at the museum. It was possible that Thurston and Eugenie were fated to meet and fated to love—but to marry? That was a different matter entirely. It was time that he wrote to his brother—time and past. Moving to his desk, he took out paper, quill, and ink. Sitting down, he stared thoughtfully into space. The missive he would send must have, he decided, the effect of a missile.

Thurston, returning to his lodgings, found Eugenie deeply asleep on the couch. It was her practice to rest before a performance, but generally she was awake before five in the afternoon. She had slept longer than usual that morning, and she had not been feeling well. She was working too hard, and for possibly the thousandth time he wished that there was some way of convincing her that dancing was too strenuous for one so delicately formed. He looked down at her adoringly and was even more incensed at his uncle's reference to these "arrangements.'' He was equally angry at his sly suggestion of trickery, as well as his mention of Cleland's infamous book!

Despite their weeks of being together, there was a touching

innocence about Eugenie that had, on occasion, filled him with
shame. They must be married and soon—even before the
season ended!

"Sir?"

Thurston turned quickly to find his valet standing behind
him. "Yes, Graves?"

"There was a letter come for you. 'Twas brought by
messenger a short time ago."

"By messenger?" Thurston questioned, feeling an odd
sinking of the heart. "Where is it?"

"I put it on the hall table, sir. I will fetch it." The valet
moved out of the room. In a moment he was back. However,
as Thurston took the envelope, Eugenie stirred and awakened.

"Oh, Thurston, you are back!" she exclaimed, smiling at
him.

Slipping the envelope inside his vest, he came to sit on the
edge of the couch. "Yes, my darling." He dropped a kiss on
her forehead. Then, suddenly aware of his valet, he added
quickly, "You may go, Graves."

"Very good, sir." The valet went quietly out of the room.

"Did you have a pleasant sleep, my love?" he asked.

"I did . . . but I fear I slept overlong." She sat up. "What
is the hour?"

He glanced at the clock on the mantelshelf. "It is past five."

"Oh, dear, I will have to get ready." She gave him a little
push. "You must rise, sir."

He got to his feet immediately. "I am at Madame's disposal,
all the days of my life." He bowed.

"Oh, you!" She rose swiftly and then put a hand to her
head.

"What is the matter?" he asked anxiously. "Do you have a
headache?"

"No, I was just a little dizzy."

"Why would you be dizzy?" He frowned.

"Oh, I beg you will not look so concerned, my love. It is
nothing."

"Are you sure? You were not well this morning."

"That is because we dine on such rich foods. I am not yet
accustomed to them. Actually I am feeling wonderfully well."
She stood on tiptoe to kiss the cleft in his chin and was
gathered into his arms.

"Oh, I do love you so much," he murmured. There was more he wanted to tell her, but now was not the time. She had to get ready for the theater. He had a fleeting wish that she might never need to go back to the theater, never dance before the appraising eyes of the ton and of the rowdy populace of the higher and lower reaches of the theater. When they were wed . . . But he could not think of that now, and perhaps it would be best to wait until the season's end.

"Love"—Eugenie moved away from him—"I must get dressed."

"Go, then." He smiled, and as she left the room he remembered the letter and took it out. He experienced a shock when he saw the direction on the envelope. The writing was so shaky, so unlike Lord Seabourne's bold, black script. Yet the ink was black, and the hand that had held the pen was indubitably that of his father. Was he ill? he wondered concernedly. He tore open the envelope and settled down to read writing that was even more shaky than that on the envelope.

My dear Thurston:

I write this from my bed. It is with great sorrow and regret that I must tell you of your brother's death. We were on our way to a reception given by Serena's parents. There had been a strong wind in the night, and our coachman, driving at a headlong pace, swerved to avoid a fallen branch in the road. The vehicle overturned. Your brother was crushed beneath the equipage, and I was thrown clear—would that it had been the other way around. I suffered only a broken arm and a concussion. Your brother died before help could be summoned.

This accident took place a week and a half ago. Had I been more myself, I would have requested that you be informed immediately, but unfortunately I remained unconscious for three days and, upon recovering my senses, was beset by fever. In the confusion that followed, none thought to send for you—but needless to say, you must come as soon as possible, for there is much to discuss, and I fear that my own time is limited. I am indeed sorry to acquaint you with this sad news, my

*dear Thurston. Please come—as soon as you receive
this communication. I remain . . .*

Your loving father.

Automatically Thurston refolded the letter and slipped it into
his vest pocket. At first he felt nothing, because it could not be
true—Tom dead and his father . . . The handwriting was so
shaky, as if overnight a man of fifty-three had become ancient,
but of course, that was ridiculous! He was not old. It was the
writing of a man who had been badly hurt and who was
grief-stricken because his oldest son, his heir, was dead, and
because he had seen it happen.

Had he?

Pray God, he had been spared that sight. And that prayer had
already been answered, had it not? His father had described a
concussion, and so had been spared the sight that suddenly
flared into horrid imagery in his own mind. Tom, crushed and
mangled beneath the overturned coach. Tom, dead—and
praise God, quickly, quickly dead. Tom, on his way to a bridal
celebration.

A sob rose in his throat. Tom. A hundred images of his
brother and himself replaced the horror he had so unwillingly
envisioned. They were two years apart. Tom had been inclined
to lord it over him, but there was always a deep affection
between them. Tom, at eight, had comforted a grieving
six-year-old when their mother had died. In happier times he
had taught him to swim, and at twelve had taught him chess.

They had run races together, had ridden hell-for-leather
through the park, had playfully jousted for the hand of Serena
Tolland, and if there had been resentment on the part of Tom
because he believed his brother better favored as to looks, it
had been no more than skin-deep. There had been some slight
unpleasantness the day before they had parted, but Tom had
been up at dawn to embrace him and see him off—with sincere
good wishes and all sorts of advice regarding life in London.
"And you must return for my wedding, for there's none other I
will have as best man," he had said warmly.

And now . . . tears rolled down Thurston's cheeks as he
realized that he would never, never again see his brother. And
what of his father, who had always enjoyed the best of health?
But from the tone of the letter and the urgency . . . of course,
there would be urgency. And, of course, he must leave as soon

as possible. Tonight—no, not tonight, the roads were not safe at night, particularly those leading out of London. He must needs leave first thing in the morning.

"Thurston, love," Eugenie called.

Eugenie.

He must take her with him but could not take her with him, not at such a time with his father ill and her commitments at the theater. Yet to leave her with Graves . . . No, he must talk to his uncle, must see that he keep an eye on her. He grimaced. His Uncle Simon was the last person on earth whom he would ordinarily trust with Eugenie, but there was no one else. However, they had had that talk this afternoon, he recalled. He had almost forgotten that. And his uncle had given him his blessings. He would have to see him . . . would see him at the theater. He did not want to go to the theater but must think of Eugenie. She would be terribly upset. He would leave money for her and return as soon as possible. It might be a fortnight, and then . . . but he could not think of the future, not in view of the terrible news he had just received. And how was it possible? Tom was only twenty-three, and with all his life before him, and Serena . . . with her bridal clothes purchased . . .

"Thurston, my love, look at me."

He looked up quickly to find Eugenie arrayed in the fur-lined pelisse he had just bought for her. He forced a smile. "Ah, that is very becoming. Are you ready, then?"

"Yes, my love, but what is the matter?" She hurried to his side and put her arms around him.

"Matter?" he repeated. "Why . . . should you imagine there was anything the matter, love? I will fetch my coat and . . ."

The arms around him stiffened. "Do not shut me out, Thurston," she begged. "I know that there is something wrong, something terribly wrong." Her arms tightened, and she stared at him anxiously.

Not for the first time her perspicacity amazed him. The truth trembled on his lips, but he must not voice it, not when she was about to dance. It would only distress her. "I have had some rather disquieting news from home, my love. My father has been taken ill. He requires my presence."

"Oh, my dearest, I am sorry," Eugenie said. "I hope it is nothing very serious."

"I am not sure," Thurston said carefully. "I will have to leave tomorrow, but I should not be home above a fortnight. And I promise that I will write each day. I am leaving Graves behind—he will see to your needs until I return."

Eugenie's hand crept to her throat. There was a pounding in it, and an inexplicable fear was creating little air bubbles, which she swallowed convulsively behind that protecting hand, for Thurston must have no inkling of her trepidation. "I see." She managed a comforting smile. "I will miss you, my love, but I do agree that you must leave as soon as possible."

"I . . . wish I might take you with me," he said regretfully. "It will not be . . . easy to be away from you. But I do not imagine you could go?"

A long sigh escaped her. "No, there . . . is the new ballet, and as you know, I am to be the lead dancer. Oh, dear, you will not see it."

"But it will be performed more than once, and perhaps it is best that you do not come at such a time." The striking of the clock startled them both. He said hastily, "I must take you to the theater. Have I told you that I will be in my uncle's box tonight?"

"Oh, I am glad. He is better, then?"

"Yes, completely recovered and anxious to see you dance. Come, my angel."

The curtain had fallen on the first act, but Simon Sorrell did not, as was his wont, stroll out of his box to speak with one or another lady of his acquaintances. Despite his estrangement from his family, the news that his nephew had imparted to him had shaken him. "God, my lad, I hardly know what to say. And you will be leaving tomorrow?"

"Tomorrow, yes," Thurston said heavily.

"I am almost inclined to think I should go with you."

"No!" Thurston said quickly, and meeting his uncle's questioning glance, he continued, "You . . . are not on good terms with father and . . . and you are needed here."

"*I* am needed?" His uncle's thin brows rose. "I do not quite understand you."

"Eugenie . . ." Thurston said on a breath. "I do not know how long I will be gone. It will depend upon my father's state of mind and his health, of course. I have told her that I will be gone a fortnight, but it could be longer. I will, of course, write each day, but she will worry. If you might visit her and comfort her . . . Graves will, of course, be with her, and I think she must have an abigail. She has refused one, saying that she can do for herself, but I think it is not right that she and Graves alone occupy my lodgings.''

"No, of course not,'' his uncle agreed. "And while I think she will find me a very poor substitute for you, I will do my best to keep her spirits up.''

"I do thank you. I will be much easier in my mind, knowing that you are within call—if she should need anything. I wish I could take her with me, but . . .''

"You are quite right not even to consider the idea,'' Simon said firmly. "It is not the time to discuss a marriage with an opera dancer.''

Thurston's face darkened. "If you feel that way, Uncle—''

"I do not feel that way,'' Simon said quickly, "but your father's sentiments are another kettle of fish, as it were. You have convinced me of her worthiness, but would you be able to do the same with my brother, especially now that you are the heir apparent?''

Thurston regarded him blankly. "The . . . heir apparent?'' He paled, saying in a low, shocked voice, "I am, am I not?''

"There is no gainsaying that, my dear lad. And while I assure you that I am yet in your corner—when it comes to your decision concerning the little Eugenie—I cannot speak for my brother. There will be shoals ahead, I fear.''

"I do not fear them,'' Thurston said emphatically. "Nothing and no one in this world can come between Eugenie and myself. I will not allow it.''

"Then, my boy, there is nothing more to be said,'' Simon murmured. "And I will certainly do my part to insure your happiness.''

CHAPTER FIVE

HE HAD RIDDEN fast, faster than ever in his life, driven by a nagging fear that his father might not be alive when he arrived, and coupled with that fear was pain, the terrible wrenching pain he had experienced upon bidding farewell to Eugenie. That she had been equally unhappy was obvious, for all she had valiantly tried to mask her anxiety. However, at the last, she had clung to him, saying over and over again, "Write, I beg you will write to me, Thurston, my very dearest."

"As if I would not, my own darling," he had groaned. "I will write you each day that I am on the road. And you know that I am leaving my heart with you."

Their parting had haunted him through the three nights and four days it took to reach Seabourne Hall. Rain had held him up on two occasions, and sitting in one or another inn watching the drops spatter against the windows and trickle in crooked rivulets to their sills, he had been driven nearly mad with anxiety and anguish. The anxiety had been for his father, but the anguish was all for Eugenie. The pain of parting with her had been like a small death, and he had an odd feeling that he would not be alive again until they were reunited. Of course, he had not translated his feelings to paper but had, instead, filled his letters with protestations of his love for her and the hope that he would soon see her.

Then, at last he was at the hall, riding between the two tall brick gateposts topped with the bronze ships that had their counterparts on the Seabourne crest. Tom had once told him that the Seabournes had Viking blood and were counted

England's enemies until the days of King Canute.

Tears started to his eyes and were blinked away as he leaned down to greet the gatekeeper, to hear himself welcomed in the old man's quavering tones, and to receive his sympathies. As he rounded the long road to the house he slowed his horse to a walk, seeing the familiar outlines of the huge mansion, which, contrary to expectations, he would someday occupy, and a small voice within him cried, "Not yet, not yet." He could not bear a second shock. Tom's death was enough, and the almost obsequious bow of the gatekeeper had frightened him, as well as his grave look when he had asked after his Lordship. " 'E be as well as can be expected, 'n' 'tis 'opeful we all are that 'e'll soon be up 'n' around again, sir."

His brother would have been buried in the small graveyard at the far end of the property, and pray God, his father would not be joining him. Finally he reached the front door of the hall. He raised the knocker, but even before he let it fall, old Wilson, the butler, had opened it, greeting him in a trembling but happy voice. "Ah, Master Thurston, you're 'ome at last."

All the while he was exchanging greetings and words of sympathy with the man, he was thinking, *This is not my home. My home is with Eugenie.* He could almost see her standing on the stairs, but there was no one on the stairs, and none but servants to greet him. When he had returned from Oxford, Tom had ridden as far as the bend in the road—the turnoff leading to the gates of the hall. He had not known it would be so odd not to see his brother come striding toward him. Yet as he looked up, he did see someone descending the stairs, a tall, young woman in black, one slender hand on the railing.

"Serena," he said with some surprise.

"Thurston, at last." She reached him and put out her hand.

Grasping it, he found it very cold. He said awkwardly, "My dear, I cannot say how very sorry I am."

She looked up at him out of wide, darkly circled eyes set in a face grown much thinner. "I thank you, Thurston. It was a very great shock to us, as you can imagine."

"It was no less of a shock to me."

"Tom loved you, you know," she said in a low voice.

"I loved him and—" He coughed, covering the sob that had risen in his throat.

"We all did. But I must not detain you longer. Your father is expecting you." Without giving him a chance to reply, she hurried to the front door and was out even before the butler could open it for her.

As he went on up the stairs he found himself puzzling over Serena's words, and as he reached the upper hall he realized that what had confounded him concerned the way she had phrased her answer to his expression of sympathy. She had said, "It was a very great shock to us all, as you can imagine." Inherent in that comment was not grief but rather a lack of it, as if, indeed, rather than being personally concerned, she was distancing herself from the fact of her fiancé's death. Before he could dwell on that matter any longer, he found himself outside his father's door. He knocked tentatively and opened it.

"Is that you, Wilson? Did I hear my son's voice below?"

Thurston paused. Standing on the threshold, it was impossible for his father to see him, but it was possible to see Lord Seabourne, to see him and be shocked by his almost spectral appearance. He was bone-thin, his cheekbones startlingly prominent in a fact that had seemingly diminished in size, and his skin had an almost grayish cast. Two strides took him to the side of the bed. "Father!" he said hoarsely.

"Ah, my dear Thurston." Lord Seabourne looked up at him. "I have been waiting for you."

"Oh, Father." Thurston knelt at the side of the bed and grasped one of Lord Seabourne's hands. "I came as quickly as I might."

"I knew . . . you would," the sick man said. "Poor lad, I . . . I wish I might be with you . . . to instruct you on all that must be done. You are young to take on such a burden . . . but I fear that cannot be."

Tears filled Thurston's eyes and ran down his cheeks. "What . . . what are you saying?"

"Can you not see, lad? There's no time for dissembling. I am . . . not likely to . . . to get any better. That is . . . the prognosis of . . . of the doctor. Oh, lad," he said quickly, as a sob escaped Thurston. "I know what a shock this . . . must be to . . . to you. But time is of the essence. We must not waste it . . . in useless regrets. Did you meet Serena?"

The question startled him. "Yes, she was coming down the stairs just as I arrived. I . . . I was able to give her my sympathies because of Tom."

"Yes, it was a shock to her and to her parents, of . . . of course, but they and she are agreed that the alliance must . . . not be broken."

"The . . . alliance, Father?" Thurston asked confusedly.

"Hear me. Tom and Serena had a . . . a liking for each other—"

"Tom loved Serena," Thurston interrupted.

"Be that as it may," Lord Seabourne said with a touch of impatience. "The marriage . . . was arranged, as you know. I would not speak of this now . . . but matters must be concluded before I go."

"Matters, sir? What matters?"

"You will inherit the title and the hall will soon be yours . . . and now I must tell you what Tom knew and you did not. There have been . . . many profligates among us . . . as far back as 1719, when your great-great-grandfather became involved in the Mississippi Bubble. Our speculations have proved debilitating if not actually dangerous to the coming generations. I need not cite your grandfather's . . ." He paused. "Pour me some water, if you please. My throat grows dry."

"Should you be talking so much, sir?" Thurston asked anxiously.

"I must. The water, please."

There was a pitcher and a glass on the table near the bed. Thurston poured out the water and handed it to his father, who drank quickly. Setting the glass back on the table, he continued, "Your grandfather had a most unfortunate experience . . ."

"The Canadian land, sir?"

"Exactly . . . entirely worthless. Then there was my brother Simon, who wasted not only his patrimony but a good deal of mine as well. He borrowed heavily from Mr. Tolland too."

"Serena's father!" Thurston exclaimed.

"Yes . . . and I, too, borrowed from him. He has it in his power to annex the hall. But he was and would be satisfied to have his daughter marry into our family. Serena, though she was badly . . . shaken by . . . by the death of Tom, is a dutiful daughter—and she is agreeable."

Thurston's heart was pounding in his throat. A white-hot flame seemed to have burned his grief away, leaving only confusion and fury. He rose swiftly, backing away from the bed, saying loudly, "You . . . you are telling me that I must marry my brother's fiancée?"

"Yes, Thurston." Lord Seabourne raised himself up as much as he could, given his diminished strength. "It might not be a marriage of love . . . but love is all too often a flame that spends itself with a puff of breath. A . . . a marriage based on birth and breeding and familiarity is . . . is greatly to be desired. You have known Serena since you were children. . . . There was even a time when I believed you envied your brother."

"No!" Thurston cried hoarsely. "No, I cannot marry her. I will not marry her. I . . . I love someone else!"

His father's eyes and tone turned glacial. "So I understand. You have chosen to take unto your bosom . . . an opera dancer."

Thurston tensed. "What . . . do you know about that?" Before Lord Seabourne could reply, he added, "I see that my Uncle Simon has betrayed his trust and put pen to paper!"

"His trust?" Lord Seabourne questioned, still in those icy tones. "My brother has seen fit to warn me about the company my son has sought. A little whore—"

"She is no whore!" Thurston said furiously. "She knew no one until she came to me."

"Ah! You had the good fortune to . . . to be her first," Lord Seabourne said sarcastically.

"Her first and last. You do not understand. I love her. I will love her until the day I die."

"And do you love the hall, Thurston? Do you . . . do you love your home or . . . or do you want to see this land where generations of Seabournes have lived put on . . . on the auction block? Do you *want* to see it sold to . . . to some greedy outsider from the city? Do you want to see the hall torn down and our graves despoiled? Will you trade it all for some nameless little waif?" Tears he could not control rolled down Lord Seabourne's sunken cheeks. "If so, let death come for me tonight!"

"Oh, father." Thurston fell to his knees beside the bed. "Oh, no, no, no, you must not die too. I . . . I could not bear it."

"I must and will . . ." Lord Seabourne sighed. "But I am

told that if my life is . . . is reasonably free from stress, I have perhaps a year. Will you deny me that year? Will you deny me the knowledge that another Seabourne has carried on our name here at the hall?''

His uncle's name trembled on his tongue, but Thurston could not utter it, could not see Simon Sorrell, the uncle, who had so cruelly and wantonly betrayed him, in residence at the hall, wasting what little substance was left to him. There seemed to be but one course open to him, but he could not bring himself to utter the words his father was obviously longing and waiting to hear. He said, "I . . . I beg you will let me think on it this night. I will give you my answer in the morning."

Lord Seabourne's sunken, weary eyes caught and held his son's gaze. "I am agreeable to that," he said. He added, "I have always known about the love you bear for the hall and . . . and so did Tom. But I will allow you this night, my lad."

"I thank you, Father." Thurston bent and kissed his cheek. Then, not trusting himself to say more, he hurried out of the room.

He had left the portrait gallery to the last, not wanting to yield to its potent spell. At the urging of Mrs. Meade, the housekeeper, who had been at the hall as long as he could remember, he consumed a small meal in the octagonal chamber that the family had always preferred to the immense dining hall, the latter being used only on so-called ceremonial occasions when neighboring families from surrounding estates were invited. He had then taken a candle and walked through the cold rooms to the state bedchamber where one Sir Roderick Seabourne had entertained Queen Elizabeth on one of her ruinous progresses.

Tradition had it that Her Majesty had been much attracted by the son of the house—and had given him a purse of gold to help defray the expenses that had come close to beggaring her host. Several years later she had conferred the title of viscount on him for services, the nature of which no one in the family was quite sure.

In the great hall there hung the tattered banner that another Seabourne had carried into battle against the upstart Duke of Richmond on Salisbury Plain only a few leagues distant from

the hall. And in the garden grew a hawthorn tree, planted by an
ancestor who had been present when the marauding Puritans
had hacked down the hawthorn supposedly planted by Joseph
of Arimathea at Glastonbury. It was a tale that had enchanted
the child he had been, and it had been told to him by Tom.

He had walked into the library, remembering with tears in
his eyes how he had envied Tom the possession of all those
books and envied him even more the equestrian painting of his
handsome young ancestor, also a Thurston, who had fought so
bravely in the name of Lady Jane Grey and died for his part in
trying to help her maintain her throne against her Papist
cousin, Mary. It was that Thurston who was supposed to walk
across the garden on the anniversary of his death carrying his
head. A ten-year-old Tom had really frightened his eight-year-
old brother with that tale.

Then, at length, because he really could not avoid it,
Thurston came to the portrait gallery, to the painting he did not
want to see. It was a large canvas and showed his beautiful
mother holding a baby in her arms, while beside her sat a
solemn Tom, aged two and a little over, with Bruno, his
father's spaniel, beside him.

Thurston's eyes, hot with unshed tears, lingered on his
mother's face, and his mind's eye furnished other images,
sitting in her lap with his arms around her neck walking with
her through the park or running in front of her while she
strolled with his father. Then there had been the painful day
when he had accompanied his father and Tom to a small Gothic
house that rose in the graveyard and was not a real house but a
mausoleum, built by his grandfather, a crony and admirer of
Sir Horace Walpole, and where his coffin was placed and also
the coffin of his dear mother. Could he abandon her—could he
abandon this house and grounds to strangers? He could not,
had known he could not even while he had argued with his
father, had known, too, that he could not marry the one
woman in the world whom he loved.

There might have been a chance had not his uncle written to
his father, for Eugenie was innately a lady, no matter what her
background. She had nothing in common with that peasant
aunt, but his uncle had foiled him with a letter, a letter that had
outdistanced him and reached the hall before he did by some
cruel quirk of fate, for it must have been sent at the same time

that he was journeying home! However, he reasoned bitterly, it was not only the letter. He must needs marry for a dowry, and that, too, he could lay at his uncle's door, his uncle who had wasted his inheritance and yet drew money from the estate.

He groaned, thinking of the money he had won and spent lavishly for lodgings; for Graves; for the abigail, Dorothy, whom he had hired, at his valet's recommendation, for Eugenie; and for the clothing and jewels he had lavished upon her—and then there were his own expenditures, not excluding the coach and horses and his own highbred stallion, purchased only last week at Tattersall's. There was very little left of his winnings—and that little must needs be sent to Eugenie. And what would happen now? Would she find some rich protector —no, he could not bear the thought! Another arrangement must be worked out, but what?

He could not think of that now, but he would write to explain. But how might he explain? He would need to see her in person. He would find some way of returning to London before the marriage—he must! He sank down in a chair and buried his face in his hands, at last giving way to the tears that had been threatening all the evening.

Eventually Thurston went to his room and settled down to write to Eugenie, but it was a long time before he could think of the right words, the words that told her only that he would see her as soon as he could leave the bedside of his sick father. She would have to hear his decision in person.

The pale light of dawn flooded Thurston's chamber. He looked at it with lackluster eyes. He had been watching the sky for hours, had seen the star-studded heavens pale, had seen the sickle moon fade, then had seen the soft, rosy glow along the horizon. Now, as his clock struck the hour of six, he slipped out of bed, dressed, and went quietly down the stairs and through a passageway to a side door and thence outside. He was tempted, sorely tempted, to go to the stables, bring forth his horse, and ride back the way he had come.

Yet he could not, would not, yield to that temptation. Instead he went to the graveyard and stood in silent communion near the mausoleum, which now held his brother as well as his mother. He had the conceit that beside them lay, equally dead, all his hopes of future happiness.

* * *

The most recent letter from his nephew lay on Simon Sorrell's desk, and despite the news it contained, he managed to look exceedingly cheerful as he faced the visitor who had intercepted it. "How is she faring, then, Graves?"

The valet said softly, "She is not well, sir. The fact that her condition has made it impossible for her to dance leaves her free to dwell on what she imagines to be Mr. Thurston's neglect."

"Has she written to him again?"

"Dorothy says not."

"I had rather expected that you would bring Dorothy with you," Simon said.

"She could not leave Miss Eugenie, sir."

"Ah, she is so ill, then? I know very little about breeding females, but I had the impression the sickness came only in the mornings."

"Of late, Miss Eugenie has been ill most of the day. She requires constant attention, sir."

Simon raised his eyebrows. "Is she in any danger, do you think?"

"Dorothy says not. She says as how Miss Eugenie, being very small and slight, might have more difficulty than a larger female. And I would say, sir, that not hearing from him has augmented the condition."

"Does she believe he has abandoned her?"

"As to that, sir, I'd not be knowing her state of mind. She's not minded toward confiding in me or in Dorothy, either."

"Ah, I would not expect such reticence from a girl of her class."

"She is quite unusual, sir," the valet said thoughtfully.

"Yes, I am aware of that. And the money he left her, Graves?"

"It is almost gone."

"And her own?"

"She is much concerned, sir."

"Has she said so?"

"No, but it is obvious to both Dorothy and myself, sir."

"Ah, then, I think it is time I called on her. You did tell her that I was out of town?"

"I did, sir."

"You are a gem, Graves." Simon opened a drawer of his

desk and took out several bank notes, handing them to the valet.

"I thank you, sir. I will bid you good afternoon."

Simon remained at his desk. To the right of a shelf containing pens and pen wipers was a carved wreath that he pressed. Immediately a panel swung back and revealed a sizable space. Reaching down, he extracted a small packet of letters, eleven in all. The last one, which he now put with the others, had contained the news he had anticipated with the first worried mention of his brother's illness. There was a draft for a hundred pounds, signed by Lord Seabourne. And in the letter a brokenhearted Thurston had written of his father's death, but more important than that was the much blotted paragraph telling Eugenie of the marriage that had taken place at the bedside of the dying man. The rest of the letter was only a repetition of several other letters. It contained frantic questions as to why he had had no response to the letters he had sent. There were also protests of undying love, and lastly there was the promise that he would see her as soon as he could. That, of course, was the most important of all and must be acted upon without delay. Pressing the wreath again, he rose and rang for his valet. He would change his clothes, and now, at last, he would call upon Eugenie.

A March wind was lashing the trees in the gardens and howling mournfully around the corners of the house. Thurston Sorrell, Viscount Seabourne, stood with Serena, his bride of three weeks, in the great hall. He was dressed for traveling, and his face was grave as he looked at an equally grave Serena, still in black. Their faces ill became a newly married pair, but as the servants—shocked by a wedding, sandwiched, as it were, between two funerals—whispered, they were not yet accustomed to marriage, since his youthful Lordship occupied the room that had been his since a lad, while his wife slept alone in the great bed where he and his brother had been born.

"Will you be gone long?" Serena asked, breaking a silence the length of which had oppressed her.

"No, my dear, not long," Thurston said after a slight pause. "But there is much unfinished business to which I must attend."

"Yes," she said, and aware of the inadequacy of the word

either as a comment or as a response, she looked up at her
husband, adding with some difficulty, "I do hope that you do
not consider me heartless. I mean concerning Tom. I do miss
him. We had always been fast friends, but the marriage was a
matter between our parents, as you know. But of course you
know. How can you not?" She spoke a little desperately, her
beautifully modulated voice less controlled than it had been
during the days that had passed since their hurried wedding and
Thurston's father's death.

"I do know," he said, and slipped an arm around her waist,
wishing then that he had not, for she had moved against him
needfully. However he let his arm remain where he had put it.
"It will be different when I return and we can put our separate
miseries behind us."

"When will you return?" she asked on a breath.

"I cannot say for sure, but it will not be over a month, and
possibly considerably less. I will write, of course."

"Please," she murmured, and for the second time in a few
minutes she wished him God's speed.

He had ridden quickly, and despite the threat of highwaymen
and other vagabonds, he had remained on the roads long into
the night, covering the miles as quickly as his horse could
gallop, while his heart, working in tandem with his brain, told
him that his journey was useless, for what more could he say
that he had not already written? But he had to know why
Eugenie had not responded, not once. That was unlike her. Her
unanticipated silence filled him with fears he could not quell.
He had written to Graves, too, and at length to his uncle, but
again, there had been no response. His uncle had not even sent
him a letter expressing his sympathies for his father's death.
The brothers had not been close, never as close as Tom and
himself, but they had been brothers—and near in age. And
why had he not heard from Eugenie?

"Why . . . why . . . why," muttered the sick man, tossing
back and forth in the wide bed. "She was gone; the rooms
were let again to a stranger. None knew where she had gone or
Graves or Dorothy, her abigail. Eugenie, Eugenie, why did
you not write . . . a line, only a line, to tell me why or
where . . ."

He sat up in bed, staring wildly, angrily, into a space filled
by what the watchers at his bed could only guess at. "Do not

speak of her in those terms, Madame de Champfleury! I will
not hear this slander. She was good, I tell you . . . good and
pure . . ."

The young woman at Thurston's bedside raised anxious eyes
to the doctor's face. "Will the fever never break?" she asked.

"If you would let me bleed him, Lady Sorrell . . ."

"No," she said decisively. "I do not hold with bleeding. It
is my opinion that it only hastened his father to his grave."

"Very well, your Ladyship," he returned coldly. "Then we
will need to let the fever run its course. He is young and strong.
We will hope for the best." He rose. "You will let me know if
there is any change, please."

"I will," she said, and saw him to the chamber door. Then,
going back to the bed, she sat down in the chair she had
occupied for a good part of the three and a half days that had
passed since Thurston came riding back to the hall, drenched to
the skin by a pounding rainstorm. He had been wild-eyed and
uncommunicative when he had come into the house. He had
also lost weight—that much she had been able to see before he
had closed his door against her well-intentioned questions.

The fever had come upon him in the night, and it was the
next morning that Serena had heard about Eugenie; had heard,
too, about a desperate search through London; had known that
he had gone from place to place looking for her. He had talked
to scores of people and received no satisfaction from anyone.
London had engulfed Eugenie.

It was Serena's opinion that the girl must have found another
protector, an opinion which, she learned, she shared with the
girl's aunt, who must have denounced her niece in no uncertain
terms. Still, though Serena was heartily glad that the little
dancer had disappeared, she had resented the woman he called
Madame de Champfleury for Thurston's sake, and again for
his sake, she had wished that he might have heard something to
put his troubled mind at rest.

She looked down at him concernedly. In the dim candle's
glow there were dark shadows under his eyes, and he was so
very thin and pale. She dared to run her hand through his
toulsed hair and then gasped, for her hand was caught and
held.

"Eugenie, my love, is it you?"

"Yes, it is, Thurston. You must sleep, my dearest," Serena
said soothingly.

"I could not find you . . . could not . . . could not . . . I thought you might have gone with Jean-Paul, but you'd not have betrayed me, I know . . . still, I . . . searched for you everywhere. Where did you go, Eugenie . . . where?"

Serena, cordially hating the elusive Eugenie, said, "I am here, my love."

"Ah, I am glad. Now we can sleep."

He felt so very weak, and he was also extremely confused. He had opened his eyes and thought he had seen the ceiling of his old room at home, bathed in the pink light of the rising sun. But he was in London, not Somerset! Now, opening his eyes again, he looked at objects that had been familiar to him since childhood. Another blinking of the eyes was enough to assure him that the images and the shreds of images that he had seen, or thought he had seen, were gone. Though he had no notion how he had come there, he was in his own room at the hall—and that was very strange, since the last thing he remembered was a muddy road and a drenching, pelting rain . . . . No, he had seen the gates of the hall, had he not? Yet he had been sure that Eugenie was at his side.

Eugenie.

With a sudden startling clarity he recalled that he had not been able to find her! She had not been in his lodgings. She no longer dwelled there. Someone else had taken the lease. He had spoken to her aunt, who, aside from castigating him roundly, had said brusquely that she did not know or care where the *prostituée* had gone and had slammed the door in his face. He had gone to the ballet and learned only that she had become ill. There had been none who had known the nature of her illness save Teresa, and she, too, had gone.

At last he had called upon his Uncle Simon, only to be told that he was visiting an old friend in Scotland. And yet he had felt her with him of late, and what had he been doing of late? He moved restlessly in his bed and had a memory of wild dreams and frightening images, which now he could not recall; but he could recall feeling weak and drained. He still felt weak and drained. Then he heard a movement beside him, and turning his head slowly, he saw that there was a woman sitting in a chair beside his bed. She was lying back wearily, her eyes closed.

"Eugenie . . ." The name emerged as a whisper. But she was not Eugenie. She was not so fair; her hair was not pale

gold but honey-colored. He knew the color, knew the face
—Serena, his old playmate, Tom's affianced bride, *not* Tom's
bride.

Tom was dead.

Serena was *his* bride. How pale and weary she appeared,
sitting in that armchair pulled up to his bed. Her bright color
was gone, and her yellow hair hung lankly about her face. And
what was she doing here? But suddenly he knew. He had been
ill, and she, his bride, had nursed him.

Disappointment was a hard lump in his throat. It had been
her voice in the night, the *nights,* and her cool hands on his
brow.

Had it been her voice alone?

Yes, for Eugenie . . . Eugenie was not to be found. Eugenie
was lost, the servants dismissed, the lodgings empty. It had
been Serena's voice alone he had heard—and what had he said
to her? He had a vague memory of crying out to someone . . .
Eugenie? Had he? And did she know about Eugenie? Of
course, she must know. He turned his face away, and in that
moment he heard her say hopefully, "Thurston, are you
awake, then?"

He did not want to look back, he did not want to hear her
reproaches, but he must, if only out of gratitude. Weakly he
turned his face toward her again. "Serena, my dear," he
whispered, and was surprised to see her eyes fill with tears.

"You . . . know me," she said.

"Yes, I do," he responded, his fears corroborated. "You
are Serena, my wife . . . and I shall not leave you again, my
dear. There is no need . . ."

"I am sorry," she said. "It was a cruel disappointment, I
know."

"It is in the past, my dear. You . . . we will not think about
it again."

"Oh, Thurston"—she leaned forward—"I must tell you
something I think you might not know."

Despite her weariness, he recognized the eager look in her
eyes, a look he remembered. He had seen it in the days when
he had gone riding with her—with Tom away at Oxford. She
had always been so glad to see him, and in those days he had
been positive that he loved her. He wondered if he could ever
summon those feelings back again. However, she had asked
him a question. "What might I not know?" he asked.

She hesitated, swallowed convulsively, and then said, "I would have been a good wife to poor Tom, you know. I was fond of him and his death hurt me sorely, but Thurston, my dearest, I . . . I have loved you all the days of my life."

"Oh, Serena," he said on a breath, not loving her but suddenly very grateful for her presence. Almost defiantly he said, "We shall be happy, you and I."

PART TWO

CHAPTER ONE

THERE WAS DEW on the grass, and the birds were just leaving their nests, their raucous cries echoing through the cool morning air. A flock of sheep nibbled at the grass, and in the distance cows lowed. However, a pair of riders, a man and a woman, galloping along the bridle paths and reaching the banks of the Serpentine at the same time, had been riding since the sun had been but a thin line of red on the eastern horizon. Now they looked at each other and laughed.

"Well, Madame la Comtesse, what do you say?" The man, slender, dark, and elegant, spoke in French.

His companion, fair and with short, curling blond hair, answered in the same language. "I say that you won by half a nose, my dear Marquis."

"Madame is disposed to be generous."

"Not in the least," she responded. "If I had won, I would have said so."

He moved his horse, a sleek chestnut gelding, closer to her black mare. "Still, the contest was close, as always. Might we assay another race?"

She shook her head. "Little Simon will be awake and wondering where I am," she said. "And perhaps Big Simon as well."

"Alas," he said, disappointed, "I expect I should be content with such morsels of time as you see fit to allow me."

"We have been riding for fully two hours," she said chidingly. "That is not a morsel, Raoul." A split second after that pronouncement, they heard the mellow chimes of a church clock announcing the half hour.

"You see?" She smiled at him. "It is thirty minutes past seven."

"Could the clock be wrong?" he asked.

"I would be wrong if I did not heed its summons. We must go in, Monsieur de Saint-Cyr."

"You called me Raoul," he said a trifle plaintively.

"It was an error."

"I'll not chide you for it. Can it not always be Raoul when we are alone?" There was an ardent look in his black eyes.

"No, it cannot be," she said firmly.

"And how is your husband's health, madame?" he demanded.

She shrugged, saying coolly, "As usual."

"One has heard that he was extremely lucky at cards some time ago."

"Yes, he won a fortune. It was shortly after we were married."

"Ah, if that is true, he had already won a fortune."

She laughed lightly. "If you persist in these compliments, Monsieur Saint-Cyr, I will cease to ride with you."

"But they are not compliments, madame. They are the simple truth," he said earnestly.

She continued to laugh. "I have a strong feeling that none of your truths are simple. But please, let us now return to the stables."

"I will race you back," he said, capitulating reluctantly.

"Good." She urged her horse forward and in a moment was several paces ahead of him. A second later he had easily outdistanced her, and they continued in their friendly competition until they reached the stables.

"Will I see you tomorrow morning?" he asked as he accompanied her to her waiting post chaise.

She shrugged. "You know that I have developed the habit of riding in the park at an early hour . . . on occasion."

He brought her hand to his lips. "Until tomorrow, then."

She smiled. "Possibly . . . as always, though, it must depend on my husband's health." With a little wave of her hand she mounted the steps her coachman had put down for her. As the vehicle drew away, the marquis stood watching it until it had disappeared around a bend in the street.

Some ten minutes later Madame's coach had stopped in front of a large house on St. James Street. As the footman let down the steps, she drew a deep breath before descending them, and another before walking up the flagstoned path to the three steps set between two white columns. She mounted the steps slowly, and before she had a chance to raise the knocker, the door was opened by Knape, the butler, a plump, gray-haired man of forty-eight with solemn blue eyes set in a grave face.

"Good morning, Knape," she said in a low voice. "Is my husband . . ."

He had nodded before she had concluded her question. "He woke betimes, Mrs. Sorrell. He has been asking for you."

She digested the information without comment. "And my son?"

The butler's lips curved into a half-smile, which quickly vanished. "He is awake, too, Mrs. Sorrell."

"I will go to him," she said decisively, and meeting the man's sudden but quickly veiled look of concern, she said soothingly, "I will take the blame for any . . . confusion that may result."

Without further comment she hurried past the butler and ran lightly up a flight of stairs to the second floor, continuing hastily along the hallway until she reached her son's chambers. Pushing open the door, she entered a small sitting room, and in another second she was in the bedroom and then almost knocked down as a small figure dashed toward her.

"Mama, Mama, Mama!" The child, a sturdy, dark-haired little boy of about six years of age, flung his arms around her. "I went into your room earlier this morning and you were not there!"

She laughed delightedly and, kneeling, put her arms around him. "But I am here now, Simple Simon, am I not?"

He nodded. "But where were you? No, I know where you were. You are wearing your riding clothes and you smell of horse! You went riding, did you not?"

"I went riding, my dear love, and I shall not smell of horse once I have had my bath." She kissed him. "Was that a horsey kiss?"

"Why didn't you take me with you?" he asked plaintively. "You promised you would." He raised huge, accusing brown eyes to her face.

"I will, my love, but not so very early. Nurse would not like it." She ran a gentle hand over his curls.

"Why *did* you go so early?" her son demanded. "Papa is very cross, Nurse said."

Her smile vanished, and a tart rejoinder trembled on her lips, but remembering her audience, she said softly, "But, my darling, it is lovely to go so very early—when the sun is newborn and the little birds are just waking."

"And," said a caustic voice from the doorway, "there is such pleasant company ready and waiting for one."

The child tensed, and his mother rose quickly, facing the sickly, emaciated man, who, clad in nightshirt and brocade dressing gown, stood bracing himself against the doorjamb. "Simon," she said on a note of protest. "You should not be out of bed."

His expression was grim, his gaze narrow, and his tone accusing as he responded, "And nor should you, Madame la Comtesse. I am told that you chose to leave this house at dawn."

"Ah, the all-seeing, all-knowing Graves," she murmured. "I begin to believe he is like a cat who sleeps with one eye open."

He glared at her. "Where did you go? I want the truth."

"Is not the truth obvious, Simon?" she demanded sarcastically. "I am dressed for riding."

"I see that I should have asked, 'With whom did you go?' "

"Ah, now, let me count them. . . ." She looked down at her hands and touched one finger. "There was Jarvis the coachman, and Enoch the footman"—she touched another finger—"*et fini . . . deux, seulement deux,* my dear Simon."

"Two . . . only two?" he questioned caustically. "Surely there is one more whom you did not mention?"

Defiance gleamed from her blue eyes and added tension to body and voice as she said coldly, "What have your spies told you, dear Simon?"

He raised a fist. "I warn you, madame—"

She laughed, a hard, crystalline sound. "The doctors have warned *you,* dear Simon, that too much exertion—and I am sure that must include the beating of your wife—might prove too much for your overworked heart, not to mention other organs."

He glared at her, all the while his thin cheeks becoming suffused with color. "Do not try me too far, Eugenie, I warn you."

"You repeat yourself, Simon, and if you are determined to quarrel with me, I beg you will spare your son a sight, which, even at his tender age, appears to distress him."

"My . . . son?" he questioned caustically. "As we know full well—"

With a lightning move Eugenie put out both hands and pushed him back into the other room, then closed the door to the child's bedroom behind her. "If you wish to bring fire to the coals of yesteryear, you will not do it in front of my boy!" she said icily.

"That is gratitude—" he began.

"And," she said, interrupting, "we will not mention gratitude. You have had your tithe, Simon, for the gracious bestowal of your name upon your nephew's bastard."

"If making me a cuckold—"

"I have not," she flashed. "I have been with no one save you in all the miserable years of our marriage."

"You are deliciously frank, my dear."

"I had an excellent teacher, one who demanded the truth every time I so much as exchanged a word with another man. He reinforced his lessons with his fists, if you will recall."

"It is a pity I did not use a cat-o'-nine-tails," he retorted. "And, by God, if you continue seeing this damned savage, Saint-Cyr, I will—"

A mocking laugh issued from her lips. "You will beat me? I am sorry, Simon, my dear, those days have passed. The exertion could kill you."

"And that, madame, is precisely what you wish, is it not?"

She shrugged. "Your death, Simon, is a matter of indifference to me."

"You little whore . . ."

"Sticks and stones, Simon." She shrugged and moved toward the door.

"Where are you going?" he demanded angrily.

"To my room. It is time that I divested myself of my riding clothes."

"Oh? And how many times have you performed that particular exercise this morning, my dear?"

He received a chill glance. "I am not in the habit of disrobing in the park, dear Simon. My days of performing were always limited to the stage."

As she moved past him, he reached out and seized her arm,

but his clasp being feeble, she pulled it away with no difficulty and continued out of the room.

Reaching her own chamber, Eugenie opened the door and closed it behind her with a quavering sigh of relief. Once, she recalled, she would have thrown herself on her bed and burst into tears. That, however, was a very long time ago. Now the white flame of anger dried her eyes before any tear could squeeze itself out. She rang for her abigail, and when the girl arrived, she said merely, "Elsie, I have it in mind to rest a bit before I leave for Lady Moberley's house."

"Yes, ma'am." The girl stared at her anxiously, and Eugenie, catching the look, guessed that her early-morning ride, the third in a week that still had two more days to run, had been the subject of gossip amongst the servants.

She smiled mockingly. She had no doubt that Elsie had been well primed on the gossip, which was not, of course, limited to this house. Servants talked, and so did their masters and mistresses; she was, she knew, a popular subject.

Though it had been four years ago that she had received word concerning the restoration of the de Villiers lands, appropriated during the Revolution, as well as the title she now bore, the household staff was quick to inform each new arrival that the Honorable Simon Sorrell had married an opera dancer!

That said opera dancer was a countess in her own right had fanned, rather than dampened, the flame of that gossip. Ironically the ton had accepted her far more easily than some of the servants. She was quite sure that there were those among the household who still chose to regard her with disdain, especially since her husband never troubled to lower his voice in the midst of his jealous rages.

"There, ma'am, may I bring you some coffee or tea?"

Eugenie looked at the girl in shock. While she had been thinking, Elsie had deftly performed the task of removing her garments and draping her in the lacy peignoir she had recently purchased at the Pantheon Bazaar. She said gratefully, "Thank you, Elsie. I think I would prefer tea this morning."

"Yes, ma'am." Elsie bobbed a curtsy and quietly left the room.

Eugenie looked after her gratefully. She was quite the best of the several girls who had been in her employ over the past seven years. The worst had been Dorothy, she thought as she settled down on her bed, leaning gratefully against the pillows.

Thurston had hired her at Simon's suggestion and . . . She paused in her thinking, realizing that she was straying far too close to a precipice. In another moment she would be falling, falling, falling, into a deep, black pit of memory, and the hatred she felt for her husband would be augmented by that which she felt for the man she had once loved to distraction!

Love and hate were closely allied. They carried with them the same symptoms—only the passion was different. She was swallowing air bubbles now, and her heart was beating faster. She was also breathing quickly, her hands were clenching and unclenching, and there was no breasting the waves that were breaking over her. The scene with Simon had, as had happened all too often, brought on the onslaught of memory she could not avoid, however hard she tried.

It came in images, images acted out on the stage of her mind. The moment when he, Thurston, had left her, his face convulsed with agony, his voice trembling as he bade her farewell not once but many times, as if he could not bear to take the step that must bring him to the door. He had promised to write, and she, believing him, had tried not to weep, but of course, she had been unsuccessful. She had wept bitterly and clung to him, and at length he had torn himself away, flinging himself out of the room, running down the stairs, seemingly in the very ecstasy of despair. How he must have laughed when he reached the outer door, and how he must have complimented himself on a display of acting worthy of an Edmund Kean!

He had promised to write. He had also given her his direction and begged her to write to him. He had told her that he would write every day he was on the road and every day he spent at home.

During that first painful week of silence she had blamed it on the uncertainty of the mails—especially when he was on the road and posting letters in small villages. However, one week became two, and fainting in rehearsal, she had been sent home. She had not been able to return. She had been too ill, an illness that did not pass in a morning but lasted most of the day.

At length, worried that he might have met with some accident on the road, she had written to the address he had left with her. She had received no answer. Then she had deluded herself again, thinking that perhaps his father had died and he was too disturbed to write. Finally she herself had written again because she was desperate, because she was with child and the money he had left her was running out. She had hated writing that begging letter, but she had still believed in him, believed that something must have happened to prevent his writing. She had decided to give him a fortnight to reply, but there had been none.

"Out of sight. Out of mind." That had been Simon's explanation. He had not stated it quite so baldly. He had been kind and considerate, or rather he had pretended to be. He had come one day to find her weeping because she was ill, her hope gone; there was no money and she knew not where to turn.

Simon had comforted her, insisting that she move out of her small and now depressing lodgings into larger quarters for which he would pay. Then, a week later he had come to her with the news that Thurston had married one Serena Tolland, whose acres matched with that of Seabourne Hall and whose dowry was large.

She had been, Simon explained, beloved of both brothers, and one of the reasons Thurston had come to London was to plunge into pleasures that might alleviate the agony he had felt over his brother Tom's imminent marriage to the lady in question. Then Tom had been killed in a carriage accident, and Thurston had wed the rich, beautiful, beloved Miss Tolland within a few days of his arrival at the hall!

"No," she had cried foolishly, as she had not heard from him all the time he had been gone. "I cannot believe it!"

"I could show you his letter, my dear, but I do not believe you ought to read it," Simon had told her, distress written large on his face.

Then the room had seemed to waver, and shortly afterward she had awakened from her swoon to find Simon bending over her, his expression distraught. "Oh, my poor, poor child," he had said with a groan. "I hold myself responsible for this."

Later, when she felt a little better, he had proposed marriage to her, comparing his situation with her own. "There was one I loved and she married another. I thought I could never care for anyone again, but I do care for you, my dearest. It was I who told my nephew about you when first he arrived in London. I told him that I had pursued you vainly, and he bet me fifty guineas that he could succeed where I had failed. I was angry, but I did not refuse the bet, because I thought you so far above us both.

''Of course, he failed to tell me that he had met you before at the British Museum—and that he had dallied with you briefly. But why belabor the matter? He is gone and I am here. My dear, I want to care for you and the child. I will give him my name and treat him as the son I never had—and indeed, we are blood kin. My dearest Eugenie, believe me that my one goal in life is to make you happy.''

She, fool that she was, had been as close to liking him as she had ever been, and also, she had been despairing, not only because of Thurston's cruel betrayal but because she, too, had been guilty of an even worse betrayal!

She had betrayed her noble blood, and like any girl of the streets, she had lived with a man, a veritable stranger, and was now bearing his illegitimate child! She was no better than poor little Mary Clare, and there had been periods when she had been tempted to kill herself, but she had been held back by the knowledge that she would have been committing a double sin, a terrible sin—murder *and* suicide! And besides, despite everything, she had felt protective of that life growing within her. Simon had offered her a name, and it was for that name alone that she had accepted the proposal—no, not entirely. He had been kind, and she had had much need of kindness then.

A vivid image of their marriage—by special license in his house—rose in her mind. She had never been so despairing, and also she had been visited by a sense of having made a most grievous error, one she would deeply regret in days to come.

It had not been days, it had been years, seven years that had seemed like seventy, as she endured the attentions he chose to dignify with the word *love*.

They had come upon her all unawares, for during the remainder of her difficult pregnancy he had left her alone in the six months it had taken her to recuperate from a condition perilously close to death. Then, when she was better, he had said, in what had seemed a jest, ''My dear, you have been a wife in name only, and it's time and past that you lived up to those promises you made on our wedding day.''

He had not been jesting.

She shuddered and shuddered again, as more images came to sully her inner vision. Simon, laughing at her protests, laughing and ignoring them. Simon, angered by her weeping, forcing compliance with his fists. Simon, teaching her to loathe and despise the very sight of him, and still the misery had continued until his collapse and illness—a heart condition, the doctor had said, brought on by too much eating, too much drinking, and, with a lewd wink, often the portion of middle-aged men who take unto themselves a young wife.

By that time she had been accepted by the ton, had been notified of efforts to restore her lands. These, unfortunately, were still underway. However, if they proved successful and the interlopers were dislodged, she would retire to her château . . . She sighed. These hopes were as yet dreams, and meanwhile Simon, grown rich through a single night of play during which he had won a fortune from a half-drunk youth, who had later killed himself, lived only, it seemed to her, to torment her.

His jealousy over her friendship with the Marquis de Saint-Cyr was totally unfounded—or was it? She did enjoy the young man's company. It was a great pleasure to go riding with him, and also very pleasurable to hear his tales of fur trapping in the Canadian wilderness whence he and his family had fled during the Terror. He was not really very happy in France—despite the restoration of his lands. He had told her that only his fortuitous meeting with her had kept him in small, confining England.

"I would like to take you to Montreal, a beautiful city, my dear."

"But Monsieur Saint-Cyr, I am married," she had responded. "I do not believe you would like my husband to accompany us."

"Your husband . . . that—" But he had not finished his sentence because she had placed her fingers lightly over his mouth, and then he had kissed them five times, one for each finger.

The marquis was exciting and charming.

Millie Moberley thought Eugenie ought to take him seriously.

"My dearest Eugenie," her best friend had said with her habitual frankness, "your horror of a husband is failing fast. I would not give him six months . . . and I know there are numerous gallants pursuing you. . . ."

"Millie," Eugenie had protested. "You ought not to—"

"I beg you will not try to prevent me from speaking what is no more than the truth, my dear. The Marquis de Saint-Cyr is the catch of the season!''

"You make him sound like a fish,'' she had said laughingly.

"And he is a very big fish indeed—handsome, rich, exciting, and madly in love with you. You deserve a Marquis de Saint-Cyr after your years of catering to that *scélérat* . . . is that not French for *scoundrel*? I have always had the very devil of a time with the tongue, but I am sure I am right.''

"You are right, Millie. I mean, about the word.''

"And about your husband I am doubly right. *Brrrrr,* the way he looks at you makes me believe in all that nonsense about the evil eye.''

If Millie could have seen and heard him that morning, she would have been even more vociferous on the subject of looks that could kill. Eugenie slid down among her lacy pillows. It was wrong, and God would punish her for wishing that the heart condition that had robbed him of strength in the last year might become as virulent as its host and destroy him.

Even though he was powerless to inflict any more physical pain on her, his very presence offended her, and in the back of her mind there was the ever-lurking fear that out of spite he might reveal the truth concerning the boy known as his son to one or another of the gossiping cronies who came to see him. And if Thurston were to guess . . . But he would not guess, unless Simon were to tell him the truth. That was unlikely. Simon was not in communication with his nephew. Indeed, there had been no word of him in all the years of her marriage.

She was startled by the opening of the door but relaxed as she realized that it was only Elsie, with her cup of tea. As she took it and thanked the girl she suddenly changed her mind concerning the rest she had craved. She did not want to be alone with the thoughts that were bombarding her, and who knew, Simon might take it into his mind to come into her chamber.

"Elsie,'' she said decisively, "I believe that I will go to see Lady Moberley, after all. Would you please help me to dress?''

"Of course, ma'am. 'Twill do you good to get out, I think.'' The abigail flushed. "If you will pardon the liberty, ma'am.''

"I will pardon it''—Eugenie smiled at her—"because I cannot call a concern for my well-being a liberty.''

Elsie flushed with pleasure. "I thank you, ma'am. And what would you be wantin' to wear?''

Eugenie was glad to turn her mind to this most important of topics. "The white muslin, I think," she said. "And the new bonnet."

"Ah, ma'am, the very thing," Elsie said admiringly, and went to the armoire.

Some forty minutes later Simon, lying exhausted on his bed, heard his wife's light step upon the stairs. She still moved like a dancer, he thought, and though she was well into her twenty-fifth year, she actually did not look much older than in those days when she had danced on the stage of the King's Theatre.

He half raised himself, but much to his annoyance, he could not summon enough strength to call her. That, of course, was entirely her fault. The scene to which she had treated him that morning had proved most debilitating—but, of course, she did not care. Indeed, despite the fact that the doctor had expounded at length on the dangers of making him angry, Eugenie had slipped out of the house to go riding with her latest lover, that so-called marquis, who was as dark as any Indian and was probably a damned half-breed!

He had forbidden her to cultivate the man, and she had ignored his strictures. Since the onslaught of his heart condition, she had paid very little heed to him. She cared only for her bastard son. In fact, he thought with a surge of fury, it was almost as though he had ceased to exist—but he did exist, and though his days were numbered, he had arrived at a decision that would give her cause to regret her current attitude! In fact, she would be regretting it all the days of her life, he thought sourly. Raising a shaking hand, he caught at the bellpull that would summon Graves.

In a short time the valet arrived. "Sir?" he asked.

"I am feeling far from well," Simon said, growling.

The valet's bland face showed no change of expression. He said merely, "Shall I summon the doctor, sir?"

"No, I wish you to summon Mr. Overbeck. Tell him that it is urgent. There are changes I wish to make in my will."

"Do you wish him to wait upon you this morning, sir?"

"If it is possible. Time, I fear, is of the essence, Graves."

"Surely not, sir," the valet said.

"Do not lapse into sentimentality, Graves. It ill becomes you," Simon said tartly. "Rest assured that you will be remembered in that particular document."

"I thank you, sir," the valet said, inclining his head.

"Go and do what I told you to do," Simon whispered. "Hurry."

"Yes, sir." Graves left the room.

Simon smiled, and then quite suddenly he laughed. " 'The cream of the jest!' " he murmured. "It is a pity that I will not be around to savor it, but at least I will die happily."

"Papa, Papa, Papa," Olivia cried. "Nurse tells me that you are going away."

"I will not be gone long, my sweetest." Thurston bent to pick up his daughter. He smiled into her dark brown eyes. "There is business to which I must needs attend."

"What is business?" the child demanded.

"Think of the tasks that Mrs. Graham sets for you to do, my love."

"Reading and writing and sums." She made a face. "I do not like sums."

"But they will be very helpful to you when you are older, my dearest." He put her down gently and ran his hand through her dark curls, thinking that she was growing very pretty. It was a pity that poor Serena could not have seen the way she had changed in the last two years. He sighed, not liking to think of Serena, or of the infant who had died with her—the son they had both wanted and who, in the end, had killed her, turning around in the womb, a breech birth, and the doctor unable to do more than shake his head and cite the number of similar cases he had witnessed.

"Papa, you look so sad," Olivia said.

"Do I, darling?" He managed a smile. "Well, if I did, 'twas because I hate to leave you behind."

"Why can I not go with you?"

He shook his head. "That would not be possible. I am not taking the post chaise. I am riding. And I will not be gone long, you may be sure of that."

"Must you go, Papa?"

He looked suddenly grim. "Yes, I must go. My uncle has summoned me."

"Your uncle?" The child looked up at him in surprise. "Do you have an uncle?"

"Yes, my love, I do. Uncle Simon, my father's younger brother."

"Is he my uncle too?"

"He is your great-uncle, my sweetest. I think Mrs. Graham is waiting for you in the schoolroom, is she not?"

"Yes, she is. Do I have to go now?"

"Yes, it is not polite to keep anyone waiting, child. Now hurry along."

"Will you come and say good-bye, Papa?"

"Yes, of course, my darling. I would never go anywhere without saying good-bye to you first," he assured her.

He watched her dart off, full of a curiosity that needed to be satisfied. He himself was similarly full of curiosity concerning his uncle's urgent letter—with its attendant note from his physician, stating that Mr. Simon Sorrell was mortally ill. Obviously his uncle had feared he would not come to London without such assurances. And that was true. They had not been in communication since the arrival of the letter informing him of the birth of the son his wife Eugenie had born him. He grimaced, reluctantly remembering his wild search for her throughout London—and all the while that he had been agonizing over her possible fate, she had been in Scotland with Simon! As her aunt had predicted, she had lost no time in finding another lover!

That letter had been a real shock, activating feelings he had thought long buried. Serena, dearest Serena, had soothed and comforted him, and it had been then that he had begun to really love her.

A long sigh escaped him. The last two years had been very difficult. They had achieved so fine an understanding and had become so very close that when she had died, he had not only lost his dear love, he had also lost his best friend.

He sighed again as he thought of the many invitations that were coming his way at present. In the four lamentably brief years of their marriage Serena had been a great favorite of all the neighboring families. However, of late, he had become aware that the support and comfort he had received after her death had undergone a less than subtle change. It had, in fact, given way to the machinations of matchmaking mothers. A titled, wealthy widower of twenty-eight was as a tower under siege. Numerous females had been introduced to him, and as he had learned, to his annoyance, these ladies and their mothers were inclined to interpret his every chancy word as a possible indication of a romantic attachment.

Of late, he had found it expedient to refuse second invitations even when proffered by those he counted among his good friends. Since nothing was ever put into words, he was unable to explain that he had no desire to marry again, that he had had two loves in his life and, through no fault of his own, had lost them both and was consequently unwilling to subject himself to further anguish. Yet the day must come when he would need to go a-courting, else Simon's son would be his heir. "But not yet. No, not yet," he muttered.

Consequently he could almost welcome his uncle's summons to a city he had not visited for seven years. Serena, bless her, had insisted that she disliked big cities, had preferred jaunts to Bath and Brighton, and had, on their delayed wedding journey to Edinburgh, protested that she had enjoyed exploring the Bastle much more than wandering about even so large a city as the Scottish capital. He blinked away a sudden wetness in his eyes and directed his steps toward the graveyard, the mausoleum, which she now shared with Tom, his father, his mother, and his grandparents. In times of stress he had often received some little comfort from a feeling that her gentle spirit might yet linger there. He was greatly in need of comfort now as he steeled himself against a meeting that must needs be attended by one who had, for a time, come perilously close to shattering his faith in all women.

"Eugenie," he muttered, and though the day was warm, he shivered as if a shadow had passed over the bright sun and the hot summer breeze had suddenly turned chill. He quickened his steps and in a few minutes had passed through the opening in the yew hedges surrounding the tall stones and the Gothic excesses of the mausoleum.

"Serena," he breathed, and again he shivered, finding no comfort here, either. If she had been with him . . . But she, too, had gone, and he was alone.

CHAPTER TWO

SUMMONED BY GRAVES, Eugenie hurried down the hall to her husband's chamber. The valet had informed her that Simon wanted to see her as soon as possible. And did he, she wondered, believe himself at death's door again? In the last few months there had been several of these false alarms —some of them coming in the middle of the night. Each time Graves had hurried to alert her to that fact, and each time she had hoped . . . but she did not like to dwell on those hopes. Even hating him as much as she did, she did not want to ill-wish him. Her years in the theater had left her with superstitions she had never been able to dismiss, however much her reason told her they were nonsense. Ill wishes were said to afflict those who uttered them. However, when she came into his bedchamber, she found her husband propped against his pillows and smiling.

"Ah, my dear," he said, "you are looking well this morning. That blue gown is most becoming—an almost perfect match for your eyes. Is it new?"

"No, it is not new," she replied. "You wished to see me, Simon?"

"Yes, my dear, I wanted to alert you to the fact that I am expecting a visitor this afternoon."

"A visitor?" she repeated in some surprise. In the last few days Simon had not wanted to see any of his diminished circle of friends on the grounds that his condition must distress them. She suspected, however, that vanity was the real reason for his decision. "You have a friend coming, after all, then?"

"Not precisely," Simon said. "I have sent for my nephew,

and Graves has just given me his note, informing me that he will wait on me this afternoon at the hour of three.''

"He . . . is coming here?" Eugenie said through stiff lips.

"As I have just said, my dear. In my condition I could hardly arrange a . . . rendezvous outside of the house, could I?''

"But why?" She stared at him uncomprehendingly.

"I have a wish to see him before I die. With the exception of little Simon, he is my only living relative, but you know that, of course."

Hot words crowded to her tongue. "And do you intend to . . . to tell him about Simon, then?''

"My dear, as I promised you long ago, that secret is sacrosanct. He will never hear the truth from my lips. That was part of our bargain, was it not?"

"I do not want him in this house," Eugenie said angrily.

Simon smiled. "I do not imagine that he will stay *here*. I have suggested that he take rooms at Stephens Hotel in Bond Street—centrally located and not too far from us. Probably he will have brought his wife with him and you will finally have an opportunity to meet her. Serena, her name is . . . good family, not as good as our own, but—''

"You have already told me about the woman he married," she said, interrupting.

"Oh, have I? One is inclined to be forgetful at times like these.''

"At what hour will they be here?"

"But I have already told you, my dear. It appears that the news has confused you. They will be here at the hour of three.''

"Why was I not told of their coming before?" she demanded coldly.

"Do you always keep me informed about your plans, my dear?''

"My . . . plans?" she repeated. "And is Thurston's arrival one of your plans, then?''

He was spared an answer by a discreet tap on the door. "Yes?" he called.

The door was opened, and Graves appeared on the threshold. "The doctor has arrived, sir.''

"Please show him in," Simon directed. As the valet left, he added, "My dear, you need not stay.''

"I will not." She hurriedly left the room. Reaching her own chamber, she sank down on the chaise longue, trying to collect thoughts scattered by Simon's announcement.

"Why is he coming?" she whispered to herself.

"I wanted to see him before I die." That had been Simon's response, but that, of course, was not his reason. He was bringing him here because he wanted to torture her with memories of the past. She had known for some days that he was planning something, her supposition based on the fact that despite his weakening condition, he had appeared to be in surprisingly good humor. She shuddered. He was never in so good a mood as when he was contemplating something hurtful. He had been in great good humor on that night when he had first claimed his marital rights. She would not let herself dwell on that. It was over, at an end, and Simon, too, was approaching the end—and dangerous or not, she wished him dead and soon!

"Let it be very soon," she murmured. "Very, very soon."

Simon was feeling ill. Propped against his pillows, he cursed his condition. The doctor's face had been grave, and as usual, he had warned against any undue excitement. Yet as he awaited his nephew's arrival, he could not help the sensations that were making his weakened heart pound heavily in his chest.

He intended to enjoy the fruits of his labors—the meeting of Thurston and Eugenie and his subsequent conversation with his nephew. He would be, he thought exultantly, putting the last brick in the wall he had erected between them, and at the same time he would be forestalling any plans that his wife might have regarding her future. Yesterday he had had a conversation with Mr. Overbeck, his lawyer, during which time he had made certain pertinent alternations in his will. These must, he was sure, discourage the Marquis de Saint-Cyr, damn his eyes.

There was a tap at the door.

Simon also damned the sudden, accelerated beating of his heart. With an effort he said, "Come."

Graves appeared in the doorway. "Lord Seabourne is here, sir."

"Ah, let him come up, and tell my wife that I desire her attendance with the boy. Where is she now?"

"She is in her bedchamber, sir."

"Good, I beg you will not let her know that my nephew has arrived.

"Very good, sir." The valet left the room, closing the door softly behind him.

Simon looked after him gratefully. He owed a great deal to Graves and would remember him generously in his will.

Thurston, mounting the stairs in the wake of the butler, looked about him in some surprise. The house was not only situated in the most fashionable part of London, it was also beautifully furnished, suggesting that his uncle had come into money. In the old days he had constantly complained about a lack of the ready. He had reached the upper hall when all of a sudden a little boy came dashing toward him. They would have collided had not the butler put out a restraining hand.

"Master Simon!" he exclaimed. "What are you doing here?"

"Simon, you naughty boy," a woman called. "How often have I—" She hurried into the hall and stopped short, staring at Thurston.

He had been looking bemusedly down at the lad. He was a sturdy, handsome child with a cap of brown curls and big brown eyes. He judged him to be between five and six years of age—but, he realized suddenly, he was over six and undoubtedly his uncle's son. However, before he could make any more assessments, she had arrived and was standing there, slender and beautiful. That was evident even in the dimly lighted hall. Her name trembled on his lips, but at the same time she saw him, and her face, which just moments before had been animated, seemed to freeze.

"My Lord," she said between stiff lips.

Eugenie. The name rose to his tongue, but he managed not to utter it. He bowed and said, "Mrs. Sorrell."

"You have come alone, then?" she asked.

"Yes." He nodded. "This is your little boy?"

"Yes," she responded coolly. She looked down at the child. "Simon, my dearest, this gentleman is your cousin, Lord Seabourne. You must greet him."

The child smiled up at him. "I am delighted to meet you, sir."

"And I am delighted to meet you, Simon," Thurston said.

The butler, a silent observer to a meeting that he, though not an imaginative man, found fraught with tensions, cleared his throat. "Mr. Sorrell is—" he began.

"Yes," Eugenie said before he could continue. "My husband is expecting you, my lord. You will come this way, please." She looked at the butler. "That will be all, Knape."

The butler bowed. "Yes, Mrs. Sorrell." He went back down the stairs.

A flood of memories had come close to engulfing him, Thurston thought. However, they had scattered as sparrows before a hawk with the mention of the man Eugenie had married. He could only be glad of that. As he accompanied her down the hall he said, "Your little boy is charming."

"I thank you, my lord," she said coolly. "Here is the door to my husband's room." She put a hand on her son's shoulder. "Simon, remember that your father is very ill. You are to be quiet."

The child nodded. "I will be very quiet, Mama."

"He has fine manners," Thurston observed.

"On occasion." She allowed herself a slight smile as she looked down at the boy. Then, as she raised her head and looked at him, the smile vanished and her coolness returned. "As I am sure you are aware that Simon is very ill. He must not be allowed to become excited."

"I understand," he responded. There was, however, much that he did not understand. Even a man less sensitive than himself must have felt the hatred that emanated from her each time she addressed him. It was an attitude that confused him. He had anticipated coldness. He had anticipated guilt and even shame, for, after all, she had deserted him, had gone to his uncle, directly upon his leaving London! However, now was not the time to dwell on it. She had just knocked on the door and, without waiting for an answer, had opened that portal, ushering him into a large sitting room. It was beautifully furnished, and with the exception of his uncle's large desk, most of the furnishings were unfamiliar. In common with what he had seen of the other rooms in the house, it was a very tasteful atmosphere, and again he had a sense of understated luxury.

The door to the inner chamber was slightly ajar, and Eugenie, beckoning to him, said, "My husband will be expecting you, my lord." Looking down at her son, she added,

"You must be very, very quiet, my dearest."

"Yes, Mama," the child responded in a low voice.

Opening the door wider, Eugenie said, "Simon, your nephew has arrived."

"Good, very good," came the quavering reply. "Please come in."

Thurston, following Eugenie into a large chamber dominated by a huge four-poster bed, had some difficulty in not bringing his handkerchief to his assaulted nostrils. The room was very close by reason of all the windows being tightly shut. The air was heavy with the odor of sickness, and his immediate thought was that the little boy should not be exposed to it or, he decided a second later, to the sight of the frail old man who lay propped against a pile of pillows in that huge bed. If he had had any doubts concerning his uncle's condition, they had fled.

At six and fifty years, the Honorable Simon Sorrell looked at least seventy! His eyes were sunken, his skin yellowed. His hair had turned gray, and the voice in which he greeted Thurston was low and rasping. However, the smile that played about his pale lips was not without its quotient of mockery as he said, "Good afternoon, my dear Eugenie. I see that you have already met Thurston. How long has it been since you have seen each other? No matter, do sit down, Thurston, we have much to discuss, and Eugenie, my dear, I think you had best take little Simon out of here now that Thurston has been introduced to his nephew. We have much to discuss."

"As you wish, Simon," she said. She dropped a small curtsy. "I will bid you good afternoon, my lord." Her son had come to stand beside her, and taking his hand, she added softly, "Come, my love. We will leave your father to his guest."

As she closed the door behind her Simon said weakly, "Does she not look blooming, my dear Thurston?"

"Indeed, she does," Thurston said evenly, his pity for his uncle warring with a resentment he had believed dead and buried.

"You . . . need not tell me that I do not look . . . blooming." Simon continued. "And I . . . beg pardon for having dismissed Eugenie so quickly, but I have little time. Doctor has waxed most grave over . . . my condition . . . suggests I might go . . . any minute."

"I am sorry to hear that, sir," Thurston said, hoping that his shock on first seeing his uncle's sunken features had not been visible.

"No matter," Simon continued, his tones growing lower and more shaky. "I . . . wanted you to . . . see my wife for a . . . purpose. She's looking very beautiful, do you not agree?"

"Very." Thurston nodded.

"I . . . am aware that you, despite your . . . happy marriage, must yet . . ." Thurston's uncle paused and coughed, his withered hand against his chest.

"May I pour you some water, sir?" Thurston asked quickly.

"No, nothing . . . beg you'll not interrupt me . . . just listen. No time, d'you see . . . no time. I was about to say that you must yet feel animosity for . . . the heartless way she treated you . . . mercenary little witch. Lud, I . . . I'll not soon forget . . . frantic summons. Three days, no more, after you left . . . said she had feeling . . . you wouldn't return . . . cast herself into my arms, crying as if her heart would break. Believed in tears, d'you see. Took her home . . . with me, wept on my shoulder . . . whole night through . . . I tried to be honorable. Told her you'd be back . . . wouldn't believe me . . . said as how she wanted to . . . to be with me. Fool that I was, I believed her. Married her . . . lived to regret it. The lad's mine . . . has Sorrell features . . . couldn't have another child . . . glad. Might not have been mine . . . no morals . . . has led me a merry dance. If I hadn't made very good investments, she'd have left me . . . years ago, but craves money . . . and will have . . . large inheritance. Want it for boy, not wasted on a lover . . . she's a countess in her own right . . . and unless deeply mistaken . . . will be marchioness or . . . French equivalent, damned fellow Saint-Cyr's her . . . latest lover . . . French." He paused, gasping for air. Then he swallowed and continued, "I know you must hate me . . . do not repine, lad. Did well to marry as . . . you did. I want you . . . to help secure my son's inheritance. Want you to be . . . his guardian . . . have taken liberty, named you in my will . . . give you control of monies. I know I can . . . trust you."

"But, Uncle Simon—" Thurston began.

"Hear me . . . know you had . . . unfortunate experience with her, know her light nature." Simon's face became suffused with color, and his eyes narrowed. "I tell you, I'll not have Saint-Cyr wasting my boy's inheritance . . . beg you . . . take lad to country . . . put him in your wife's care . . . want him brought up in . . . decent household. If he's half French, he is also a Sorrell."

Simon was breathing shallowly. His face was even more flushed, and he was obviously far too excited as he weakly clutched Thurston's arm. "Promise me, you and your wife will care for my poor boy . . . promise me, please."

"Sir, it is best that you make other arrangements," Thurston said gently. "I have no wife . . . Serena is dead these four years past."

"Dead?" Simon rasped, looking at Thurston with a mixture of fear and anger. "Dead, you say? Why . . . why, had I no word of this? Four years dead and no . . . no word?"

"You forget, sir. We have exchanged no word since—" He broke off as his uncle, sitting straight up in bed, shook his fists at him.

"Damn you to hell." He snarled weakly. "Damn you . . ." A long, rattling sigh escaped him, and he fell back against the pillows.

Shocked and confused, Thurston stared down at him. Simon was lying very still. He hardly needed to put an ear against his chest. Even before he made that futile move, he was aware that Simon Sorrell's heart had stopped beating. It was a moment before he could bring himself to close his uncle's staring eyes and pull the sheet over his face. He wished he might feel pity or grief, but he felt nothing; not even his old anger stirred as he stared down at the sheeted figure of his late uncle. Moving away from the bed, he started toward the door. He would have to find a servant who would break the news to Eugenie.

St. James Church was only partially filled. Eugenie, clad in her widow's weeds, sat near the altar, her little boy beside her, and as next of kin, Thurston sat on her other side. It was an arrangement neither of them fancied. However, Lady Moberley, Eugenie's best friend, had insisted that the amenities be observed. In her frank way she had said to Eugenie, "You, my dearest, have always been the subject of gossip. For your own sake and for the sake of little Simon, you must play or dance the role of Caesar's wife."

Thurston, informed that he was required to sit in the family pew, had made no objections. Now, as the minister spoke a eulogy based largely on his own imagination, since he had seldom seen his late parishoner, Thurston cast a side glance at Eugenie. In her black garments and with a black veil covering her face, she seemed the very image of sorrow. Yet on that day, half a week earlier, when he, emerging from his uncle's chamber, half bemused by the suddenness of Simon's demise, had met her in the hall and blurted out, "Uncle Simon is dead," her reaction had shocked him.

She had come to a stop mid-step, her eyes narrowing and her slender body tensing. Yet rather than the expressions of shock and grief he had anticipated, she had said, quite composedly, "I must tell my boy, and I would be grateful if you would, on your way out, instruct Knape to summon the doctor."

Then, as if she had only at that moment become aware that he was more than a mere bearer of bad tidings, she had added, "Ought I to proffer my sympathies, my lord?"

Her chilly acceptance of the news, coupled with a question that appeared to be edged with mockery, had shocked him and, at the same time, had underscored his uncle's confidences. Had it been at that moment that he had decided not to renounce the duties thrust upon him by the late Mr. Sorrell? It little mattered when, he decided. By his silence he had tacitly accepted them, and on the morrow, the reading of the will would take place.

A wry smile played at the corners of his mouth, and he quickly sucked it in. Despite the fact that he was far more in the mood for smiling, it was a time for grieving—or at least a show of it. Fortunately he had learned to mask his emotions, emotions which, at this time, might have given rise to gossip were there any present who knew that his late uncle's wife had once been his nephew's mistress.

He frowned, trying to understand, as he had for the three days since his uncle's death, why Simon had evolved so strange a plan. Had his marriage cut him off from his friends to the point that there was none other he might entrust with the guardianship of his son? And who was this Saint-Cyr? On entering the church, he had scanned the several people who had come to offer their sympathies to the widow. They had numbered among their ranks several distinguished, elderly gentlemen and a few ladies, one of whom, a Lady Moberley, was with her husband and seated in their same pew. Obviously Eugenie had a place in London society, and if she also had a lover, he had been wise enough not to make an appearance at her husband's funeral.

Eugenie, her eyes hidden by a veil that darkened but did not obscure her vision, darted a side glance at Thurston and wished that she had been granted an ability said to be possessed by seers. Why had her husband summoned him from the country? To torture her, of course. And what had passed between them? Had Thurston been partially responsible for the death she had so long anticipated and for which she had prayed? Yet to pray for a death and have that prayer granted was frightening. Even more frightening was the arrival of the man she hated second only to Simon. Now that Simon was dead, he stood alone, a dark memory come to life.

As she had not been able to do on the day of his arrival, she cast surreptitious glances at his profile. As she had noticed on that first day, he looked older. He would look older. He had been one and twenty when they met and was now twenty-eight. Surprisingly there were strands of white in his dark hair. There was also an air of settled melancholy about him. She had also noted that on the day of his arrival—noticed it without noticing it, she realized. Or, she thought, perhaps the unhappiness was not as settled as she had imagined. Perhaps he was merely missing his wife. And why had he left the lady behind?

Simon had expected that he would bring her with him. He had said with a laugh, "You will now have an opportunity to meet your rival, my love. I understand she is very beautiful and, of course, a lady of high degree. But do not imagine that I am denigrating your heritage, my sweet. It is just that we English have these odd prejudices about women who exhibit themselves on the stage in various degrees of undress. But, of course, it was your unfortunate circumstances forced you to it, was it not? And then there was your grand passion for my unworthy nephew, which resulted in your . . . er, final fall from grace. Consequently, even if you had had a dowry, Thurston could not have wed you." His face had darkened then, and he had added, "I beg you will not let such falls become a habit after I am gone, my dear. After all, you bear my name."

She bit her lip, wishing that she could not remember so many of his sneering comments. And she need never to have been a party to them at all if . . . Her bosom swelled with a caught breath as she glanced at the man who had been responsible for all, all, all that had happened to her—the man who had professed a love he had not felt at all! He and his uncle were two of a kind—and why had Simon summoned him, and why, since Simon was dead, had he remained?

Bitterness prowled through her brain—bitterness like a caged animal in the Tower menagerie—paced back and forth, fretting at the barriers that kept it imprisoned, kept her imprisoned by custom! In the days to come, she would be clad in mourning cloth, she who could only rejoice that Simon's voice was stilled. No longer could he revile her or threaten her with revelations that must disgrace her and brand her son with the bar sinister. Yet despite the removal of that threat, she must pretend a grief that she did not feel.

"Mama, everyone is leaving. May we leave too?" little Simon asked.

Eugenie looked up and saw that the people were filing out. She glanced to her left and found Thurston standing near the pew. She said, "Of course, my love, we will go. There will be guests at home to whom we must see." She looked at Thurston again and said what courtesy demanded. "Will you come with us, my lord?"

He shook his head. "I thank you . . ." He hesitated and then continued, "I have letters to write, Mrs. Sorrell."

She loosed a breath of relief. "Very well." Again courtesy demanded another question. "Will we be seeing you again before you leave?"

He was about to answer when a darkly handsome young man came forward. "Ah, my dear Madame Sorrell," he said. "I have been wondering where you were. I arrived late. May I tell you how very sorry I am to hear of your bereavement?"

Eugenie, meeting his dark, dancing eyes, flushed. "I thank you, Monsieur Saint-Cyr." She glanced at Thurston. "I do not believe you have met my husband's nephew, Lord Seabourne. My lord, this is the Marquis de Saint-Cyr."

"Ah, no, I have not had the pleasure." The marquis turned to Thurston. "My deepest sympathies, my lord."

"I thank you, monsieur," Thurston said stiffly. He turned to Eugenie. "I will say farewell for the nonce, Mrs. Sorrell, but I will be there tomorrow."

Surprise went through her, but before she could question him further, Saint-Cyr was offering her his arm, and other friends were crowding around her, expressing their sympathy.

Much to her annoyance, Thurston did not linger. Consequently she could not question him as to why he found it necessary to call upon her again. However, if he did, she would tell him in no uncertain terms that he was not welcome in her house. It was her house now, she realized, and she was free to decide who she would welcome. Thurston would learn before he was very much older that he would never be welcome.

CHAPTER THREE

"BUT WHY?" EUGENIE said in tones uncharacteristically high. She was confronting the tall, heavyset, grave-faced man she had always privately called "overbearing, overweening Overbeck."

"Why has my husband's nephew been invited to attend the reading of the will?" There was another question she longed to ask, but that must needs be put to Thurston. Why had he given her no inkling of the reasons he had remained in the city? He could easily have told her yesterday at the funeral. She glared at the lawyer and repeated. "Why was I not told?"

The lawyer regarded her coldly. He was well aware of her background, and unlike the ton, he was not so ready to forgive and forget a past that had included a lengthy stint as an opera dancer. He wondered if she had not also been an actress, for certainly she was treating him to some high-pitched histrionics. And even though he was aware of her lineage, he had no liking for the French. Had not one of their number been responsible for half a world of turmoil—and the Battle of Waterloo as well? They were all the same! However, he must needs remember that he might remain in her employ, if indeed she chose to use his services now that the Honorable Simon Sorrell had been gathered to his maker. Consequently, with a gentleness he was far from feeling, he said, "It was your husband's wish, ma'am."

"So you have said!" she retorted. "But as I have already explained, I do not feel that my husband's nephew should be present!"

"The late Mr. Sorrell specified—"

"Yes, yes, yes, I know what he specified, but still I would like to have an advance look at the will and so spare myself another meeting with this . . . this man!"

She had made the word *man* sound like an epithet, Mr. Overbeck thought, and given his opinion of her, it was with some little satisfaction that he said, "I am afraid that is not possible, ma'am."

She was silent a moment, then, raising tear-washed blue eyes, she said softly, at last, "Could you not make this one exception?"

The lawyer's lip curled. She was now resorting to other tactics, but his many years of dealing with the angry relatives of late clients had steeled him against any and all forms of persuasion or, in her case, barefaced blandishments. Since right and might—if that will could be so construed—were on his side, he stood his ground. "I have my instructions, Mrs. Sorrell. I cannot deviate from them."

"Then there is no more to be said?"

"I am afraid not, Mrs. Sorrell." However, having made his point and stuck to it, he could afford to be a little magnanimous, he decided. "You will not need to remain in Lord Seabourne's society long—the will reading should be at an end very quickly." He swallowed convulsively, being suddenly reminded of the new instructions contained in that same document. However, they were only of peripheral concern to him.

Meanwhile the young woman, whom in his own mind he still called "the opera dancer," gave him a look of such concentrated virulence that he shivered and felt some compassion for young Lord Seabourne. At the same time he decided that he could quite understand Mr. Sorrell's decision regarding his wife. He said, "Would you mind, Madame, if I were to repair to the library? I must sort out my papers pending the reading."

"Yes, you may," she said coldly. "I will have Mr. Knape accompany you."

The clock, striking the half hour between one and two, caused Eugenie to start and also to wish for perhaps the thousandth time that her late husband had possessed numerous relatives. The fact that these worthies must needs have been mentioned in his will did not concern her. They would have kept her from needing to talk overmuch to Thurston. Unfortunately there would be no barriers between them. They would occupy the two chairs drawn up to the desk in the library. Behind them would be those servants who were mentioned in the will. He had not included the entire household staff, he had told her—only those who had been with him the longest. These included Mr. Knape, the butler; Mrs. Yates, the house-keeper; Mrs. Peebles, the cook; and, of course, Graves, her husband's valet, whom she disliked heartily if only because he had once served in that same capacity when she was living with Thurston.

No, that was not entirely true. There was something about Graves she did not like, had never liked. He had a way of looking at her that contrasted greatly with a manner bordering on the servile. Indeed, he gave her a feeling that were she to question him, he could reveal much that was hidden. However, she would need to pay for that information . . . and why was she thinking of such things? She had an answer for that. She did not want to dwell on the imminent arrival of Thurston, who should have, she thought with a little thrill of anger, told her why he would be present today. And why had Simon summoned him? It was cruel of him to thrust his nephew at her after all these years, and just as cruel for Thurston to have answered that summons. He should not have been there. He was part of a past that she had, with infinite difficulty, buried.

"I tell you yet again Banquo's buried. He cannot come out of his grave." But Banquo had come out of his grave to haunt the guilty Macbeth—and the analogy was wrong. She ought not be haunted; she should be the haunter, and, of course, she was thinking along nonsensical lines. It was equally nonsensical to wish that the reading of her husband's will might be carried on in the garden where she could wear her veil. Yet, on second thought, she had no need to hide from Thurston. It was he who ought to hide, he who had made so many promises and all of them lies! It was a pity that he was no actor, for certainly he had played the part of a distracted lover to the hilt!

Hard on that thought, Knape came into the drawing room. "Lord Seabourne," he announced.

Eugenie rose. "You will show him into the library, please," she said. "I will join them in a minute."

As the butler withdrew, she cast a glance in the mirror that hung near the double doors. She was momentarily taken aback. Her veil was so very dark! It obscured her hair too. Indeed, she looked not unlike one of the black-clad Furies of *Alcestis* and was immediately angry with herself for the analogy. Still, she could not help remembering that later that same night, she had met the handsome young man to whom she had spoken so briefly at the British Museum—the young man who had later bet his uncle fifty guineas that he could seduce her.

She turned away quickly, wondering why she had been afflicted with that particular memory at a time like this. She left the drawing room and went down the hall, hesitating as she reached the library, but Knape was just emerging and he moved quickly to hold the door open for her. Head held high, she entered swiftly and, having seen the chair she was to take, came to it and nodded at the lawyer, now ensconced himself behind the desk. She forced herself to greet Thurston, who had immediately stood up.

"Good morning, Lord Seabourne."

His face was grave as he said, "Good morning, Mrs. Sorrell. I hope you are feeling better. I know how trying a time this must be for you."

She would have dearly loved to tell him that the time was not in the least trying and that her health had not been affected by her husband's death and that, on the contrary, she was happier than she had been in years. However, these sentiments could not be confided, especially to the man whose presence she resented so bitterly. Praise God he would be gone once the reading was at an end. She said merely, "I am well, thank you."

As she, and then Thurston, took their seats, the lawyer cleared his throat and picked up a document before him. Clearing his throat a second time, he said, "As you are aware, those present are here to attend the reading of the last will and testament of my late and much lamented client, the Honorable Simon Sorrell." He looked up and surveyed the people in the room. "The order of the will is reversed. My late client wished to name first those of his household who have served him faithfully over the years. To Mr. Theobald Knape, his butler, he leaves the sum of . . ."

Eugenie hardly heard him. Anger was a hard lump in her throat. It was so very like Simon to leave her so-called fate to the last. And why, she wondered, as she had been wondering ever since his arrival, why, why, why was Thurston present? Thurston, whom Simon had never mentioned without an accompanying sneer or a curse.

Had he brought him from his home in Somerset merely to turn the knife, as it were, in wounds previously inflicted by that same nephew, or had he another more malefic purpose in mind? Knowing the man she had reluctantly called husband for the last seven years and longer, she was quite sure it was the latter. And what further indignity did he hope to visit upon her? Did he have it in mind to make Lord Seabourne his beneficiary? She doubted that. Simon had bitterly resented the quirk of fate that had made him the younger rather than the older son, and he had not scrupled to tell her that he was envious of Thurston's luck in brothers.

"A man of his character does not deserve such good fortune," he had said more than once.

No, she was sure that he would not willingly increase his nephew's fat inheritance.

These ruminations were interrupted by Mr. Overbeck, who said, "That ends the bequests to the servants. I think that everyone—with, of course, the exception of Mrs. Sorrell and Lord Seabourne—may now leave the room."

There were murmurs of gratitude as the servants filed out. Then Mr. Overbeck, waiting until the door had closed behind the last of them, said, "We will now concern ourselves with the final part of this document."

Eugenie stiffened. Was it her imagination, or had there been an ominous note in the lawyer's voice? Rigorously she quelled a desire to glance at the man sitting so quietly at her side. Lifting her chin, she fastened her eyes on the lawyer's egg-shaped countenance, thinking irrelevantly that she had never liked men with small eyes and full, pouting lips under wispy mustaches. She clasped her hands and, a second later, realizing then that she was clenching them until the knuckles showed white, she unclasped them.

"I, Simon Alexander Sorrell, being of sound mind . . ." Mr. Overbeck's voice had taken on the deep, mellow accents of a minister in a pulpit, complete with falling inflection, Eugenie thought, and paused in her thinking as the lawyer continued. ". . . do give and bequeath, with the exception of the aforementioned bequests, all my worldly goods and proper-ties to my wife, Eugenie de Villiers Sorrell." The lawyer stared at Eugenie, and then, clearing his throat, he said, "Mr. Sorrell has further stipulated as follows: 'If my wife, Eugenie de Villiers Sorrell, marries before the age of thirty, her inheritance, comprising all monies and properties, will be conferred upon our son, who will remain in the care and under the guardianship of my nephew until he reaches the age of twenty-one. His mother will forfeit all claim to him.''

''Nom d'un nom, I will not have it!'' Eugenie leapt to her feet a second time and turned to face the man beside her. She glared at him. ''I will not have it. I will not have you the . . . the guardian of my son.'' Her hot gaze turned on the lawyer. ''It is not possible!''

''Madame,'' the lawyer said coolly, ''I did not have the composing of the document. It was framed by your husband, and I fear you have no choice but to abide by the stipulations contained therein.''

''I will not, I tell you! I would rather die!'' she cried.

''Eugenie . . . Mrs. Sorrell.'' Thurston was also on his feet. He turned toward her. ''I suggest that before you consider such . . . er . . . drastic measures, we discuss what can be done.'' Addressing the lawyer, he continued, ''I, myself, am not in agreement with my uncle's bequests, and I would appreciate it if we might have another meeting in your chambers, sir.''

''You may, of course, Your Lordship, but it would be well nigh impossible to make any alterations in this document.''

''It must be altered!'' Eugenie said furiously.

''In what circumstances might it be changed?'' Thurston asked evenly.

''If my client proved to be of unsound mind, there would be a reason to look into the matter, but if you will examine the document, you will see that it is signed by three witnesses. They were his doctor, his lawyer, and a Captain Harlock, who is in the service of the Regent. All of them are agreed that the late Mr. Simon Sorrell was aware that his decision might be questioned and that he consulted his doctor, who provided an affidavit attesting that the said Mr. Sorrell was of sound mind at the time the will was drawn up. Mrs. Sorrell, I think you have no choice but to let this document stand as composed.'' The lawyer spoke with the faintest touch of complacency.

''And may you . . .'' she began furiously, then paused, swallowing her words with an almost palpable effort. She continued, ''I am sorry if I have seemed discourteous, Mr. Overbeck, but I hope you can appreciate my surprise. This clause concerning my possible remarriage . . . what drove my husband to assume that I would choose someone unworthy, provided another marriage were in my mind, which, at present, it is not.''

"Again, madame, Mr. Sorrell feared that your youth and inexperience might lead you—''

"I disagree," she said, interrupting. "He felt that . . .'' She paused, again stifling words that must thoroughly acquaint the man beside her with the misery of her marriage, the marriage for which he, with his clever lies and ultimate evasions, was, in effect, responsible. As calmly as she might, she continued, "I fear that I am in no condition to discuss this matter at present. I would prefer to arrange another meeting when I have consulted other authorities.''

"I am at your disposal, of course," the lawyer said, gathering his papers together. "I will leave you a copy of the will, and there is one for you, also, my lord.'' He produced the documents.

"I thank you, Mr. Overbeck." Thurston bowed.

"You are welcome, my lord," the lawyer responded with a touch of the obsequiousness due a peer of the realm. He turned back to Eugenie. "If there is nothing more that you wish to tell me, madame, I will take my leave.''

"There is nothing more at this time," she said coldly.

"And I, too, will leave," Thurston said.

"No!" she exclaimed, and was immediately angry at herself for a response that had the ring of a protest as if, indeed, she might want him to stay for reasons other than the obvious. She continued coldly. "I feel that there is more we must discuss, Lord Seabourne.''

"As you choose, Mrs. Sorrell," he said in tones as chilly as her own. "I am, of course, at your disposal until this matter can be brought to a satisfactory conclusion.''

Mr. Overbeck; as he later told a wife avid for as many details as he might provide of a meeting that had intrigued her far more than his other cases, was aware of actual electricity in the air. "'Twas no more than I expected, of course.''

"And was she angry, that French wench?" Mrs. Overbeck demanded with a sneer.

"Mad as fire! It is obvious that she hates young Lord Seabourne. I expect, however, that she would feel the same about anyone that Mr. Sorrell had appointed.''

"Aye, and where there's smoke, there's fire. Probably she has his successor already picked out, and he knew it, poor soul. But what man would wed her without money?''

Thurston was unconsciously in agreement with Mrs. Overbeck. The name Saint-Cyr was large in his mind as he stood alone in the library while the lawyer was taking his leave. Even though Eugenie had, as much as was possible in the circumstances, avoided looking at him, he had occasionally been able to see the play of emotions on her face. By turns, she had appeared puzzled, angry, and confused, but the anger, or rather the fury, appeared to outweigh everything else. Furthermore, he could not help but feel that a great deal of that fury had been directed at him. And yet was it fury or the proddings of a guilty conscience, provided that this woman, who had pretended to love him to distraction and who had answered none of his letters and had wasted no time in running to his uncle and, in a sense, seduced him, possessed a conscience.

His uncle's will appeared to give the lie to that. It seemed very likely that he had, in effect, taken a cuckold's revenge by inventing stipulations that literally kept his guilty spouse from making a second marriage. He must have known that such plans were already under way. He, himself, did not find this hard to believe, as again he hearkened back to Eugenie's glib vows of love and fidelity to him. Had they been completely false? Had she been planning, even as she kissed him good-bye, to put herself under his uncle's protection? He grimaced, wondering what she must have thought when she'd learned he had come into the title?

"Lord Seabourne."

He turned quickly, to find Eugenie standing in the doorway, her blue eyes as cold as if, indeed, he thought angrily, he, rather than she, was the one who had not kept faith. However, he had already expended far too much thought on a past that, until he had read the summons that had brought him here, he had largely succeeded in putting out of his mind.

"Yes, ma'am," he said, unwilling for reasons he did not wish to examine too closely to call her "Mrs. Sorrell," and why, he wondered, had she been called Eugenie de Villiers Sorrell in the will when her name had been de Montfalçon? It did not matter, he decided. He continued. "It is time we discussed this matter."

"Past time," she agreed coldly. She indicated a chair. "Will you not be seated, my lord?"

"I thank you." He sat down, and, looking in her direction, found she had taken the lawyer's seat behind the desk. The chair, thronelike in structure, had the effect of diminishing her. He had forgotten that she was so small, so delicately made, a porcelain figure, save that it had a pleasant, insipid expression. Certainly there was nothing pleasant about the face she turned in his direction. Anger had brightened her eyes and brought a twist to her lips. With a hope of avoiding a possible quarrel he said quickly. "How may I be of service in this matter?"

There was a moment's pause before she responded. "You will please tell me how my husband came to choose you as the guardian of my son?" Before he could respond, she continued hastily, "I am told that you have a family of your own. I cannot imagine that your wife would also want the responsibility of my little boy."

"My wife, ma'am, died four years ago."

Her eyes widened. "Oh, I am sorry, my lord. I was not informed of your bereavement."

"It is not common knowledge here in London, ma'am. As I think you must know, I have not been in communication with my uncle over the past few years." He leaned forward. "I knew nothing of his illness until I arrived in London the other day."

"And will you say that you knew nothing of his plans regarding my son and the inheritance?" she demanded icily.

"No," he said slowly, "I cannot say that. He told me of his intention on the day of his demise. I tried to argue with him. I pointed out that I, being a widower, was ill equipped to undertake the care of the lad—"

"The care of my son," she said, interrupting. "And how did he suggest that you care for him, my lord?"

Thurston flushed. "He appeared to believe that I should take him to the country in the advent of a second marriage. I was in the midst of explaining my cavils when he had his seizure. You know the rest."

"In other words, you were minded to refuse the guardianship?"

"At that time, yes. But he would not hear of it. He seemed exceedingly concerned for the welfare of his son."

"On the grounds that I once danced in the opera?" she demanded sarcastically.

Unwillingly Thurston suddenly saw in his mind's eye an image that had remained there on and off during the twenty-four hours that had passed since she had introduced him to the all but smiling Marquis de Saint-Cyr. On leaving the church, he had lingered by the gates and seen her come out with a tall young woman, the same woman who had been sitting next to her in the pew. There had also been another man, probably that woman's husband, and directly behind them had been the Marquis de Saint-Cyr! He had seen Eugenie look back at him. Saint-Cyr had been really smiling then. It had hardly been the mien for one attending a funeral! Was his attitude based on the fact that his mistress's husband had conveniently died? Suddenly he wondered at his lack of perspicacity. That, he feared, had been the result of seeing Eugenie again and experiencing a welter of forgotten feelings. It had resulted in a confusion that was finally fading away. Indeed, he felt as if blinders had suddenly been removed from his eyes and that without them he was suddenly seeing her clearly and remembering his uncle's very reasonable concern. He was also aware that he must needs answer her question.

He said coldly, "No, he was concerned over a future marriage."

"A future marriage?" she questioned angrily. "Was he more specific on that point, my lord?"

"As it happens, Mrs. Sorrell, he was. He seemed to believe that you planned to form a connection with the Marquis de Saint-Cyr."

Eugenie pushed her chair back from the desk and rose swiftly. "Damn him," she said loudly. "Is it possible that he thought a marquis was not good enough for me?"

"I think, Mrs. Sorrell"—Thurston also rose—"that he was considering the welfare of his son."

"His son!" She laughed angrily. "He did not care for his son, my lord, he cared only to rule my life as he has done for the past seven years."

"I beg to differ with you, Mrs. Sorrell. He appeared to have the greatest concern for his boy."

"For his boy?" she echoed, glaring at him. "And if I were to tell you that he had no feelings for him, none at all, what would you say?"

"I fear I would not believe you," he said coldly.

His words hit her like a shower of little daggers. That Thurston Sorrell could speak to her like that and look at her with such animosity, such disdain, when . . . But she would not consider the "when"; she would not consider the past at all! This was the present. This was the man who, in effect, was responsible for all the misery she had suffered for seven years, seven years that had seemed more like seven centuries! If there were only some way that she might hurt him as he had hurt her, she thought furiously. Indeed, she longed to throw something at him—that paperweight, for instance. It might break his head—but no, she must match his coldness with her own.

She said, "I have every intention of contesting that will."

"I am afraid that you will not be successful," he said. "And I find that, after all, I am quite willing to undertake those duties that my uncle conferred upon me."

She glared at him. "We will see what the judge rules, Lord Seabourne."

He considered her in silence for a moment before saying, "I am inclined to believe, Mrs. Sorrell, that the judge will probably refer back to the time when you were an opera dancer. I have the feeling that is common knowledge. Now, if you will excuse me, I will take my leave."

"You . . ." she began furiously, but she was speaking to the air, for he had left the room.

CHAPTER FOUR

"BUT HE IS a monster!" Lady Moberley protested. "Another Simon, indeed!"

Eugenie, sitting in the snug little parlor where Lady Moberley invited only her most intimate friends, moved to the window, staring into the blooming garden. "I never realized how very like his uncle he is."

"My poor Eugenie." Lady Moberely sighed, her large brown eyes warm with sympathy. "And this is the man you once loved?"

Eugenie nodded. "He is completely changed. Or rather, he did not change, it was only that I never really knew him." She raised dark-circled eyes. "Oh, Millie, what am I to do? He has it in mind that I am a light woman because . . . but you know."

"These men"—Lady Moberley sighed again—"they think of us as objects of their passion. They take what they may and then do all that is in their power to destroy us . . . and then they dare to have contempt for that which they themselves are responsible."

"He does have contempt for me." Eugenie turned to face her. "It is obvious."

"And you, my love?" Lady Moberley stared at her intently.

"I hate him!" Eugenie took a turn around the room. "He has not done enough to me; he will take my son from me also."

"If it comes to a magistrate's court, my love, you will have witnesses who will speak in your behalf."

"I thank you, Millie, you have always been my good friend—despite my background."

"You have many good friends among the ton."

"You were the first," Eugenie reminded her. "The others came after my titles were restored, but you never derided the fact that I was once an opera dancer."

"My dearest Eugenie, anyone with half an eye can see that you are not cut from common cloth. He is a very handsome young man."

"Who?" Eugenie demanded, startled by this sudden change of subject.

"Your in-law, Lord Seabourne. I was able to obtain a good look at him coming in and going out. He bears no resemblance to his uncle, surely—but handsome is as handsome does, I expect."

"He is another like his uncle!" Eugenie said bitterly. "Oh, dear, it is horrid being a widow."

"I am sure it must be, though black is most becoming to blondes. If I were a widow, I would insist on gray . . . black blots me out. Oh, dear, what am I saying?" Lady Moberley gasped. "If anything happened to Moberley, I should be utterly devastated."

"Dear Lord Moberley seems to be quite robust." Despite her current state of depression, Eugenie smiled. "I do not think you are in any danger of becoming a widow—especially since your husband is but two and thirty."

"One is always in danger, especially in London's streets. The pace at which some of these Corinthians drive their curricles . . . it appears to be fashionable to see how close you can come to some coach without engaging your wheels. But I am quite put off by what I meant to say. It is a pity that you need to wear mourning for Simon, despite the fact that it is *becoming.* You do look well in colors, particularly that beautiful blue lutestring with the fuller body that you bought at the Royal Opera Arcade last month. I have heard it said that skirts are going to get fuller . . . we might even eventually wear gowns like those our grandmothers donned. Can you imagine waltzing around a ballroom in those wide skirts, your hair combed into an actual edifice, complete with a ship in full sail or a bird cage on top? Oh, dear, how did I get so diverted? That, again, is not what I meant to say.

"Regarding marriage, perhaps you can go to France. Does not the marquis have an estate in the Loire Valley, which is, I understand, one of the most beautiful parts of the country? You could live there quite happily and with no one the wiser

. . . and there is, of course, his beloved Canada, though I do not see how *anyone* could love Canada. I had a cousin who was sent out there, a wild lad, you understand . . . his parents were in despair and there were wolves and Indians . . ."

"Millie," Eugenie felt it incumbent upon her to say, "we have not discussed marriage."

"Oh, but he will. He obviously adores you. If he did not, I would not be allowing this meeting. And he is extremely charming, as well as quite divinely handsome, and so tall for a Frenchman. I expect it was growing up in Canada and trapping all those animals, though that could have had nothing to do with his features. I just like to look at him, but never fear, I will not. I have instructed Matilda to summon me from the room five minutes after he arrives. You will allow me those five minutes, will you not, Eugenie?"

In spite of her inner trepidation, Eugenie had to laugh. "Of course, dear, dear Millie—need you ask? You are kind letting him come here."

"Well, you could not receive him at home," Millie said reasonably. "Oh, dear, these strictures concerning the proper behavior of widows are ridiculous. Think of all those poor girls who are married for their dowries and whose husbands are never at home save to encumber them with another child. I am sorry if I sound indelicate, but it is no more than the simple truth. Then let the husband be killed while racing his curricle, or shot while dueling over the dubious charms of his latest mistress—and 'tis the wife who must needs swath herself in black and act like a nun for two years straight! I . . ." She paused at a discreet tap on the door, and in that same moment the clock on the mantelshelf chimed the hour of three. "There, I am sure that is your marquis, and to the minutes. I wonder how long it will take him to offer for you? I give him twenty minutes and not a second more."

As Lady Moberley had predicted, the knock on the door was the butler, announcing the arrival of the marquis. Surprise flickered in his eyes as his mistress instructed him to show the guest to the parlor.

"Oh, dear." Lady Moberley sighed as the butler closed the door behind him. "You can rest assured that the servants will have grist for their gossip mill. It is fortunate that Lord Seabourne is staying in a hotel—where the tittle-tattle is unlikely to penetrate."

"Oh, dear." Eugenie looked concerned. "Is there nothing one can do to stem the gossip?"

"Not as long as there are masters and servants, my love, but it depends on whose ears it reaches. As I have said, it is unlikely that your new watchdog, however much he might stroll past your house, as you say he has been doing, will have his nose to that particular wind, and with his limited acquaintance in the city, he'll not have his ear to that particular plot of ground, either!"

"Yet to see him out there at various times during the last two days"—Eugenie clenched her fists—"I have been hard put not to have one of the servants warn him off."

"That would not have been wise, my love. There's no law against strolling for pleasure, as it were."

"There's a difference between strolling and patrolling," Eugenie snapped.

"True, but . . . ah," Lady Moberley murmured at another tap on the door. "Come in, please," she called.

The butler opened the door. "The Marquis de Saint-Cyr," he announced.

He entered swiftly, his dark eyes gleaming with the smile that curved his well-shaped mouth. Moving to his hostess, he kissed her hand. "Ah, Lady Moberley, how is it possible to thank you?"

"It is not possible, monsieur." She smiled "I beg you will not refine overmuch on a very small service."

"It is not small, and well you know it." He crossed to Eugenie and lifted her hand to his lips. "My dear, I have been in agony these two days past, not knowing how I could speak to you without alerting your . . . guard. And I ask myself, what right has he to be so vigilant?"

"My late husband, in naming him the guardian of my son and, in effect, of myself, conferred that right upon him." Eugenie explained in a tight little voice.

"Ah, that one, a monster indeed. They are both monsters, I think."

"Yes," Eugenie agreed bitterly. "Both."

"But we must needs see that you are not troubled by them, my dear, and . . ." He paused at a knock on the door.

Lady Moberley answered it. "Yes, Matilda, is anything the matter?"

"Oh, yes," the abigail said from beyond the door. "Little

Max has hurt his knee and is crying for you, milady. Might you . . .''

"But of course. I will come immediately, Matilda." Lady Moberley turned back to her guests. "I do hope you will excuse me, but as you must have heard . . ."

"Of course, we will excuse you, dear Lady Moberley," the marquis said.

"Yes, please go and attend to Max." Eugenie bit down a smile with some little difficulty.

Directly when she had gone, the marquis laughed. "What a very good friend she is, to be sure—and so now we may really converse, my dearest," he continued in French. Moving closer to her, he added, "I hope you do not think I am too familiar. I am sure you know how I feel about you."

"Yes, Raoul"—she smiled fleetingly—"but I—"

"But," he said, interrupting, "you will not put any more barriers between us now that they have finally fallen, now that our monster is dead and you are free."

Eugenie edged away from him. "But I am not free," she said emphatically. "Did you not receive my note concerning the terms of my husband's will?"

"Yes, of course I received it, and I confess myself astounded that he would confer such powers upon his nephew. Are you not guardian enough for your son? But I think you need not answer that. It is only more of the cruelty that Lady Moberley has already described to me."

"Has she?" Eugenie frowned. "I did not know."

"It was inadvertent, I assure you. She is your true friend, and true friends are hard put not to confide in other true friends—such as myself. And she knows that I am more than your friend, and will you tell me that you are not aware of it also?"

Meeting his ardent gaze, she said, "Yes, I am aware of it, Raoul, but—"

"But," he said, interrupting, "will you say you have no feeling for me?"

"I cannot say that, but—"

"But? Again, but? There can be no 'buts.'" He seized her hands, kissing one and then the other.

She regarded him ruefully. "There are. I have not told you all that is in my husband's will."

"What, my love, has he cut you off without a cent? That

would mean nothing to me. I am without parents who would demand a dowry. I am rich and—''

''You are more than generous, Raoul,'' she said, interrupting. ''I am aware of that, but . . .'' She gently withdrew her hands and, rising, moved restlessly around the room. ''My husband has made an arrangement whereby my son can be taken away from me.''

''What?'' He rose, too, and came to her side. ''How could he do that?''

In a small voice that she vainly tried to keep cool and dispassionate, Eugenie acquainted him with the terms of the will.

''Five years!'' The marquis exploded. ''But the man is a monster! Can you not contest it?''

''You are aware of my past,'' she said simply.

''I care nothing for that.''

''I am told by my husband's nephew that the courts *will* care. And Raoul, there is more you do not know about Lord Seabourne.''

''More?'' he questioned.

Eugenie nodded. ''It is not a nice story, but I owe you the truth.''

He gave her a strange look, ''I think, my love, that I might know some of that story. And I would not condemn you for whatever happened. You had no choice, I think.''

She regarded him in astonishment. ''How . . . who told you . . . not . . .'' Inadvertently she looked toward the door.

''No, no, no, my love, I did not hear it from the good Millie. You have, I think, a cousin—one Etienne de Champfleury?''

''Etienne?'' she repeated, staring at him in consternation. ''You have met Etienne?''

''Yes, in Canada. It was in April of 1816. He entered the fur trade as I was about to forsake it. He spoke of having all his titles restored, as did we all who could claim them. It was discussing our ancestry that brought us together. For a short time we were comrades, and in trading tales of how we happened to be in the wilderness, he told me a strange story of having had his life made miserable because his cousin, whose dancing at the King's Theatre had been the mainstay of the household, had been thrust from their home by his mother. Consequently he, who was blamed for the situation, was forced to fend for himself.''

"Great heaven!" Eugenie exclaimed. "You will never tell me that Etienne was turned out of his home!"

"Not entirely, but it seems that his mother had been in a royal rage at the time she had thrown the girl out. After she calmed down and realized what she had done, she turned her anger on him. Evidently she was a real virago, and he fled to Canada so that he could put a sea and half a world between them. So, you see, my dear, I knew of you even there, and then I came here and met you. I did not know immediately that you were the Eugenie that your cousin had mentioned. But your name struck me—and I had heard, also, that you had once been an opera dancer." He paused and said ruefully, "I am sorry to acquaint you with the fact that there is still gossip."

"But I know that," she assured him.

"Etienne told me also that Thurston Sorrell was the name of the man who became your lover . . . and so the fact that you were wed to one Simon Sorrell—"

"You do not know the facts connected with that marriage," she said hastily.

"I knew the difference between the names Simon and Thurston, and so I made inquiries. Eventually I learned that Simon Sorrell was wont to haunt the theater whenever you performed. I learned, too, that his nephew had stolen the prize and then suddenly left town . . . and just as suddenly you married his uncle."

She looked away, saying in a low voice, "That is not all the story."

"Knowing you, I am sure it cannot be all the story," he said strongly. Then his eyes brightened with anger. "And now —this rogue, this Thurston Sorrell—is daring to control the life he attempted to ruin? Ah, it is very strange. I can understand his uncle, but I cannot understand him."

Eugenie flushed. "Yes, it is very strange. It is also very strange that you should have known my cousin Etienne. Is he yet in Canada?"

"I do not know." The marquis shrugged. "He found the fur trade very rough and not to his liking, I know that much. Shortly after our meeting I lost sight of him. Canada is very large, you know. Also, it is very beautiful. I should like to take you there—you and your son. We could go and lose ourselves in the great forests, or we could live in Montreal."

"Raoul, my dear," Eugenie said warmly, "have you not

told me that you are very happy to be back in France, where it is civilized, and that you have made many plans for the reconstruction of your château?''

"The château would mean less than nothing to me, were I to occupy it without the woman I love. I love you, Eugenie, and you have said—''

"Please, Raoul,'' she said, protesting softly, "I cannot speak of love at such a time.''

He stared at her, saying bitterly, "If this man had not entered your life again, would it have been different?'' Without waiting for her answer he continued. "But of course it would be different.''

"Yes,'' she said, thinking of all that had happened seven years earlier. "Yes, it would have been very different, indeed. But we cannot turn back time as we might the hands of a clock, dear Raoul. And so you see that now . . . I can make no decisions.''

"Yes, I can see that you are momentarily impeded by this scoundrel. However, in this life, nothing ever remains the same. I can attest to that and so can you.''

"Yes,'' she said, and strangely there appeared in her mind's eye the small suite of rooms where she had once been so very happy. Anger thrilled through her and was reflected in her eyes. "Nothing remains the same.''

"We must find a way to fight this will,'' he said decisively.

"If it is possible.'' She nodded.

"Did your husband appoint another guardian, one to take his nephew's place if, say, anything were to happen to him?''

She gave him a startled look. "No, but nothing is liable to happen to Thurston. He is only eight and twenty.''

"It is possible that he could meet with an accident.''

She tensed. "What are you implying, Raoul?''

"Nothing, my love, save that this life can be very uncertain, can it not? And he is young to have held the title of viscount for seven years and more.''

"His brother was killed in an accident.''

"You see . . . ?'' Raoul murmured. "And his father?''

"He was hurt in that same accident and . . . but I do not want to talk about that, Raoul,'' she continued quickly, as she suddenly thought of all the ramifications attendant upon that pair of accidents. It had not only changed Thurston's life, but also it had changed her life. Much to her annoyance, she felt the prick of tears in her eyes and turned away quickly. "It is getting late. It seems to me that Lady Moberley said she had an appointment, and I must also be getting home. My son will wonder where I am. I hope you do not mind."

He smiled ruefully. "Of course I mind. These last mornings have been very difficult for me—riding in the park alone. It is always difficult when I do not see you. Still, I quite understand that you must be with little Simon as much as possible. He is fortunate, indeed."

"Fortunate?" she echoed. "He has lost his father, you know."

"But he has you for a mother, and pardon me if I am talking out of turn, but I have received the impression that the late Mr. Sorrell was a less than fond parent."

An affirmative answer trembled on Eugenie's lips, but she was suddenly confronted with the fact that she had already said far too much. "Simon was not young, and my son is a very active little boy."

"And"—the marquis smiled—"in consequence deserves the experience of having a young stepfather. Surely you must agree?"

Something in the back of Eugenie's mind stirred and amazingly whispered, "But he *has* a young father." Anger edged with pain smote her. As she had on other occasions, she felt as if she had been suddenly divided, and one part of her brain was in the possession of a stubborn stranger, a stranger she must needs defy. She said strongly, "Yes, I must agree with you. Youth is certainly more patient with youth than age can ever be."

"Ah." As he had when he had arrived, the marquis seized both her hands and kissed one and then the other. Looking deep into her eyes, he added, "Would you allow me the liberty of embracing you, my dearest Eugenie?"

"No." She determinedly pulled her hands from his tightening hold. "There must be no more liberties, Raoul."

He did not release her. "But we are alone, my love."

"Liberties, sir, can become a habit, and this is one I dare not encourage at the time."

Reluctantly he dropped his arms and moved back. "And so, we are encumbered by custom." He sighed.

"And courtesy, sir. I cannot abuse the hospitality of my dear friend." The moment those words left her lips, she regretted them. She had, in effect, allowed him to imagine that there would be another time when she would be more lenient and, she realized with some little annoyance, that she was not in the mood for surreptitious encounters. "I mean . . ." she began.

"Your meaning was entirely clear to me, my dearest Eugenie," he said softly. "I can be patient if I am not required to be patient too long."

She said firmly, "There must be a mourning period, sir. And now I do think you had better go."

"Can we not at least go together?"

She said determinedly, "I am sure, sir, that you are well enough versed in the customs of this island to know that we can do nothing together as yet."

"Ah, yes," he said with a grimace. "In India I am told that they have a most unfortunate practice. They burn the widow on the pyre with her husband. Here they suffocate her with antiquated customs. We must think of a way to circumvent them, my love. And so, farewell." He bowed over her hand, and turning, he went swiftly out of the room.

Though she had been glad to see him, Eugenie found herself equally glad to bid him farewell. At this moment in time she had found his passion and his urgency almost as trying as Simon's jealousy. Indeed, she wanted nothing so much as to be left alone with her little son and, in effect, to enjoy some part of the period the marquis had decried. Her eyes gleamed as she realized that for the first time in many years she need not be answerable to any man.

Lady Moberley came back into the room. "I watched him leave from the upstairs window," she said excitedly. "He was here for quite a while. Was it a . . . pleasant visit?"

"Very pleasant," Eugenie said. She was aware that Millie was eagerly waiting to hear more, but she was not willing to divulge more. However, it was necessary to satisfy some of her friend's curiosity. "We agreed that there could be no decisions at this time."

"Ah, then, decisions were discussed?" Lady Moberley pursued.

"Yes, they were discussed, certainly."

"My dear, I am delighted. I could wish nothing better for you." She embraced Eugenie.

"I do thank you, Millie. And I will go now. There is another gentleman who awaits me.''

"*Another* gentleman?" Lady Moberley's tone was edged with suspicion. "And who might that be?"

Eugenie was taken aback. Did Millie, for all their long friendship, suspect her of arranging and, as it were, boasting of other clandestine meetings? She said softly, "I was referring to my son.''

"Oh, of course, your son." Lady Moberley laughed. "I confess I am not yet used to thinking of him as a . . . gentleman.''

"At present he must needs don that mantle, for he is the gentleman of the house." Eugenie smiled. "Again, Millie, let me thank you for your hospitality.''

"You are entirely welcome, my dear," her friend said warmly. "I only hope that something positive may come of it.''

Eugenie favored her with another more enigmatic smile. "At this point I can, as I have told you, say nothing."

She was relieved as she came down the steps of Lady Moberley's Georgian mansion. She had committed herself to neither her dear friend nor the marquis. As she entered her waiting carriage she experienced another moment of delicious liberty, a moment that was particularly sweet to her when she recalled the myriad times she had gone shopping with Millie or with some other lady of her acquaintance or had attended a lecture or a concert only to be summoned into the library the moment she set foot in the house—there to be interrogated as if, indeed, she were some manner of malefactor! It also occurred to her as she gave the coachman the direction to drive her home that for the first time in the six years they had been residing there, the house had taken on the lineaments of a home.

In consequence of those feelings of freedom and release, Eugenie was far from pleased to be informed by Knape that Lord Seabourne was awaiting her in the library. As soon as she had divested herself of her outer garments, she hurried in that direction, but as she neared the library she was arrested by her son's delighted laughter. Air bubbles rose in her throat, for what reason she could not tell, and in another second she had pulled open the door to the library just as another shriek of laughter issued from her son's throat.

Eugenie came to a dead stop on the threshold to find

Thurston on his hands and knees, while little Simon rode on his back, his arms around his neck. "And this, my boy, is the way the camels walk"—he swayed from side to side —"because in addition to his two humps he must carry people on his back."

"Oh, I should like to see a camel!" the child said eagerly.

"One day . . ." In that same moment Thurston looked up and reddened, saying hastily, "Here is your mother. It is time that we both behaved like gentlemen."

"Don't want to be a gentleman," the child protested. "You would show me how a seal walks."

"Another time, young man." Thurston remained kneeling until the little boy climbed off his back. As he rose, little Simon regarded him with great approval. "That was fun, sir."

"It was fun for me, too, lad." Thurston flushed a deeper red as he looked at Eugenie. "It is a game my little daughter enjoys."

For some reason her heart began to beat heavily. She said rather breathlessly, "Oh, you have a daughter, then, my lord?"

He nodded, but before he could say anything more, Simon said importantly, "Her name's Olivia-Serena and she is almost six."

Almost six, born not long after Simon. Almost six and the daughter of Serena, his great love and also the half sister of the son he knew nothing about. Bitterness was a hard lump in Eugenie's throat. She had to speak over it, had to say calmly, "Ah, how nice for you, my lord."

"She is my second cousin," Simon said knowledgeably. "And he says that he is my first cousin." He gave Thurston a warm smile. "I did not know that I had *any* cousins, Mama."

She would have given much to deny that relationship, but that, of course, was not possible. "Oh, yes, everyone has cousins," she said casually. She added, "I think, Simon, dear, that you must be with Nanny now. I will bring you up to the nursery. If you will excuse me, my lord." She turned toward Thurston and experienced a shock. His face was flushed and his hair disarranged. One lock, loosed from its pomaded perfection, hung over his forehead. She had not noticed that when she came in and now realized that up until this moment she had not looked directly at him. Now, against her will, memories came rushing back. In his semidisheveled state he

did not look like a guest. Indeed, he could have been the man
of the house. He could have been her husband and was, she
reminded herself, the father of her son. She swallowed a lump
in her throat that had no business being there and managed to
say coolly, "I will be back in a few moments. Simon, my dear,
say good-bye to your cousin . . . Thurston."

"Good-bye, sir." The child put out his hand. "I did enjoy
myself ever so much."

Thurston grasped the proffered hand and held it for a
minute. "And so did I, Cousin Simon."

As she took the child upstairs to the nursery she barely
listened to his excited comments concerning the nice gentleman, who had played with him the way his own father never
had and, from the very first, had not spoken even one cross
word to him. Her heart was still pounding in her chest, and she
was thinking of Thurston's daughter. There were no sons,
then, no other children, else he would have mentioned them.
He had a daughter only, and she had a son who must be his
heir, unless, of course, he were to marry again for the heir of
which his uncle, in effect, had deprived him.

It was a strange situation,—a diabolical situation, indeed
—for Simon to make Thurston the guardian of his own son.
She conjured up an image of him on the floor, his little boy
riding so happily on his back. In that moment, too, he had
seemed like the man she had once loved—but that man, she
must needs remind herself, had never existed. The words he
had spoken to her were all lies, as false as his promises, and he
had no right to be in *her* house and with her son!

Much to her annoyance and anger, she found her vision
blurred and decided that the tears she hastily blinked away rose
not from the past, but from the present when, due to her
husband's will, she must needs be encumbered with one who
had treated her so cruelly. If there were such things as ghosts,
how he must be enjoying her untenable position—but, she told
herself, hotly, she was no longer subservient to his whims and
his commands. Indeed, she could almost wish he were a ghost,
a form without substance, unable to wield the power he had
once had over her. And guardian or no guardian, Thurston had
no power over her, either!

She opened the door to the nursery and met the cold gaze of
Mrs. Hooten, his nurse. "Ah, Master Simon," she said
coldly. "You were a very naughty boy—running away from

me and bothering that gentleman.''

The child raised indignant eyes. "I did not bother him. He said that he liked me."

Mrs. Hooten ignored his remark and said to Eugenie, "He darted away from me, Mrs. Sorrell. I tried to catch him, but the gentleman took him to the study. Since he is his guardian, I did not feel that I could interfere."

"That is quite right, Mrs. Hooten," Eugenie said, annoyed now because she was, in a sense, siding with Thurston. However, she had never liked the woman and in fact, had been pleased that she had been called away at the time of Simon's death. Otherwise she must have filled little Simon's head with all sorts of pious homilies. She said, "You will see that he has his bath, please. I will be back later to be with him while he eats his supper."

"Very well, Mrs. Sorrell." The woman had a disapproving look on her face. No doubt she missed her late employer, who had sharply protested when Eugenie interfered with nursery discipline.

Eugenie stifled an urge to tell the woman she could take another leave of absence—one that would be permanent. Instead, she went down the hall to her chamber to remove her coat and bonnet and have Elsie comb out her short curls.

Seated before her mirror, she was glad that she had cut the long, fair strands of hair that Thurston had once been wont to kiss and fondle. She was also pleased because it seemed to her that the face that stared back at her from the glass was almost totally different from when they had been together.

The eyes were certainly wiser. She had learned wisdom in a hard school. The mouth was firmer, she thought, but she could not remain up here contemplating the present in the terms of the past, a past that she had once thought dead and buried—was dead and buried, inhabited only by specters that had no more substance than that she had just attributed to her late and unlamented husband.

A short time later Eugenie came down the stairs, her hand caressing the balustrade. She was remembering that will or no will, it was her house, and that if she chose, she could ask Thurston to leave and he must needs obey.

She walked slowly along the passageway to the library, and as she reached the door she was once more assailed by an image of father and son playing on the floor. Thurston must love children. That had been very evident in his attitude. Probably he would have liked to have a son such as little Simon.

Well, she had craved revenge, and it suddenly occurred to her that she had it in the form of the child he believed to be his uncle's son—his uncle's son and her son. Her only fear lay in the letters she had sent to him, the loving and ultimately frantic letters that he had ignored, being involved with his new or, rather, as Simon had explained, his old love, cruelly promised to his brother but released by the latter's death. Might he not one day put two and two together and guess that the child she had mentioned in the last of those letters might possibly be his? No, she told herself quickly, because obviously he had paid little or no attention to them. He had been too happy with his inherited bride!

She came into the library and found him standing at the window. "You wished to see me, my lord?" she asked coldly.

He turned swiftly, and she was surprised to find his gaze as chilly as her own. The tone in which he responded—"Yes, I did"—matched it. "I have been giving some thought to your son."

She tensed, wondering if indeed he were questioning the resemblance between himself and the boy. However, the child might be said to resemble his so-called father as well. "Yes?" she asked.

"I was wondering if he might not be happier in the country for the nonce?"

"In the country, Lord Seabourne? Where in the country, pray?"

"With a child of much his own age. As I have told you, Mrs. Sorrell, my daughter is nearly six. And . . . we have a large acreage. As they are cousins, it would be nice for them to get to know each other."

"I agree, my lord." She forced a smile. "But as it happens, I have other plans for him at this particular time."

"I wonder if you are aware that it was practically your husband's last wish that I take little Simon to Seabourne Hall directly after the funeral."

A spate of angry words rose to her lips. She had an eerie sensation that Simon was reaching out from the grave to speak with Thurston's tongue. And, in a sense, that was exactly what he was doing in mouthing Simon's malevolent desires. Not content with making her miserable in life, he was using the medium of his nephew to inflict more pain upon her. However, anger would not prevail with Thurston. She must needs remember that old saying about the soft answer that turneth away wrath. She said gently, "I have other plans for him, my lord. As it happens, I am taking him to our estate in Kent, and we shall be there until Simon has recovered from the shock of his father's death. But I do thank you for the offer."

His eyes widened, and he seemed on the point of remonstrating. However, he merely said, "In that case I have nothing more to say."

Though she was surprised and a little wary of his sudden and unexpected capitulation, she managed a smile. "I am delighted that we have reached an agreement, my lord."

"As am I, Mrs. Sorrell. I will take my leave, then."

"Will you be remaining in the city, sir?"

"I think that I might return to the hall." His eyes lingered on her face for a moment. "I try not to stay away too long at any given time. My daughter misses me when I am not in residence."

"I am sure she must, my lord."

"However, Mrs. Sorrell, I will come back to London from time to time."

Eugenie tensed. It seemed to her that there was an implied threat in that statement as if, indeed, he were tacitly telling her that he meant to see if she were carrying out the terms of the will . . . and was he also suggesting that he expected to have a say in the raising of his so-called nephew? Hot words rose to her lips. She would have dearly liked to point out that he was not Simon's guardian yet. However, again, she managed to quell that impulse. She said merely, "London is a very pleasant city. I find it difficult to remain away from it for very long."

"I expect that is understandable, since you have spent so very much of your life here, Mrs. Sorrell. I will bid you good afternoon."

"Will you be returning to the hall tomorrow?"

"That is my intention, Mrs. Sorrell."

"Then I wish you a most pleasant journey, my lord."

"And I wish the same for you. When are you planning to go to the country?"

"At the end of the week, I imagine. There are still some

pressing matters to which I must attend before I leave.''

"You will be shutting up the house, I expect?"

"Yes, for the time being, my lord.''

Finally he left, finally, finally, finally. She had been afraid that their desultory conversation must needs have continued another twenty minutes. She bit down a small smile. She had, however, helped prolong it—in the interests of gathering information. Had that been his objective as well? Of course it had! He was taking his duties very seriously, but they were not duties, not yet. He was not little Simon's guardian, and if she had to remain alone for the rest of her life, he never would be!

Hurrying up the stairs, she went into her chamber, and standing at the window that faced the street, she was in time to see Thurston climb into his post chaise. She watched until the vehicle had rolled away before ordering her housekeeper to prepare for an immediate move to the country.

She was able to alleviate Mrs. Yates's pain by some degree by telling her that they would take only a skeleton staff. Still, the intelligence that she wanted to leave at half past six in the morning was enough to send the lady into strong hysterics, which Eugenie soothed with the mention of a higher wage.

In the midst of these hurried preparations she suddenly thought of the marquis. It was hardly right to leave for her estates without informing him of her intentions. Yet what if he took it into his mind to follow her?

She frowned. She did not relish the thought, but actually was rather sure that he would not want to leave London. Raoul enjoyed the dances, the routs, and the theater. He was much in demand. A prejudice against those of French extraction had not extended to one who had suffered in the terror and had made a fortune in Canada—spending it lavishly in London.

There were many ambitious mothers with nubile daughters who extended invitations to him. While he appeared impervious to these, Eugenie was sure that he had other interests, which included the theater and the opera. Being a passionate young man, he was not one to let his needs go unsatisfied. His years in the wilderness had whetted his tastes for the frivolities of life, and though he had professed himself quite willing to brave the wilds of Canada with her, she was not at all sure he meant it. Men who fancied themselves in love were wont to make the most extravagant claims, only to forget them conveniently once the object of desire was secured. None knew that better than she, she thought with a little shiver as she unwillingly recalled Simon's many promises.

He had been so kind during the first eighteen months of their marriage. How proud he had appeared at the christening of the child to whom he had so generously given his name. He had acted as if the lad were his own son. Consequently his about-face had proved the more startling and frightening. He had not been content with merely possessing her body—he had seemed to crave access to her very soul. If she were to smile at some remembered witticism, he would demand that she tell him what she was thinking, and he would question her, probing, probing, probing, as a magistrate with an arrested felon, a magistrate used to dealing with criminals and never, never believing their protestations of innocence! He had worn a look, a smile, or a greeting from one or another gentleman met at some rout or banquet into the ground and, she thought with a little shudder, there had been that same sort of suspicion mirrored in Thurston's eyes.

It was possible, she thought bitterly, that he was judging her by himself. Those who practiced duplicity could never trust anyone. And who would have thought all those years ago that *Thurston* could look at her that way? Angrily she thrust her encroaching memories back . . . she was almost free of the Sorrells, and tomorrow she would be loosening another of the chains that bound her. With that in mind, she settled down to write her note to the marquis.

CHAPTER FIVE

THURSTON, SITTING IN his hotel room, was writing a letter to his daughter in simple words that she would understand. She could read amazingly well, he thought fondly, but the smile that played about his mouth at the thought of her vanished as he slipped the letter into an envelope.

Olivia's image had been replaced by that of Eugenie, conniving, lying Eugenie, who was, if she but knew it, as much his ward as her son. Despite the fact that her titles had been restored and her place in society assured, she was at heart the mercenary little dancer who had once meant more to him than life itself. Even now that he knew her beauty and charm were only a facade, she still had the power to attract him. However, he was no longer a naïve young man of twenty-one. He had lost that vulnerability that had made him her victim as well as her lover! It had gone with the certain knowledge that his enchanting little mistress had waited less than a week to fly to the arms of his uncle, a man she had once professed to dislike.

He, who had once hated his uncle, now felt very sorry for him. Despite his greater knowledge of the world, he, too, had been cozened by Eugenie. He could well understand the late Simon Sorrell's fears for his son. He loosed a long, quavering breath. He had not been impressed by the Marquis de Saint-Cyr. The man was handsome and well spoken, but he had a roving eye, and certainly he was not the sort of a stepfather that little Simon should have! He was a bonny lad, but he would receive scant attention from the marquis, he was sure.

Yet unless something happened to prevent it, he and Eugenie would marry.

He smiled grimly, wondering what she would have said had she known that he, primed by his uncle's suspicions, had watched the house for the past three days and had ultimately been rewarded by the sight of Eugenie leaving it. He had followed her carriage in his post chaise and seen her go into a house on Arlington Street. He had waited outside and had been half ashamed of himself for what could only be termed spying; but then he had been rewarded a second time—if one could call what had happened a reward. He had seen the Marquis de Saint-Cyr arrive and go into the same house. He had waited for a goodly amount of time, but the marquis had not reemerged. It had been, of course, an assignation. He had had a wild notion of following him into that house and confronting Eugenie—but that, of course, would have been madness.

He had gone to her house, intending to wait and confront her with what he had seen, but instead he had met little Simon, such an adorable little boy! It was amazing that his uncle could have fathered so delightful a child. He had taken to him immediately, and the lad had seemed to like him too. The child had, in fact, completely appropriated all of Thurston's attention. He had actually forgotten Eugenie's perfidy. Indeed, it had occurred to him that if he and Eugenie had had a child, he might have looked a great deal like little Simon.

He did not resemble his father quite so much, but the Sorrell features had a way of skipping generations—as witness himself and poor Tom. Simon was one of the reasons he would not be returning home. In fact, he had it in mind to accompany Eugenie to Kent. If indeed she intended to meet Saint-Cyr there, he would have all the proof he needed and could make arrangements to secure the guardianship of the lad. She would hate him for that, but she hated him already. That was only too obvious.

Why?

He had an answer for that too. She must be embarrassed at seeing him—after her shameless flight to his uncle's arms. How, he wondered bitterly, could he have been so blind, believing that she loved him when her words had been as false as she? Yet he could only be grateful for the experience, because now he knew her for what she was: a heartless little schemer. And he had once thought her so far above the other ballet girls with whom she had associated. She was not above them. She was an opera dancer through and through, beautiful, beguiling, and for sale to the highest bidder!

He groaned and found his eyes suddenly wet. He rubbed them furiously—he was being a damned fool. He would go to the opera that night, repair to the Green Room, and would meet there a thousand Eugenies and take one of them to supper and to bed. He knew how to do it. He had learned from an expert just how to please these women. Gold. Gold would open any door.

They were finally on their way—a caravan of coaches, if one could use so large a word for the three vehicles, two carrying goods, chattels, and staff while the third and last in line was given over to Eugenie, little Simon, and Elsie. Much to her unspoken ire, Mrs. Hooten had been left behind, Eugenie having insisted that she would share her chores with a willing Elsie.

As they reached the highway Eugenie was thinking about Mrs. Hooten, who had glared at her and firmed her mouth until it appeared almost lipless. It was an expression she had seen all too often on the woman's face as she had reproved little Simon for some infraction of her rules. With the exception of her abigail, Mrs. Hooten and all the staff had been handpicked by the butler, under her husband's careful supervision. Mrs. Hooten was a stern disciplinarian. Simon had seen to that.

Outwardly a doting parent, he had resented his "son" and made that resentment extremely apparent in the days before his illness had turned his attention completely to himself. He had done his best to keep Eugenie from coddling the child, as it were. He had used Simon to bring her to terms whenever she had protested his hurtful intimacies, reminding her that without his intervention she might have dropped "her brat" in a workhouse.

On several occasions he had threatened to leave the child in the country the year round, and when Eugenie had protested, he had said, "I ask myself, my dear, what does a ballet dancer know about rearing a child? To my certain knowledge, most of 'em farm out their bastards and are damned glad to get rid of 'em. Of course, yours is a 'love' child in every sense of the word, is he not?"

She had lived with that threat for the half year until his

illness had ended or, rather, had seemed to end the subtle tortures he had inflicted upon her, but, of course, they were *not* at an end. He had done the unexpected and the unthinkable! He had brought his hated nephew Thurston back to be her mentor in his place. She shuddered. That had been the very essence of cruelty.

Had it been at Simon's suggestion that Thurston had offered to take her boy to the country? Had he suggested, also, that she was an unfit mother? That seemed more than likely, and Thurston, who unfortunately resembled his uncle in more ways than she ever would have believed, appeared very willing to undertake that guardianship. Had he no conscience? It was a marvel that he could even face her, given his heartless desertion of her.

Unbidden, a memory of father and son on the library floor rose to her mind. Much as she hated him, or rather loathed him, she did have to admit that he seemed to have a way with children. And what would he have said had he known that the child in question was his own son, half brother to the little girl of whom he seemed so fond? To use one of Simon's favorite expressions, it was the "very cream of the jest." Simon, she was positive, must have found it very funny indeed. However, he who laughs last, laughs best. Simon's laughter was stilled forever!

She stared at the passing landscape. She was not in the mood for laughter yet, but it was delightful to think that they were putting some two hundred and fifty miles between herself and London. And for once the prospect of going to the beautiful old house that lay in its own park outside of the village of Fordwich, which, in turn, was not far from Canterbury, could be viewed with unmitigated pleasure, mainly because it would be the first time that they were going there without Simon.

She winced, assailed by an unwelcome memory of the previous summer, with her husband already ill and angry at her because she was in the best of health. However, it was better not to dwell on that. Instead she would concentrate on the great house. It had originally belonged to the Fitzhugh family, now died out. Old Sir Arthur Fitzhugh, the last owner, himself at death's door, had sold it to Simon.

It had been an abbey, and much of it had been ruthlessly pulled down at the behest of Henry VIII. However, the cloisters had remained, and so had the refectory and a part of the chapter house. These were incorporated into a brick building erected over some two centuries, starting in the time of Henry VIII and continuing through the reigns of Mary I, Elizabeth I, James I, and Charles I.

Ironically it had stood completed and beautiful for the first time in a hundred and eleven years, and then had come the zealous Puritans to batter and destroy the homes of the Cavaliers—especially those that were Papist-wrought. The house, called by its owners the Sanctuary, had proved a particularly beguiling target—especially since the owner of the house, Sir James Fitzhugh, had fought bravely for his king and eluded capture, fleeing to France with his wife and his ten-year-old son.

Twelve years later the son, Sir Anthony Fitzhugh, had returned to survey and decry the devastation that had obliterated the last vestiges of Papistry in the cross, the sundial that had stood in the garden, and the stained-glass windows in the small chapel. These had been smashed to smithereens, and the beautifully carved altar had met a similar fate. The pews had been burned for firewood, and the whole of the chapel had reeked of manure from the horses stabled within.

Eugenie remembered that old Sir Arthur Fitzhugh had spoken of this destruction as sorrowfully as if he had witnessed it with his own eyes. Yet, he had admitted, albeit reluctantly, that on the whole they had been fortunate, since the building, having been used as a field headquarters for Cromwell's troops, had escaped the cudgel and the torch.

The house had been, of course, remodeled since the days of the Civil Wars. Sir Anthony had married one Anthea Hazeltine, a court beauty not unacquainted with Charles II, a fact unknown to her husband until after the premature birth of their first child, a daughter whose dark hair and eyes proved startling to at least one of her parents. Oddly enough, Sir Anthony had not seemed to regret his marriage. As a ward of the crown, his bride had come to him with a very large dowry, which he had used to repair and rebuild the house. The beautiful Anthea had subsequently produced a child a year for nine years, dying shortly after the birth of the last infant, her health and beauty gone. According to the family chronicles, she had looked many years older than the dates on her tombstone, which had given her age as twenty-seven.

Sir Arthur, Eugenie remembered, had been surprised and

shocked by the laughter with which Simon had greeted what he obviously believed to be a melancholy tale. When they were alone, Simon had remarked, "It is a pity that all cuckolds have not the means to react in kind."

Reminded that he had not been a cuckold, he had shrugged and said, "But, of course, my dear, I was not referring to *our* situation. I was aware of your sweet sin before we were wed. It was rather obvious by then, was it not?"

"You were aware only because I told you of my condition," she had flashed.

"Yes, yes, you were entirely honest, my dear love, but how could you not be in the circumstances?" he had demanded with one of his hard, hurtful embraces.

Eugenie, with a retrospective shudder, remembered how glad she had been that the subsequent family history had been merely commonplace, thus depriving her husband of more opportunities for his barbed comparisons. And, she thought defiantly, the succeeding generations had had reason to be grateful to poor little Anthea. In addition to the outward repairs, there were also improvements by Robert Hooke, who had redesigned the library and the dining room. These were beautiful, and later generations had concentrated on the gardens with the help of Capability Brown, who had utilized the stream that flowed through the grounds and widened it, accomplishing a most magnificent view from the front windows.

The gardens had become Eugenie's real sanctuary on those occasions when she had managed to escape from Simon and go wandering through them, a stroll delightful enough to make up for the inevitable questions and the accusations she had faced when she returned.

How had she been able to weather the years of her marriage, she wondered, with each day beginning or ending with her husband's unwanted, hurtful attentions, or bisected by his unfounded suspicious and subsequent furies? Actually the torment had not lasted for the length of her marriage. She had to remember that during the first eighteen months of their marriage he had been kind, and the final year had belonged to her and her son while Simon had either slept or suffered, railing at his nurses, their expertise being preferable to her care. She had seen him only nights and mornings, and for that year she had thankfully slept alone and would sleep alone here, as peacefully as any of the monks who had dwelled in their abbey three centuries earlier. Yet, contrary to her own situation, their peace had fled at the last—and they, much as they had in France during the Terror, had been turned out of their monasteries and the nuns out of their convents—or perhaps France had followed the English example.

She wondered why she had once more cast her mind back to those days of upheaval? She, at last, was free from turmoil, free to spend a few weeks, or possibly more, at the Sanctuary, where she and little Simon would not need to fear her husband's sudden, hurtful rages or the possible arrival of Thurston. He would be on his way home, never knowing that she had come here this day. She blinked against unexpected tears. Thurston had changed very little, actually. He still looked very much like the man she had loved, and again, she must needs tell herself that that man had never existed. He had been like all the others, those who had taken as their mistresses opera dancers.

Mary Clare was a case in point. She winced. She had not thought of her in a long time. Poor, poor girl—but still, it was a pity that she had killed herself, thus depriving her unborn child of life. That was the greatest tragedy of all, not having known the joy of a baby at her breast.

Eugenie smiled down at little Simon, and then her smile vanished as she remembered Simon's will and Thurston's suggestion that he take her child to the country. However, there was no reason to dwell on her husband's perfidy. He was dead, and she was on her way to a house that she might now, with impunity, call a sanctuary.

In the end, Thurston had not gone to the Green Room. The ballet dancers had been young and pretty and accomplished. He had not seen one who had attracted him. He had gone, instead, to Brooks. He had been a member in years past and had, almost before he knew it, settled down to a game of piquet. He won consistently and was consequently five hundred pounds richer by the end of an evening that had somehow slid into morning—when he finally left the establishment, the sky was light and he weary enough to sleep until noon.

Not surprisingly, he had dreamed of Eugenie—not as she was now, cold and reserved, but the Eugenie who had danced through his dreams, had turned a smiling face in his direction,

had looked at him adoringly, had drawn him into the dance,
and then the visions had become fragmented and he had, at
length, found himself alone in a desolate landscape filled with
broken statuary under a slate-gray sky. He was no seer. He
could not generally interpret dreams, but that particular dream
had been easy enough to understand, pointing up shattered
beliefs and the perfidy of the woman he had once loved more
than life itself. Had he? He had been a mere twenty-one at the
time and, despite a few adventures, almost totally inexperi-
enced in the ways of females, particularly the wanton demoi-
selles of the ballet. He had been grist to her mill, but there was
no use concentrating on the past. He had promised himself that
he would call on her that morning—in his role of appointed
guardian. He would like to see the boy again. He had found
him delightful and very bright. The children of older fathers
were said to be uncommonly intelligent, and the child certainly
seemed to bear out that particular notion.

It was close to two in the afternoon by the time he had
arrived at the house on St. James's Street. He hoped that
Eugenie would be out shopping, or possibly at some secluded
rendezvous with Saint-Cyr. That would give him time with
little Simon. It was amazing how much he was drawn to one
who was the child of parents he despised. He was smiling as he
descended from his post chaise, came up the steps, and gave
the knocker a hearty slam.

It was a matter of several minutes before the door was
opened, and by a man he recognized. "Graves!" he exclaimed.

His onetime valet showed no surprise. "Good afternoon,
Your Lordship," he said in the cool accents Thurston remembered so well.

"You are employed here?" Thurston demanded.

"I was valet to the late Mr. Sorrell," he replied.

Thurston digested this information without comment. He
said, "I have come to see Mrs. Sorrell."

"I am sorry, my lord, but Mrs. Sorrell is not at home."

"I would be glad to wait for her, and meanwhile I should
like to see my nephew."

"Actually, sir, he is not in residence. Mrs. Sorrell and her
son left for the country early this morning. Mrs. Sorrell did not
mention a time when they would return."

Thurston was conscious of an anger that gave every sign of

developing into a full-fledged fury. It was on the tip of his tongue to inquire if someone other than her son had also accompanied her, but he managed to restrain himself. He said merely, "I see. Would you have any notion as to what part of the country she intended to go?"

The valet hesitated. "I have been requested not to divulge that information, Your Lordship."

Graves's hesitation had not escaped Thurston. It seemed to hint at indecision. "Would two guineas prove an inducement?" he asked bluntly.

The valet hesitated again, "Shall we say . . . twice that amount, my lord?"

"I am entirely amenable," Thurston returned coldly. Producing his wallet, he counted out the money.

"I do thank you, my lord," he murmured. "They will be in Kent. The estate is known as the Sanctuary. It is located outside the village of Fordwich. Though I have been there once or twice, I fear I am not observant enough to give you the exact location, but any one of the villagers will provide the information you desire."

"Thank you, Graves. Might I know one more thing?"

The valet tensed. "My lord?"

"At what hour did Mrs. Sorrell depart?"

"They left at the hour of seven, my lord."

"Ah, thank you, Graves. I will bid you good afternoon."

"Good afternoon, my lord."

As he returned to his waiting carriage Thurston found himself cold with rage. A momentary surprise had given way to the conviction that he ought not to be surprised at anything Eugenie did, given her character or, rather, the lack of it. He also cursed himself for not suspecting that she was contemplating something of that nature. Indeed, he could compare these actions with those of seven years ago when she had woefully, tearfully bade him farewell only to throw herself into his uncle's arms. And what had been the reason for her secrecy? The answer was simple—it went by the name of Saint-Cyr. And if he found them together, he *would* assume full guardianship of that unfortunate child!

They had made good time, and they arrived at the Sanctuary a few minutes after one on the afternoon of the third day of their journey, missing a threatening cloudburst by a good half hour.

The two coaches containing the staff had reached the house well ahead of them, and it was delightful to step into a hall in which a fire was already burning on an immense hearth. It had been her husband's contention that one of the reasons the monks had ultimately been expelled from their abbeys had been the number of creature comforts they had managed to enjoy in the course of their supposedly austere existence.

"I can well imagine half a tree burning in that fireplace," he had said, "and I am quite sure that they baked whole oxen in the kitchens." Eugenie wished that she had not been reminded of Simon's dry comments. However, she reasoned philosophically, one could not dismiss seven years in the space of a week. She had spent a relatively short time with Thurston and . . . but she would not think about him, would not have been thinking about him at all, had it not been for Simon's incredibly cruel decision!

"Little Simon seems that tired, ma'am," Elsie said. "The road was monstrous bumpy afore we turned into the carriageway."

"It certainly was. You may put him to bed. However, he will have to have supper first."

"Mama"—the child caught Eugenie's hand—"may I sleep with you tonight?"

She looked down at him and saw that he was frightened. She knelt quickly and put her arms around him, realizing that too much had happened to him in a relatively short space of time. "Of course, you may, my love," she said. "But I will not be retiring for quite some time. Will you mind waiting for me in my room?"

"Oh, no, Mama, if you promise you will be with me. Nurse says that I should not ask, but she's not here tonight."

"That is right, dearest, she is not here tonight, and she was wrong to tell you that you should not ask. We will be cozy as two bugs in a rug!"

"Oh, Mama." He flung his arms around her neck. "I do love you so much."

"And I love you, my heart's darling." She kissed him. "But you must go to bed now for a little nap, and afterwards we will have supper in my room. You will like that, *mon enfant?*"

"Oui, Mama, je . . . would like it . . . *très bien."*

"Oh, my sweet." She kissed him again. "Now go with Elsie, *vite, vite."*

"Come, little love." Elsie took his hand, and they went out of the room.

Eugenie, divesting herself of her wraps, frowned, thinking of Mrs. Hooten. She would dismiss her as soon as they returned to town. She had never approved of the harsh way in which she had treated the child. Furthermore she had protested Simon's wish to occasionally sleep with his mother, hinting that it was unhealthy. Her husband, of course, agreed with her. With the onslaught of his illness he had applauded anything that might cause her pain, but that was over, over, over, and his cruelties no more than a memory she would exorcise in time.

Coming into the hall, she watched as Elsie and Simon rounded the bend in the stairs, and then she moved into the drawing room. It was a cold room—the heavy furnishings had been purchased from the previous owner. They were not her taste, but she had not been consulted. Her husband had decried the gilt chairs and the tapestries the French enjoyed. She was at liberty to employ her own taste now, could redecorate the entire house to her liking and then spend more time here. It would be nice for little Simon. He was entered into Eton, but it would be six years before she need think of sending him to school. Meanwhile she could be with him as much as she chose, without being harassed by her husband's barbed comments and the threat—always the threat—of acquainting the child with his true parentage.

She raised both hands to her head, wishing that she could exorcise the past. Coming to the window, she stared into the misty distances. It was still light, as it always was during the long evenings of summer, but the rain was coming down heavily now, forming small rivulets on the windowpanes, and pools in what she could glimpse of the gardens. It was lovely just to stand there and watch without fear of being summoned by Simon. There had been times when he had reminded her of a wayward child with a pet cat—always rousing it from its sleep to play with it, pulling its tail and tweaking its whiskers—with the one difference that the cat had claws and could use them. She had had no defenses.

"I will not think of him," she whispered fiercely. "He is gone, I am free, and I will remain free!"

Unbidden, an image of the marquis rose before her inner eyes. She was particularly glad to be away from him, mainly because her conscience had begun to trouble her whenever he was present. Originally she had encouraged him mainly because her husband had appeared to dislike him. Her rides in the park, and even the meeting at Lady Moberley's, had been acts of defiance.

She did like him, but after considerable reflection, most of it taking place on the way down to the Sanctuary, she had to admit that she did not love him. Had she tried to love him? It was very difficult to sort out her feelings, and there was a reason for that: *Thurston.*

He was so dreadfully changed, changed enough to cause her to wonder if indeed she had ever really known him. No, obviously she had not! The man she believed she loved could never have been so utterly cruel! Consequently she had been mistaken in her feelings, had mistaken his feelings—and could she not be mistaken again? If Raoul and she were married, might she not have just as shattering an awakening? Love was dangerously deceptive. She must needs put the love for a man out of her mind and instead concentrate on raising her son—being both mother and father to him. And he need fear his stepfather no longer, would not be sent supperless to bed for the slightest infraction of rules that Simon often invented on the spur of the moment. On occasion she had been hard put not to challenge his authority. However, on the one occasion that she had defiantly defended him, his punishment had been the harder: locked in his room for two days, cut off from all the household save his nurse, who had not scrupled to tell her that she had interfered with his discipline. She had longed to answer back in words the woman would not soon forget, but she had held her tongue for fear that she might bring even more trouble to her child.

"How did I stand it?" she murmured. However, she reminded herself wryly, she had been well trained in the art of forbearance. She had lived with her Aunt Vivienne, and that was one ghost she need not consider. She started, hearing a distant pounding, metal on metal. Where? The hall, of course; there was someone at the door.

She hurried into the entrance hall and reached it just as the butler admitted a tall man, wrapped in a wet cloak. The hat he had doffed was also wet, and his dark hair was plastered against his head. However, gallantry knowing no hindrances, he bowed and said, "My dear Mrs. Sorrell, I beg you will pardon my appearance, but it being summer and the weather clement when I began my journey, I decided to ride here on horseback."

Eugenie's hand crept to her throat. "Raoul . . . I did not expect you."

"Did you not?" He seemed surprised. "Then why did you send me a note acquainting me with your direction?"

Against her will, Eugenie had to laugh. Despite all her precautions, she had erred. Living her whole life in England, she had largely forgotten the French mentality. She said, "I will have the housekeeper prepare a room for you, Raoul. Certainly I cannot turn you away tonight—but tomorrow . . ."

He surprised her by saying, "I quite understand, my dearest Eugenie. Tomorrow I will be glad to seek a village inn. However, I did not want you to await me in vain."

Another laugh rose and was hastily stifled as she said, "I beg you will get out of those wet clothes, Raoul. If you do not have a change of garments with you, there are here some clothes of my husband, if you do not mind donning them."

"I do have fresh garments in my saddlebags," he said. "However, were they not with me, I could think of nothing more to my liking than . . . donning your husband's clothes, my dearest Eugenie."

CHAPTER SIX

SHE OUGHT TO have awakened with a sense of freedom, the sort she had experienced on first arriving at the Sanctuary yesterday afternoon. However, Eugenie, rising early, felt oppressed and angry. She slid out of bed with a fond and regretful look at her son, curled into a ball on the far side of the bed. She must remand him to the care of Elsie and see to the needs of her unwanted, unexpected guest, with whom she had been, out of courtesy, forced to converse far longer the previous night than she had wished.

Thinking back on their conversation, she made a little face. It had been full of innuendo. He had not tried to make love to her, but he had appeared annoyingly positive that her foolish mention of her direction had been, in effect, an open invitation! She had longed to tell him that she had, by mentioning her location and the fact that it was a two- to three-day journey, hoped to discourage him. She had learned her error all too quickly. On her reference to the length of his ride he had merely laughed and told her that to himself, used as he was to the vast distances between one Canadian township and another, this had seemed hardly longer than a London street.

Accused of exaggeration, he had shrugged. "If it had been from London to the moon, be assured that I would have come, my dearest Eugenie, but you are entirely aware of that, I am sure."

Had it not been for the fact that despite his brave words he was obviously bone-weary, she would have made a point of taking umbrage at a remark that seemed to suggest she had issued an elliptically worded invitation that he join her. Indeed, it was on the tip of her tongue to order him to leave and at once, but pity had triumphed over discretion and she had let him remain. However, that morning, she was far more in command of herself and the situation than she had been the previous night—and she would be firm! She had no intention of allowing him to remain and burden her with his lovemaking. She might start by pleading a headache and remaining in her room. No, that would be cowardly, and besides, a glance out of her window had brought her the welcome sight of blue skies, a bright sun, and gardens that looked especially enticing.

They could stroll through the gardens—no, no, no, that would only be inviting trouble. Her best device was to ride with him over the property—if the grounds were not too wet. Did widows ride? It hardly mattered. This particular widow would ride even though she did not as yet have any black garments for riding. That, she decided defiantly, did not matter! They would not be straying off the estate—at least she would not be straying, and consequently there would be no Mrs. Grundy to observe and protest.

Yes, that was by far the best solution to the problem of the marquis. On horseback she would be far safer than on the ground, and furthermore they could not converse over much. She rang for Elsie.

She had expected some protest from her abigail when she had helped her to don her habit. It was not a new one. It had been fashioned by Mrs. Bell, the wife of the publisher of *La Belle Assemblée*. That gentleman's barefaced advertisements for his wife's dressmaking establishment via the "fashion pages" was the laugh of London. However, everyone read the magazine, and a great many females swore by her designs and by her great invention, the Circassian corset.

Eugenie, however, had not been drawn to the lady. Mrs. Bell had been extremely full of herself and not a little condescending to one who had been an opera dancer. However, the riding habit of pelisse cloth in a pale blue that matched her eyes was very flattering, and Elsie, evidently not at all disturbed by its hue, said, "Oh, ma'am, it's still that fetching, and I am glad you are going riding. 'Tis a fine morning for it. Himself'll be joinin' you, I expect."

"I expect that he will," Eugenie admitted reluctantly. Meeting Elsie's sympathetic gaze in her mirror, she added, "I had wanted to be free of complications while we were here."

The girl nodded. "But 'e be ever so 'andsome 'n' young, milady."

"He is very young," Eugenie agreed. "He is not out of his twenties."

"And neither are you, ma'am," Elsie said pointedly. "You be younger 'n 'im."

"Am I? I do not feel young, Elsie." She stared into the mirror and was surprised to see the face that looked back at her. If there was a pensive droop to the mouth, the skin was unlined and her bright eyes gave no hint of her interior conviction that youth had gone seven years back, in those lonely rooms where she had waited in vain for Thurston's letters; but she must not, would not, think of Thurston!

"Mama, Mama, Mama." Her son came bouncing into her dressing room. "Oh, Mama, are we going riding, then?"

She looked at him regretfully and held out her arms. "Good morning, my love, did you sleep well?"

He embraced her joyfully. "I slept very well, Mama. When are we going riding?"

"We will not be going riding this morning, my dearest. We have a guest. You remember the gentleman who came last night?"

"I do not like him." Simon grimaced.

"Master Simon!" Elsie protested. "What a face! How would you like it if 'twas to freeze that way?"

The little boy's ill humor vanished. "Oh, Elsie, it won't." He turned back to his mother. "I want to go riding now."

"But you 'aven't 'ad yer breakfast," Elsie said. "An' not yer bath, neither. You 'ave to eat 'n' be washed, 'n' afterward us'll go for a nice walk an' look for rabbit 'oles."

"Rabbit holes?" he demanded interestedly. "Are there rabbits around here, Elsie?"

"Rabbits 'n' 'edge 'ogs 'n' all manner o' animals. Master Simon, I know where to find 'em."

"Oh, do you, Elsie? Oh, I should like to see them!" the child said eagerly.

"We will." The girl smiled then looked at Eugenie. " 'Ave I yer leave to take 'im for a walk, then, ma'am?"

"You have, and I do thank you, Elsie." Eugenie looked at her fondly. A half-formed resolution came to full fruition. Elsie would be her lad's nurse, and Mrs. Hooten would be dismissed as soon as they returned to London. No, she would not wait that long. She would write to her directly, enclosing a draft for her final payment and some extra money to sustain her until she found another position. She had never liked the woman, and of course the feeling was entirely mutual. Mrs. Hooten had never scrupled to conceal her contempt for a onetime dancer, and she had let Eugenie know that she took orders only from her master. Simon had enjoyed her discomfort. She winced as she remembered him saying, "You must agree with me, my love, that little Simon's heritage is not of the best. If he is not to become like his father, he will need discipline."

She expelled a long sigh. It was so entirely useless to dwell on the past, especially at a moment when she had more immediate problems or, rather, a *problem*—in the person of her unwanted, unexpected guest! She could not continue to be burdened with him throughout her stay at the Sanctuary. She must needs insist that he recognize the fact that she was officially in mourning and that if she were to retain her reputation, she must absent herself from society and from dalliance for the requisite year—at the very least. It was unfortunate that he was fully aware of her feelings for the man she was ostensibly mourning. She had also made the mistake of . . . *Had* she encouraged him?

Unfortunately she had, or was it more accurate to say that she had not precisely discouraged him? He was charming and had lived an extremely exciting life. She had loved to hear his tales of the Canadian wilderness and its attendant dangers. She had been living in such a state of misery when they met, and she had found him most attractive. It had been pleasant to bask in the admiration of a *young* man, a man whom other females did not scruple to pursue. Furthermore he was wealthy and eager to wed her. As Millie had said more than once, he was an excellent prospect. She had gone as far as to counsel her that it would be wiser to brave the scandal that must needs result from a possible marriage than to wait a year.

She remembered when she had received that piece of worldly advice. It had been before Simon's death. In fact, it had been proffered just after the doctor had informed her that there was no hope of his recovery. She, confiding this news to Millie, had been shocked at her friend's reaction.

"Marry the dear marquis and travel to Canada on your wedding trip. By the time you return, no one will be the wiser as to whether or not you were a proper widow. Oh, you will be discussed, and there will be a small scandal, of course, but another scandal will arrive to take its place—we can always depend on one of the princes can we not? Meanwhile you will be quite forgotten in a month, my love."

Yet if she had been shocked, she had not been entirely averse to the idea. The marquis had attracted her. They had much in common—both being displaced French aristocrats with the same sad history behind them. Had she let him know that she was attracted to him? A negative rose in her mind and was reluctantly banished. She *had* flirted with him. She had gone for those long rides in the park. She had even accepted Millie's invitation to make one of a foursome to attend the yearly opening of the Vauxhall Gardens. She had known that the marquis was invited, and of course it was inevitable that they should absent themselves from their table and stroll down a sequestered path and that he should kiss her and that she would allow it. They had been masked, of course, and she had not permitted any other intimacies. Unfortunately these were enough.

"I was a fool!" she whispered.

Yes, she had been a fool, but she had been so frustrated, so unhappy, and had loathed her husband so. Indeed, in the months before his illness had worsened, she had longed for the courage to kill herself, and if it had not been for little Simon . . . She shook herself. She must not remembered those days. They were at an end, and for the time being, the marquis must be persuaded not to pursue her. He would not take kindly to that persuasion. He might, in fact, turn away from her completely. Would she miss him? Possibly. But the alternative was too terrible to contemplate—he could not compete against her son. And now, for the first time, she was going to have a chance to be with Simon without her husband's hateful interference, without his constant threats and barbed remarks. Yet Simon cast a long shadow, and if Thurston, who also appeared to hate her, were to learn that she and the marquis had been together at the Sanctuary, he could—and would—take the child away. She dared not run that risk. Servants talked. Word spread.

As she came down the stairs she saw the butler in the hall. His eyes widened and then narrowed, and she guessed that her garb must have shocked him. However, she need not make any excuses to him. She said, "Good morning, Knape."

"Good morning, ma'am," he said coolly.

Again she was impelled to explain her attire, and again she curbed the impulse. "Is Monsieur Saint-Cyr down yet?"

"He is, Mrs. Sorrell. He is in the library, I believe." Knape's tones had taken on another degree of frost.

"No, I must correct you, Knape. I am not in the library." The marquis came down the hall, and to Eugenie's relief he was wearing his own garments again. He smiled at her. "Ah, Mrs. Sorrell, you look as fresh as a morning breeze."

"I thank you, Raoul." She glanced at the butler and found that he was moving toward the outer hall. "Knape," she called, "will you have Timothy bring the horses round—that of Monsieur Saint-Cyr, and I will be riding Antigone."

"Yes, Mrs. Sorrell, at once." The butler went on out.

"Are we going riding, then?" the marquis asked.

"I will ride with you as far as our border," she said firmly. "And I will explain the direction to Fordwich. I expect you will want to stay there at some inn before undertaking the long ride back to London."

He frowned. "In other words, you are inviting me to leave, Eugenie. That is hardly hospitable."

"I did not invite you to come. It was your assumption only that I did."

"Last night," he said in hurt tones, "you told me—"

"Last night, Raoul," she said, interrupting, "you were extremely weary and uncomfortable. I did not want to add to your discomfort by expressing my feelings. However, I must tell you that it is of the utmost importance that you go. If rumors of your visit should reach . . . the wrong ears, we would be sharing in an *on dit* that would prove most harmful to me."

"My dear Eugenie." His frown deepend. "Surely you are enlarging upon this . . ."

"I assure you that I am not. I am a new widow and . . ."

"And do new widows wear blue?" he asked lightly. "I beg you will not imagine that I disapprove. Blue is most certainly your color."

She flushed. For the moment she had forgotten about her habit. She said, "I will not be wearing blue for very long, I assure you. I've not had an opportunity to visit the mantua maker and have another riding habit made. I will directly, you may be sure."

"It will be a pity. Black, of course, becomes you, but blue—no one but yourself should wear it, and you should always wear it. But I fear I repeat myself."

It occurred to Eugenie that she was in no mood for persiflage. Another few moments and he would be openly flirting with her. She was about to give him a set-down when the butler returned. "Yes, Knape?" she asked.

"The horses are at the door, Mrs. Sorrell."

"Ah." She started toward the hall and stopped. "But we must fetch your luggage, Raoul."

The marquis reddened. "I . . . brought very little with me. I am wearing it."

Eugenie regarded him quizzically and was suddenly suspicious. It was entirely possible that he was staying at one or another hostelry in this location. Her burgeoning ire increased, but she managed to quell it. "I see, then we can go." Decisively she moved ahead of him.

Timothy, the groom, was waiting with the horses. The marquis was riding Venus, the spirited black mare, who had won many an impromptu race in the park. She was pleased that she had chosen to ride Antigone, a chesnut that had been stabled at the Sanctuary. The sight of one of the London steeds might have encouraged a flood of the sort of sentimental reminiscences she dearly hoped to avoid. She said, "I know a shortcut through the woods. Shall we go that way?"

"We may go any way you choose," the marquis said coldly.

She avoided looking at him as Tim helped her into her saddle. "Very well, we will take the shortcut." Having gained her point, she gave him a brief smile. The path was narrow, and for most of the way they would need to go single file. "I will take the lead," she added.

"You know the territory, I do not," he responded ungraciously.

As they struck out across the park, the marquis was silent, and Eugenie, recognizing an ominous silence spiked with indignation, wished heartily that she had not encouraged him. She had been very foolish.

"By God!" the marquis exclaimed suddenly, "what is that?"

Eugenie's mare snorted indignantly as she reined her in. "What is the matter?" She turned and was surprised to find the marquis standing on the ground, the reins wound around his hand. "What happened?" she asked anxiously. "Did you fall?"

"No, but what is this stone? It is shaped like a female!"

"Oh." Eugenie glanced in the direction he was pointing. "That is the witch-stone."

"The witch . . . stone?" he repeated. "Is this a place of covens as well as monks?"

"No, it is a legend associated with the abbey that used to stand here. It seems that a witch fell in love with a handsome young monk and sought to cast a spell on him so that he would forsake his faith and become her lover. However, the Virgin Mary, shocked at this sacrilege, turned the witch to stone."

"I see." He stared quizzically at her. "And was it the Virgin who turned you to stone, Eugenie?"

She tensed. "I do not understand you."

He moved toward her. "Do you not? I do not think that I believe you." Before she could guess what he was about, he had suddenly pulled her down from her horse, catching the startled animal's reins, as he did, but holding her with one powerful arm.

"Raoul!" Eugenie cried indignantly as she vainly tried to pull away from him. "Have you gone mad?"

"Possibly," he rasped, "for you are like to drive a man mad. What has changed you? You are as cold as that stone!"

She finally managed to free herself. "I have not to answer you. You are aware of my circumstances. The will . . ."

"Damn the will! Where there's a will, there's a way to circumvent it!"

"I dare not consider it at this time. I have already explained that my husband's nephew is another like his uncle. He will be waiting for me to make some misstep that he can enlarge into a scandal. I am sure of it."

"He cannot wait in Canada."

"I am not ready to go to Canada yet, Raoul. I need time to be alone with my son. He enjoys it here."

"He would enjoy it even more in Canada."

"He has been uprooted once already. Surely you understand

that I cannot think of myself at this time!''

''Eugenie,'' he cried. ''Why have you changed toward me?''

''I have not changed, Raoul,'' she said impatiently. ''You have changed. I have enjoyed our friendship, yes, but I never led you to believe it was anything more than . . . than what it is!''

''That is not true and you know it,'' he retorted hotly. ''I have been involved in many light flirtations, but this was more, much more. Why will you not admit it? Certainly your actions led me to believe that you were not indifferent to me!''

''We never spoke of love!'' she exclaimed.

''Did we need to speak of it? Did we, Eugenie? There were indications.''

She glared at him. ''If there were, they were not intended.''

''Do not tell me that you've not changed.'' His eyes were full of pain. ''You have. What has come between us? Or whom?''

''No one,'' she cried. ''Why will you not understand? I have been locked into a miserable marriage for the last seven years, and now that I am free, I want to remain free. I do not want to answer to anyone.''

''And do you think I would chain you to a wall with gyves on both wrists? I am not the beast you married. I love you, and no matter what you say now, you have given me the reason to believe that you were not indifferent to me and now . . . now that freedom is within our grasp, you turn away. Once more, I ask you, what has changed you?''

''Do you not understand, Raoul? We have talked of freedom, yes, but it is now only a word. The will is binding. If I marry before the age of thirty, I will lose my son and my inheritance. The latter means nothing to me, but little Simon is my life. Why cannot you understand that?''

''Because I have money enough for us both! Because your so-called nemesis would not follow us to Canada, and if he did, he would not find you.'' There was a hurt look in his eyes as he added, ''I love you, I need you.'' He reached out his free arm and pulled her against him. His kiss was passionate and invading, and though she struggled to free herself, she could not escape. Finally his hold relaxed. Lifting his head, he said passionately, ''Now what have you to tell me, my stubborn little love?''

"Oh!" She glared at him, rubbing a hand across her mouth. "You are no different than . . . than Simon. I have told you what I feel, but my needs are as nothing to you." Running to her horse, she found a small boulder and was able to stand on it and fling herself on the animal's back. She flicked the reins, turning in the direction of the Sanctuary, and urged the mare into a canter, not looking behind her, intent only on returning home. It was not until she had emerged from the trees that she was aware that the marquis was following her. She clenched her teeth. Once she reached her stables, she would have the men throw him out.

By the time they had gained the carriageway, Eugenie was a little calmer and her common sense had tunneled through her emotions to tell her that she was, in a sense, partially responsible for Saint-Cyr's confusion. There was no denying that she had given him reason to believe that she was not uninterested. Now, however, for reasons she could not fathom, she felt none of the excitement he had once aroused in her. It was really ironic . . . Her thoughts scattered as, riding up the road, she saw a man standing a short distance away, watching her.

"Eugenie." The marquis caught up with her, and leaning toward her, he said hoarsely, "Will you ever forgive me? I did not know what I was doing. It is only that I love you so desperately. Please, Eugenie, I beg you . . ."

She barely heard him. The man was some distance away. She could not make out his features, but she knew who it was, knew what he must be thinking, could imagine what he had been told by a disapproving butler, and now, with his own eyes, he was seeing everything for himself—he was seeing a woman who had lost her husband no more than a week ago, a *widow*, garbed in a blue riding habit, accompanied by the man who, he must be aware, had spent the previous night at the Sanctuary and now, since she had inadvertently loosened her grip on the reins, her horse was inexorably bearing her forward, to confront her husband's appointed guardian —Thurston Sorrell, Lord Seabourne!

There were pounding hooves behind her. The marquis was once more at her side. She glanced at him, but she was not looking at him with *her* eyes; she was seeing him as Thurston must be seeing him—and thinking what he must be thinking. Her heart was pounding in her throat, and now she was close enough to see his cold, brown gaze. She could not face him at this moment, could not speak to him. She spurred her horse forward, passing him on her way to the stables, and again the marquis was behind her.

By the time she reached the stable yard, her burgeoning fears had been replaced by pure anger. She dismounted hastily and faced the marquis who had, in that same moment, also dismounted. "It seems that I have another uninvited guest," she said coldly. He flushed, but without waiting for his reply she turned to one of the stable hands. "When did His Lordship arrive, John?"

"Weren't more 'n 'alf hour since, ma'am. Come on 'orseback 'e did 'n' the poor beast were that lathered. 'E were in a rare takin', 'e were."

Her mind swiftly furnished reasons. Thurston had suspected that she had not told him the truth regarding her plans as detailed to him when he came to see her. He must have paid her another visit on the day she had left, and someone in the house had informed him of her destination, the destination she had adjured her remaining staff not to divulge.

Who could have informed on her? Mrs. Hooten? No, it would have been Graves, another whom she planned to dismiss. She had never quite trusted him, and his presence had always been unwelcome because of his connection with Thurston in the days she had tried to forget. And, she remembered furiously, he had solemnly promised that he would give her direction to no one—no one save her worst enemy, he should have said!

"Will there be anything else you'll be wantin', ma'am?" John asked.

"No thank you." She turned to the marquis. "You know the terms of the will, Raoul. Have you any suggestions for me?" she asked crisply.

He had been looking both angry and ashamed, but in the face of her own anger he said placatingly, "I will speak for you, Eugenie. I will tell him that my presence here was none of your desiring." His face darkened as he added bitterly, "I shall be telling him no more than the truth, it seems."

"I doubt that he will believe you." She could not restrain a deep sigh.

"Why would you think that, Mrs. Sorrell?" inquired a cold voice behind them. "Tell me what you both believe I should hear? Tell me that you did not plan to flee to the country without telling anyone, that you did not intend to meet your lover at the house of your late husband?''

Eugenie whirled to face Thurston. ''I planned nothing!'' she snapped. ''I had no more to do with his arrival than I have with yours—and neither of you are welcome here.''

''Indeed?'' he questioned coldly. ''And yet you gave this 'unwelcome' guest a room for the night.''

''I—'' Eugenie began, but the marquis spoke over her.

''I stayed the night here, yes. I arrived here in a pounding rainstorm, and Mrs. Sorrell was kind enough to allow me to remain until morning—and no longer.''

''And yet you are still here, Monsieur Saint-Cyr,'' Thurston observed caustically.

''And if he is, how does that concern you?'' Eugenie flashed. ''This is my house, and I determine who and who does not come here. I would appreciate it if you both went back the way you came!''

Thurston's eyes were hard. ''I must compliment you on your mourning attire, Mrs. Sorrell. I am sure it must reflect your sentiments well enough.''

She was saved from responding by the marquis, who said sharply, ''Mrs. Sorrell has not had an opportunity to have her new garments made, though I cannot see why any explanation is due you.''

''You seem very well acquainted with Mrs. Sorrell's affairs,'' Thurston retorted. ''That does not surprise me. I imagine that you are one of the reasons—if not the main one—that my uncle wanted a guardian for his son.''

''Just what are you suggesting, my lord?'' Eugenie demanded icily.

''I should not think that was hard to fathom, ma'am.''

''Your uncle's son is in very good hands, my lord!'' the marquis said sharply.

''And he will remain in them,'' Eugenie said coldly. ''You have obviously reached conclusions that are erroneous, my lord. Monsieur Saint-Cyr and I—''

''Yes?'' Thurston said, interrupting freezingly. ''Do tell me about yourself and Monsieur Saint-Cyr.''

Eugenie drew herself up. In tones that matched his own she said, ''I need not tell you anything, Lord Seabourne. I will tell you, however, that I do not like your attitude. I will also tell

you once more that you are not wanted here. I suggest that you
leave—immediately.''

"I am sure that a third person is not to your liking, ma'am. I
have already given instructions that your son's clothing be
packed. I am sure that his presence here can only add another
unwanted third to so cozy a menage.''

"How dare you come into my house and issue orders?"
Eugenie demanded furiously. "You have no right, no right
here at all. And I assure you that that order will be swiftly
countermanded.''

"And I assure you that it will not be. I have every right to
issue it. It was conferred upon me by my late uncle, who
obviously knew whereof he spoke. He warned me of your . . .
connection with Saint-Cyr.''

"He lied!" Eugenie retorted. "He was half mad with
jealousy because—''

"And did that jealousy have no foundation, ma'am?"
Despite your titles and your position in society, you've not
changed. You still have the . . . the morals of an opera
dancer!''

"That is enough, Lord Seabourne!" The marquis slapped
him across the face. "Name your seconds, damn you!''

Eugenie paled. She caught the marquis's arm. "No, Raoul,
I beg you will not fight! I beg you'll not be so stupid, either of
you.'' She moved away from the marquis and whirled to face
the two angry young men. "Though you little deserve it, Lord
Seabourne, there is a reasonable explanation!''

"It is too late for reasonable explanations, ma'am,"
Thurston said with an anger that surpassed even that of the
marquis. "That you invited him here when—''

Anger she could not suppress colored Eugenie's tone once
more. "I did not invite him here, but if I had, I would not need
to answer to you or to anyone! This is my house and I will have
no dueling here. That is final. Now go, go, go—both of you!''

Quite as if she had not spoken, Thurston turned to the
marquis. "I choose pistols, Monsieur Saint-Cyr.''

"Very good. I have a brace of them in my saddlebags," the
marquis responded sharply. "I suggest that we keep this
meeting amongst ourselves. I will name a second from yon
stable, and you may do the same if you are agreeable.''

"I am agreeable, monsieur," Thurston said.

"No, I tell you, I will not have it! It is all a misunderstanding. Raoul?'' Eugenie turned to the marquis. ''Can you not be satisfied with an apology?''

''For myself, perhaps, but it was you he insulted, and I have no intention of letting him cry off.''

''I have no intention of crying off, damn you!'' Thurston retorted.

''Mama, Mama!'' Little Simon ran into the stable yard. ''Where were you? I saw you ride back. I thought you'd come inside.'' He looked up at Thurston and smiled beatifically. ''Oh, it is you, Cousin Thurston. I did hope I would see you again.''

Making a valiant effort to subdue his anger, Thurston managed a smile. ''Well, here I am, my dear lad.''

''Have you come to visit us? Oh, I do hope so, and will you show me how a seal walks?''

''Not at this precise moment, my lad, but later.''

''Simon, dearest, where is Elsie?'' Eugenie demanded.

''I do not know . . . she is somewhere.'' The child still looked at Thurston.

''Well, we must find her. Come, my love.'' Eugenie took his hand and, glancing at the two men, added, ''We must talk further. I charge you, wait for me here.''

''We will wait,'' the marquis said after a slight hesitation.

''Why can I not remain with my cousin?'' Simon demanded plaintively.

''You may see me—'' Thurston began.

''Simon!'' Eugenie said, interrupting sharply. ''You are to come with me now.'' Seizing his hand, she started forward, and meeting resistance from him, she lifted him in her arms and hurried in the direction of the house.

''I wanted to stay with him,'' Simon said sulkily as they came inside. ''I like him.''

''Simon, I have never known you to be so naughty!'' Eugenie said reprovingly. ''Now where is Elsie?'' She looked about her. ''And where is Knape?''

''I don't know,'' the child said sulkily as she set him down and tried to catch her breath.

Eugenie eyed the long staircase in annoyance and thought of going to the servant's hall, but that was even farther away, and meanwhile she must take her son to the nursery. ''Come,'' she said, ''we will go upstairs.'' Then, as little Simon made no move to obey her, she thrust him ahead of her. ''Go on upstairs.'' she ordered.

Simon, who often took the stairs two at a time, walked up very slowly, ignoring his mother's impatient promptings. She was hard put not to carry him and run the rest of the way, but he had proved far too heavy for her and there was a chance she might drop him.

Coming into the nursery, she found Elsie peering into an open bandbox. She had put a few things into it, but she was looking extremely distressed. As Eugenie and Simon appeared, she cried, ''Oh, Mrs. Sorrell, I were 'opin' ye'd be back. I didn't know wot to do. 'Is Lordship 'n' Knape said as 'ow I should pack 'is clothes 'n' all, but—''

''You may unpack them, Elsie,'' Eugenie ordered sharply. ''And I charge you, come into the hall with me, please. There's something I must tell you.''

''I want to come with you, Mama,'' little Simon shrilled. ''Why cannot I go down and see that nice gentleman who says he is my cousin. I love him.''

''Because I say you cannot.'' Eugenie was amazed that she could speak so calmly, given the anger or, rather, the rage that had risen in her breast at Thurston's arbitrary assumption of authority in her house. Far from trying to interfere in the duel, she should let the marquis have his way with this man, who had dared to give such instructions to her servants. She was equally enraged with Knape, who, she did not doubt, had filled Thurston's ears with an account of the marquis's arrival the previous night. However, as she and Elsie moved into the hall, she managed to subdue some of that rage. She could not let that ridiculous duel take place. If word of it were to leak out—and, of course, it would—there would be no living in this community and . . . She swallowed a sudden obstruction in her throat. There was a chance that the marquis might try to hurt Thurston. Unbidden, a memory of something Raoul had once mentioned came back to her.

''He might meet with an accident,'' he had said.

There was now a pounding in her throat, and suddenly she was quite certain that the marquis meant to kill him, thus removing the obstruction to their marriage—as he must believe.

''No,'' she whispered. ''No!''

''I beg your pardon, ma'am. I did not 'ear you.'' Elsie said.

''Elsie.'' Eugenie clutched her arm. ''Tell Knape that he

must send for the constable.''

"The . . . constable, ma'am?'' The girl stared at her in surprise.

"Yes, and hurry. I am in hopes that I can stop this, but if I cannot . . . No matter, do as I say and keep an eye on Simon. I am wasting time. I must go back to the stable and try to talk some sense into them." She started for the stairs.

"But, ma'am." Elsie hurried after her. "Wot's 'e to tell the constable?''

"Say that there might be . . . no, tell him that there is going to be a duel and he must stop it." Eugenie dashed down the stairs. She was out the front door in a trice, cursing the fact that the stables were not nearer. Finally she reached the yard, but as she had feared or, rather, as she had known, neither of the men she sought was there, and it hardly needed a second look to tell her that only two stable lads were present of the four that had been there earlier. She ran to one of them. "Where did they go, Zak?" she demanded.

He was a tall, lean boy with a shock of red hair, round eyes, and a mouth that always seemed to be open. He regarded her owlishly. "Oo'd ye be meanin', ma'am?''

"The marquis and Lord Seabourne—and where are Tim and Matt?''

He gazed at her dully. "Don't rightly know, ma'am.''

"Damn and blast it," she cried, unconsciously using one of Simon's favorite expressions. "They must have told you!''

"Ma'am''—John had come out of one of the stalls—"isn't no use askin' 'im nothin'. 'E be slow in the noggin fer all 'e's so good wi' 'orses. Got kicked in the 'ead, don't you know.''

"Never mind his infirmities. Where are their lordships, John?''

"I don't rightly know, ma'am." John's glance was evasive.

"John," Eugenie said sternly, "if you have been instructed not to tell me, I must remind you that you are in my employ and owe your first loyalty to me, and I want to know! Better yet, I want you to take me wherever they went. Now.''

"Well . . .'' he began hesitantly.

"Do you wish to remain in my employ, John?''

"Oh, yes, ma'am." He paused and then said, "They be at the old Bowlin' Green, wot lies at the edge o' yer woods back o' these stables aways. 'Tis pretty well grown-over, but 'tis secluded 'n' the ground be flat.''

"The Bowling Green, yes. I am not sure of its exact location. Could we ride there?"

"Aye, us could. 'Tis about three-quarter mile from 'ere. They took their 'orses."

Her heart was beginning to pound heavily again. "They . . . they've not been gone long, have they?"

"No, ma'am, not above a quarter hour."

A quarter of an hour, she thought despairingly, while she had been taking an unusually stubborn Simon back to the house, while she had been conversing with Elsie and had Knape sent for the constable. But he would not know where to go. Ought she . . . no, time was of the essence.

"Come, then," she said urgently. A second later she paused, staring at the other stable hand. "Is Zak capable?"

" 'E's not capable o' much that 'asn't to do wi' feedin' 'n' curryin' 'orses, ma'am."

A half-formed idea of also sending him for the constable died. "Then let us hurry, for God's sake."

Much to Eugenie's distress, the Bowling Green proved farther away than she had anticipated, but finally they reached it and she, not even trying to tether her horse, leapt down and dashed toward that stretch of grass that once must have been kept well clipped but was now high and filled with weeds. Simon had never been interested in such sports. She dismissed him from her mind as she saw the two men, standing apart from each other, and one of the stable lads, his hand raised to give the fatal signal. They were taking aim!

Hardly knowing what she was doing, Eugenie ran swiftly toward Thurston, throwing herself in front of him as she screamed, "Nooooo!" at the same time that the boy cried, "Fire."

"God in heaven," came a cry, and at the same time, Thurston clutched her with his free hand, staring down at her incredulously.

"You might have been killed," she cried. "He meant to k-kill you . . . I know he did."

"Oh, God, Eugenie." Thurston's voice was quivering with emotion. "How could you . . . *you* might have . . . have been killed."

The marquis had covered the distance between them in seconds. "What . . . is the meaning of this?" he demanded in a shaken voice.

Brought to her senses by the shock and anguish in his tones, Eugenie flushed and moved quickly away from Thurston, her heart pounding heavily and explanations crowding to her tongue concerning a reaction she herself could no longer understand. She said shakily, "You . . . you were both being so f-foolish and—" She broke off as she saw a tall, gray-haired man striding across the green. He was followed by Elsie.

"Oh, ma'am." The girl ran to Eugenie. "I couldn't find Knape, so I went for 'im . . . the constable, ma'am."

"Well." The constable bent down and picked up Thurston's fallen pistol. He then turned an irate eye on the marquis. "What am I to deduce from this, er . . . meeting? Dueling, gentlemen, I need not tell you, is against the law."

A small silence was broken by the marquis. "But we were not dueling, sir. We came here for mere practice. That tree over there was our target." He pointed to a lightning-struck oak.

"Target practice?" The constable's suspicious gaze traveled from the marquis to Thurston and then to Eugenie. "That is not what this young woman told me." His last glance was for Elsie.

"What did she tell you?" the marquis asked.

"I beg that you will excuse me." Eugenie looked at the constable. "I fear all of this was my fault. These gentlemen had had words earlier this morning over some trifling matter. I feared . . . but I was wrong."

"Good God, Mrs. Sorrell!" The marquis looked at her with some little annoyance. "I have never been one to settle a . . . minor argument with a pistol. I have heard that Lord Seabourne was a notable shot, and I but wanted to test his mettle."

"That is the truth of it." Thurston also addressed the constable. Then, turning back to Eugenie, he added, "My cousin, here, is inclined to act first and think later."

Despite her increasing confusion, Eugenie managed to pout slightly and say, "You both looked so fierce. Oh, dear, I am sorry that we brought you here on a wild-goose chase, sir." She fixed regretful eyes on the constable's face.

His expression was dubious, and there was a moment's silence while his glance moved from Eugenie to Thurston and then to the marquis. Then he said, with some little ire, "I hope, ma'am, that the next time there is an argument, you will wait to see the outcome rather than routing me from my office!''

"Oh, I will.'' She managed a smile. "I promise you that, sir.''

"Then I will ride back to the village.'' He visited another look upon them and then added, "I think you'd best give that dummy who works in your stables a piece of your mind, Mrs. Sorrell. 'Twas he who told us where to find you—and he seemed sure that you was off to halt a duel.''

"The . . . dummy?'' Eugenie regarded him with unfeigned amazement.

"Aye, tall lad he was, currying a horse.''

"Oh,'' she said quickly, "but as you have already pointed out, Constable, he's not quite right in his head.''

"That 'e isn't.'' John stepped forward. "Gets things all twisted up, 'e does.''

"Um.'' The constable grunted. He said sourly, "And I might add that if I had had proof of a duel, I'd not have hesitated to clap both of Your Worships in jail.'' He bent an eye on Elsie. "You can show me how to find my way back, please, miss.''

"Oh, yes, sir,'' she said.

As they strode off, a small silence that had fallen between the three of them was broken by the marquis. "I think I had best take my leave, Mrs. Sorrell,'' he said coolly. He looked from Eugenie to Thurston. "It seems that I have been under a strong misapprehension.''

"I . . . do not approve of duels,'' Eugenie said rather lamely.

He nodded. "You have made yourself abundantly clear on that subject, ma'am. And I am in agreement with you.'' He glanced at Thurston and then turned back to Eugenie. "Duels should have a purpose. They are generally fought because of an offense or a defense. I am convinced that neither was applicable to this present situation. Consequently I must beg your pardon, ma'am.''

"Oh, Raoul,'' she said remorsefully. "I do not know what to . . . say.''

His regretful gaze lingered on her face. "I think,'' he said at last, "that it is not necessary to say more than farewell, Eugenie.''

She nodded. "Farewell, then, Raoul. God be with you.''

"And with you, my dear." Taking her hand, he brought it to his lips and then, quickly releasing it, he strode to his horse and leapt on its back, urging it into a fast canter.

John, looking after him, came to Eugenie's side. "Is it all right if us goes back to the stables, ma'am?"

"Yes, of course. Please." She had half a mind to tell them that she would be joining them—save that she had no wish to ride in the same direction as Raoul. She had not looked at Thurston since that moment when, obeying an impulse she could no longer understand, she had run to him. She still could not bring herself to face him.

In an amazingly short time the green was free of people. There were only herself and Thurston. Why was he so silent? And where was he? She would not favor him with a word. He would speak to her in his own good time, and she, now that she had managed to gather some of her wits together, was finding it even more difficult to understand why she had risked her life for him.

"Eugenie," Thurston finally said, had finally come to stand before her to ask that one question for which she still had no answer. "How could you have done anything so foolish?"

She raised her eyes to his face. The answer flew into her mind and pleased her. "I want you to go . . . I want you to go with them," she said freezingly. "You must not imagine that because I wished to prevent this barbarism, I have changed my mind concerning your cruel desertion of me!"

The moment those ill-considered words left her lips, Eugenie longed to call them back. Never should she have said "cruel desertion"! That suggested that she was still suffering over it, and of course, she was not. It was on the tip of her tongue to tell him so, but it was too late, for he was answering her, his own eyes ablaze with anger.

"My desertion! I do not understand you. Surely you might have taken into account the time it took me to reach my home. Yet I was told by my uncle that three days after we parted, three little days, you came to him and wept in his arms and . . . and later in his bed!"

"*He told you that?*" She looked at him aghast, and then her anger rose again. "It's a lie. You are lying to me. Three days? I waited weeks and weeks and weeks, and each day passed like the one before it, and I heard nothing, nothing, nothing! Finally, when I could not dance anymore and the child was on the way and there was very little money left . . ."

"The child!" he exclaimed. "There was a child?"

"Do not tell me you did not know!" she flashed. "I wrote to you at your home. I did not want to but I was desperate, and still there was no answer, and when your uncle came to see me, he was kind, or seemed to be, and I was so desperate and you had not written—"

"I did write to you!" he cried hotly. "I wrote nearly every day, and I never had one letter from you, not one!"

"Nor I from you!" she retorted, caught firmly now in the grip of that old grief. "And I did write to you." Tears rolled down her cheeks. "And there was no answer, and then S-Simon came to . . . to tell me that you were married. And that you had married practically the moment you arrived home . . . that you had married your great love—Serena, her name was—and she was to . . . to marry your brother and your heart had . . . had been broken and . . . and that was why you took up with me!"

"Lies, lies, lies," he said furiously. "He lied, Eugenie." He put his hands on her shoulders, staring down into her face. "Listen to me. I did marry Serena at my father's insistence, and it broke my heart to consent but I had no choice. Oh, God, heed me, I will do my best to explain it to you."

Eugenie was very silent while Thurston brokenly explained the conditions attendant upon his marriage. It sounded plausible enough. And from what she knew of Simon . . . But Thurston was still talking, and she must needs hear every word. "After we were wed I . . . I could not be with her. My marriage vows meant nothing to me because I had not exchanged them with you. And she was understanding when I told her I must needs know her better before we consummated the marriage. She was understanding, too, when I said I must return to London. Oh, God, Eugenie, I sent you a hundred pounds, and you will tell me you never received it?"

"Never, I received nothing. You came to . . . to London?"

"Yes, I looked for you everywhere—I searched all London, and you were nowhere to be found. I even went to your aunt. Oh, God, who was it did this to us . . . who was it had our letters intercepted? But need I ask? It was my uncle, who had spoken so highly of the beautiful Mademoiselle de Montfalçon of the opera ballet. He had always coveted you, and then on his deathbed he still tried to separate us with his lies . . . speaking of your perfidy and the marquis. He wanted me to take the child—'' He broke off, staring at her. ''The child . . . his son. Eugenie, is Simon my uncle's child?''

She hesitated. She was as shaken as he, and yet, could she be entirely certain that he was telling the truth? There had been so many, many lies, and all of them had sounded truthful. Yet there was no doubting the agony in his eyes, and no doubting the tears that were still running down his face. She was suddenly seized by a fugitive memory . . . Thurston, as he left her that morning, all those years ago. There had been the same agony in his eyes. She could not doubt it now. She could not doubt his tears. She said, ''Little Simon is my child and yours, Thurston.''

''Oh, my love, my poor love.'' He put his arms around her and, drawing her against him, sank down in the deep, wild grass. ''All those lost years . . . I will make them up to you, I will, and as for my uncle . . .'' He shuddered. ''To . . . to make me the guardian of my own son . . . that was, to use his favorite expression, the very cream of the jest! It is wrong to speak ill of the dead, but—''

Eugenie put her fingers to his lips. ''Do not, my love, he is nothing to us anymore.''

''No, nothing, my beautiful Eugenie,'' he agreed, and caught her in an embrace that acknowledged and dismissed their long separation in the most satisfying way imaginable.

EPILOGUE

THE GUEST, HAVING SEEN both children and agreeing that despite the fact that they had different mothers, there was a strong family resemblance, pronounced herself delighted that after so many years Eugenie had finally found happiness and a family life she could enjoy—and had enjoyed for the past two and a half years.

She also admired the house where generations of Thurston's family had been born. In the midst of these encomiums there was an ominous roll of thunder that brought her to the window to study the massing gray clouds.

"I am glad that we will be staying the night, my dear!" she exclaimed, and then put her hands up to her ears at an especially loud crash of thunder. Subsequently she visited a mischievous smile upon her hostess. "I am half inclined to think it is your late husband expressing his displeasure."

"There are no ghosts in this house, Millie," Eugenie said firmly.

"But there are ghosts in London, and that is why you will not return?" Lady Moberley asked, and then, before Eugenie could respond, she added, "But if you are still laboring under the fear that the ton has not forgiven you for marrying within a fortnight of Simon's death, I assure you that among a thousand other scandals there was that dreadful business about Queen Caroline and the coronation. Did you hear this ditty?

> " 'Most gracious queen, we thee implore,
> To go away and sin no more;

Or if that effort be too great,
To go away at any rate.'''

"No, I did not." Eugenie laughed and then sobered. "The poor thing . . . the prince treated her very badly."

"I beg you will not weep for her . . . the way she comported herself in Europe—with all her lovers and dancing about half naked, but of course, she must be half daft. But what I really mean to say is that no one will remember anything about you and Thurston, either here or there, by which I mean Paris. Did you not tell me that your Aunt Vivienne died?"

"Yes, she is dead," Eugenie said.

"And that news came to you from the marquis. That was kind of him. Does he continue happy in his marriage?"

"He is ecstatic, and so is she." Eugenie smiled. "They are in Montreal this year."

"Ugh." Lady Moberley pulled a face. "Better they than I. After our voyage to Tahiti last year I have come to loathe anything connected with rural climes, excepting, of course, the English countryside. Did I tell you that I am of the opinion that you have wrought miracles in the garden?"

"With the help of the gardener and his several accomplished assistants," Eugenie said modestly. "You must take my husband's words with several grains of salt, you know."

"Oh, lovely!" Lady Moberley exclaimed.

"What?" Eugenie looked at her confusedly.

"I am talking about the loving way in which you pronounced the word *husband*—and after two and a half years. Do you ever quarrel?"

Eugenie giggled. "We do not actually quarrel, but we do have rather strong disagreements."

"I do not believe it. The way he looks at you, Eugenie, as if he were having difficulty convincing himself that you are real."

"Oh"—Eugenie winked at her—"I think he needs no convincing on that count."

Lady Moberley blushed. "You French!" she said, chiding teasingly. "You can say more with the lift of an eyebrow or the droop of an eyelid than we with several sentences." She sobered. "And speaking about sentences, I knew I had something to tell you that you might have difficulty believing."

"Really?" Eugenie regarded her curiously. "Tell me. It is a long time since I have heard one of your wicked *on dits*."

"This is not one of mine, and it does not concern any of our friends, either. I was thinking of that rascally Graves, the valet. My gracious, what a story that was, and what a pity that the late Mr. Sorrell could not be called to account as well. How did you feel when little Simon found the catch to that drawer?"

Eugenie was silent a moment, seeing in her mind's eye a whole parade of images. The episode to which Lady Moberley had referred had taken place shortly after she and Thurston were married. They had returned to the London house, and while they were going through the rooms deciding what furniture they would take with them, they had been startled by a howl of fright from their son.

Having ascertained the location, they had hurried down to the library to find the child vainly trying to hide a hole in the desk and looking the picture of guilt. "I . . . I did not d-do anything to it," he had sobbed. "It . . . it just went and . . . opened up."

It had been Thurston who had gently pried his hands away, saying with a meaningful look at her, "What's broken can usually be mended, lad, and this, I think, is not your fault. It is a secret compartment. You must have pushed something that made it open."

Eugenie had asked curiously, "And what will be inside? Jewels?"

"Let us see . . ." Thurston had reached down into the compartment. "No, it's paper. Bank notes, perhaps. Was my late uncle a miser?"

But it had not been bank notes, it had been letters, fifteen letters, twelve from Thurston and three from Eugenie, the lost letters, the stolen letters that had left in their wake such grief and pain.

Unmindful of the boy, they had, once they had ascertained what they were, fallen into each other's arms, both weeping out of a long remembered pain, mixed now with their present joy. Later, they had found other notes in Graves's careful handwriting, describing Eugenie's growing despair because she had heard nothing from "the other," which was the way Graves had chosen to describe his young master.

"Eugenie." Lady Moberley snapped her fingers in front of her friend's eyes. "Where have you gone?"

Eugenie laughed self-consciously. "I am sorry, I was thinking. You mentioned Graves?"

"Yes, you remember that you were not able to get him arrested because it was too long after the fact?"

Eugenie nodded. "We did dismiss him without references, though."

"I thought you had. It's my notion that he must have forged some, because he found another position with one Sir Hartley Manners."

"Oh, how did you discover that?" Eugenie asked curiously.

"Ah," Lady Moberley said with some satisfaction. "I was positive that the news had not yet reached Somerset."

"Millie!" Eugenie exclaimed impatiently, "I accuse you of being purposely provocative. What about Graves, pray?"

"Well, it seems that he was caught rifling through Sir Hartley's desk. Among other items he had taken a valuable stamp box, malachite, and gold. Naturally he was sent to jail, and he has been sentenced to be transported to New South Wales."

"Oh, really." Eugenie's eyes gleamed. "I must tell Thurston. You know that Graves narrowly escaped being murdered. Thurston was primed for it, I can tell you."

"When was I primed to murder anyone?" Thurston came in. "Good afternoon, Millie, that is a fetching gown. Green becomes you. Did I tell you that we are delighted to have you here?"

"You did, my dear, and I am delighted to be here. Gracious Thurston, love, you do look rather wet. I thought you and Moberley would have come in before the rains started."

"We were too far out in the gardens," he explained.

"Oh, dear, I hope he packed the physic . . . colds make him dreadfully irritable. I will have to see to him at once. He does nothing for himself. Will you excuse me, my dear?"

"Of course," Thurston said, but he spoke to the air, Lady Moberley having already rushed past him.

"And you, too, must have physic," Eugenie said determinedly. She rose.

"Wait," he pleaded. "You must tell me why I was primed to murder anyone."

"We were discussing Graves."

"Oh?" Thurston frowned. "Why? I thought Millie was well acquainted with that tale."

"She is, but this is something else entirely. Graves, as it happens, is in . . . grave difficulties."

He cocked an amused eye at her. "Would you be telling me, I hope, that our Graves is in a grave?"

"Not quite, but he is being transported to New South Wales."

"Ah, that is graves news indeed," he said solemnly.

"Oh, you! For such a dreadful pun I must punish you," she exclaimed, leaping to her feet and advancing on him threateningly.

"Pun and punish? I think we are even, or will be soon."

"Soon, my love?" She smiled up at him.

"Now, I mean." He drew her into a long embrace.

"Goodness," she said laughingly as he finally released her. "Now we are both extremely wet!"

He cocked an eye at her. "Have you any objections if we—er, dry off together?

"None in the world, my dearest. I will race you up the stairs."

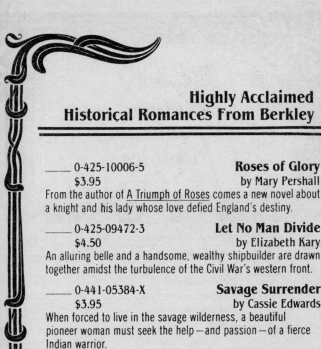